SC

The Indigo Lounge Series, Volume 4

Zara Cox

Published by Zara Cox, 2014.

This is a work of fiction. Similarities to real people, places, or events are entirely coincidental.

SOAR

First edition. September 29, 2014.

Copyright © 2014 Zara Cox.

Written by Zara Cox.

SOAR
THE INDIGO LOUNGE SERIES #4
BY
ZARA COX

ONE

No. *No, no, no.*

"Fuck no."

Time suspended, then kicked into slow motion. Noah waited for the denial. Waited for the nightmare that flashed across his vision to subside. A muffled whimper came from beside him.

Leia Michaels. The most important thing in his life right now stood next to him. The one person he had woken up this morning thanking his lucky stars for. The one he should be looking at. Taking care of. Hanging onto so she wasn't dragged into this bedlam.

But he couldn't look at her. Couldn't force his gaze from Ashley Maitland, the woman sitting cross-legged on his living room sofa. The woman whose lips parted, ready to utter words he knew would change his life forever.

"Oh yes. One hundred percent, yes. You are going to be a father, Noah."

"Dear God. Ashley what...*why?*"

"Why? Because you're supposed to be my husband and the father of my children," she said with the same unapologetic assurance that stated the world owed her a living. A trait he'd once thought sexy.

Bitterness coating his mouth, he sliced a hand through his hair, resisting the urge to pull the damn strands out. The grenade she'd detonated in his life had done more than enough to unbalance him. The last thing he intended to do was grant her the satisfaction of knowing she'd turned his life inside out.

"We're no longer together, Ashley." He sucked in a deep breath, struggling for a civil tone in the face of her ridiculous assertion. "I'm no expert on pregnancy—that is if you really are pregnant—but I think baby brain is supposed to kick in *after* you have the baby. Unless you're claiming amnesia on top of everything else that you're making up right now?"

Her features tightened for a second before settling back into the serene look she liked to present to the world. Noah hadn't noticed how creepy that transformation was before now.

"Why would I make up something that you can check in two minutes? I may be many things, but I'm not stupid. This is happening. I get that you need to take a moment, but Noah...it's happening."

Her gaze slid to Leia and back to him. The clear smugness in her eyes made him swallow hard.

Jesus. If she was telling the truth...

He was going to be a father. With the one woman he detested more than any other in the world.

His vision clouded for several seconds. He concentrated on getting air into his lungs and his brain. He needed to, so he could wrap his head around the insanity of the situation.

But even though the facts were clear, he couldn't believe the enormity of the transgression.

He forced his hands into his pockets, to resist striding across the room and strangling her with them. "So let me get this straight. You used my sperm without my permission and got yourself knocked up so what...we could play happy families?"

Her smile widened, one slender shoulder lifting in a careless shrug. Despite her outwardly relaxed impression, Noah caught a dart of apprehension in her eyes. "You should never have left me. What happened two years ago was just to bring you to your senses. Even after you left, I thought you'd come back. We weren't supposed to be apart for this long. You've dragged things out too far. It's time for us to be together again."

The choked sound came from beside him again. Head spinning, he glanced at Leia. Her face was ashen, her beautiful eyes a dark, haunted grey that stared back at him in bleak resignation.

No.

He moved toward her.

She took a step back.

His heart clenched. "Don't do that. Don't retreat from me," he pleaded. With everything going to shit around him, he couldn't take a world without Leia. He took her hand and, thankfully, her fingers closed around his.

From the corner of his eye, he saw movement. Warren Snyder - Leia's ex-guardian and the other unwanted equation in this whole despicable debacle - rose to his feet. Again, the slimy bastard's eyes slid to Leia in a way that made Noah want to cause him serious and permanent damage.

A tiny frozen part of him was quite impressed at how his two nemeses had orchestrated this meeting. Hell, he couldn't have planned it better.

That didn't alter the fact that they were seriously messing with the one thing in the world most precious to him.

Leia.

He turned to her as she pulled her hand away. She folded her arms across her midriff the way he'd come to recognize as a self-preservation tactic. This time he didn't stop with one step. He took her arms, pulling her close, crowding her. When she refused to look at him, he captured her nape and forced her to face him.

"Don't you dare leave me here in the fucking Twilight Zone all by myself." It was a fucked up time to be making jokes. But the very blatant reality that she was pulling away from him threatened to send him down a tunnel he didn't want to contemplate.

"Leia—"

Noah twisted round, unable to stop the snarl surging from his throat. "Do not say her name. You have two options, Snyder, you either sit down and shut the fuck up or you leave right now. You know where the hell the door is. You don't control her any more. Got that?"

Warren Snyder's demeanor remained the same. Cold, non-reactive dead eyes, which sent an uneasy sensation down Noah's spine. But to his credit, Snyder sat back down, crossed his legs and steepled his fingers together.

Noah turned back to Leia. Her eyes met his. He breathed a sigh of relief to see that the haunted look had dissipated somewhat.

"I need to go," she said.

Anxiety rose to mingle with the shitload of emotions coursing through him. She was reeling, he got that. But the irrational part of him, which suggested she was giving in to what Snyder wanted, rose and slapped him in the face. "No you don't." His response was rough with anger. "We had plans."

Her mouth dropped open. "Are you serious?"

His grip tightened on her arm in acknowledgement of her disbelief. "Jesus, I don't know what the hell I am, but I know I don't want you to leave. Not now." *Not ever.*

She shook her head and closed her eyes. The look that washed over her face cut right through him. "Noah, I can't stay. You know that, right?"

"Says who?"

"She's right, Noah. What we need to discuss is just between you and—"

"Shut the hell up, Ashley."

Unable to stand the look on Leia's face, he slid his hand down her arm and dragged her to the sliding doors. Stabbing the button that parted them, he led her to the terrace. The crisp and fresh breeze from the ocean promised a bright new day.

After the night he'd spent with Leia, their fiery row and their even more tempestuous making up, it was a day that should've harkened a new and glorious beginning. It had all right. Except, he'd never have foreseen this version of it in his wildest dreams.

He stopped beside the gleaming pool and looked down at her. She'd grown paler, and her lips trembled before she pursed them.

"Leia, I know this was a curveball neither of us expected. Hell, I can't even begin to think straight about any of this, but leaving isn't going to solve anything. It's selfish, I know, but I'm asking you to stay."

"Why? What good could I possibly offer here? Warren is right—"

"You fucking agree with anything Snyder has to say about us, and I won't be responsible for what happens next," he said through jaws clenched so tight he expected them to snap in half.

"I'm sorry, I know you don't like him—"

He snorted, cutting her off.

"And I know I've been blind to certain indicators," she continued with a small frown. "But he's right."

His vision threatened to cloud again. He pinched the bridge of his nose and sucked in breath. "No, he's not. He's a goddamn—"

"Noah, you're going to be a father." The words were hushed, dropped into the middle of his rage with soft, agonized, whispers.

He froze, unable to look away from the anguish in her eyes.

Reality rose in twenty-foot waves. Regardless of how he felt about Ashley, she was most likely carrying his child. She wouldn't be so bold, so smug, if there wasn't some truth to her assertion.

"Do you even know how you feel about that?" Leia shook her head. "You don't need me around. I'd only confuse issues."

"What the hell is that supposed to mean? I want you here. You belong with me."

"I can't be here, Noah. I can't be the support you need." Her voice broke. She tried to move away again.

He caught her to him, selfishly drawing on her warmth, on the memory of last night and what he'd felt in her arms. She'd tried to leave then, too, thinking she wouldn't be enough for him.

But she'd been the promise of everything he wanted come to life. He'd convinced her to stay and she had. With every atom in his body, he wanted to be back in that place, in that time with her.

But he was already losing her. She'd retreated into herself, to a place where he couldn't touch her. He tried to understand. She needed to regroup the same way he did. Hell, he needed more than to regroup, he needed to get to the bottom of what was going on. Speak to his lawyers...find out how the hell this had ever happened. But first he had to deal with Ashley.

Mingled anger and disbelief scythed through him at the thought of what she'd done. But with it came the realization of what was happening.

He'd never given much thought to children in the immediate future. Before last week, work and sex had been his life.

Leia had quickly taken precedence over those priorities.

Now this...

"Fine." He kissed her because he couldn't help himself. Because he needed her in ways he still hadn't been able to fathom. Ways he couldn't communicate with anything but his touch, his kiss.

He kissed her because he was at a loss as to how to stop her from retreating. Because he could still feel her pulling away. He deepened the kiss. Her lips puckered beneath his, opened up and let him in. With a groan of relief, he tasted her long and hard. The crazy receded until there was only the two of them, wrapped in their own world, their chemistry a clawing hunger that demanded to be satisfied.

She grabbed his nape, scraped her long fingernails along his scalp, threading that fine line between pleasure and pain that was their own unique aphrodisiac, their own nirvana. He slammed her back against the solid outside wall, heard her moan of pleasure at the rough treatment. He wedged a thigh between hers and slid one hand to grip her throat. Then they fell deeper into the kiss, their need for each other escalating to the point where he lost touch with reality.

It took several seconds to realize she was pushing him away, not forcefully but with enough strength to remind him where they were, what shitty chaos they were treading neck-deep in.

He sighed, released her and dropped his forehead against hers. Sliding his thumb down her cheek in a soft caress, he quickly calculated. "Give me a few hours to deal with this. I'll reschedule our meeting with the investigator for this evening." He hadn't lost sight of the fact that Leia's stepfather, Stephen Willoughby - the man who'd violently raped her when she was seventeen - was out there, released from prison early and determined to make her life a living hell once more. Protecting Leia was still his highest priority right now. "God, this is nuts. I don't want you to leave. Stay here, baby. I'd go crazy wondering if you're okay if you leave."

She started to shake her head before he'd finished. "No, I can't stay."

"Dammit, I really wish you wouldn't fight me on this, Leia."

She turned her head, and he caught the renewed anguish on her face. "You don't understand. I'm not leaving now to return later. We won't be meeting your investigator together. When I leave, I'm not coming back, Noah."

He leaned back, frowning. "What do you mean you're not coming back? Leia, your stepfather is out there and he needs to be found. We will meet with the investigator tonight. There's no way I'm calling off the search for Willoughby. Not until he's found and back behind bars where he belongs. In case I didn't make myself clear, your safety is non-negotiable. So yes, if you don't want to stay here, I'll let you have a few hours in that bastard Snyder's care, but you're coming back here tonight. Understood?"

Firm hands pushed him back harder. "You're not going to make this easy, are you?"

"I didn't realize that what I was asking was so damn impossible."

She shot him an incredulous look. "Noah, there's a woman sitting no more than twenty feet away who says she's carrying your baby. Why don't you focus on that instead of throwing down ultimatums at me? I'm the last thing you should be worrying about."

"Wrong. You're the most important thing in my life."

She froze. Her grey eyes rounded, first with shock, then with a tiny glaze of hope before they dulled again. Noah wanted to shake her, wanted to demand to know what was going on in her mind. But she was already shaking her head, withdrawing even further away from him.

When he reached for her, she slapped him away. "No. I'm leaving, Noah. And you won't stop me. Goodbye."

She took three steps before he realized exactly what she meant. "Wait a sec. Just so I get this straight, are you leaving this place or are you leaving *me*?"

She turned. "I can't compete with this, Noah. I'd fight for you with anything else, but not this."

"This?" Thoughts crashed into one another, but one blazed through them all. *She was leaving him.* "What the hell do you mean by *this*?" he demanded fiercely.

Her mouth wobbled for a second. "A child, Noah. I won't compete with your child."

TWO

Leia had thought her pain couldn't get any worse. She'd really imagined, considering her own circumstances, that the single most heart-ripping news she could face was that the man she loved was about to have a child with another woman. Until she'd caught a glimpse of Noah's reaction to the news of his impending fatherhood.

She was dead certain he hadn't even realized the naked emotion emblazoned on his face a split second after Ashley had told him about the baby.

Wonder and elation.

It had dissipated very quickly, of course. The circumstances were nothing if not fucked up.

Now, the combination of shock and confusion had rendered his normally vibrant skin sickly grey. His brows clamped together. His hands trembled before he tightened his hold on her.

"You're leaving me? Is that what you're trying to tell me? Even before I verify there's any truth to what that bitch is saying, you're leaving? And what the hell do you mean by *competing*?"

"You know it's the right thing for me to do, Noah," she forced out through her pain.

He stepped back, unclamping his hands from her arm. "No, I fucking don't. All I know is that a few short hours after promising me you wouldn't, you're running again."

"Don't say that. Please."

"Please? Then tell me what it is you're doing. I'm seriously confused, Leia. Enlighten me in plain fucking English so I get that you're not walking away from me because I'm...I'm..." His jaws clenched tight and he closed his eyes. Shoving a hand through his hair, he breathed in deep. "I may not have known you for a long time, but I know you're not walking away because of this. So tell me, what the hell is it?"

She opened her mouth to remind him that she was only half a woman, that what her stepfather had done to her had damaged more than her spirit, but the pain shredding her heart stopped her.

She shook her head. "I deluded myself into thinking that we could make this work. God, I don't know what I was thinking. My last relationship was just before I turned *seventeen*, Noah. And I can't even call that a proper relationship. I was little more than a spoiled teenager with a rebellious streak, testing my boundaries. I had no idea what I was doing then. And this... this is way more than I can deal with. I'm going to fuck it up for you. You have to let me go."

"You want to be able to pick and choose your battles, is that it? To retreat from the world the way you've done for the last five years and only come out when you think it's safe and *comfortable*?" he grated at her.

A cold shiver chased down her spine. "Why are you doing this?"

"Why am I standing here fighting for you instead of letting you chicken out and walk away? Is that what you're seriously asking me?"

She crossed her arms over her midriff, desperately wanting to cling to the *fighting for you* part. Letting Noah take control, convince her that walking away wasn't the right thing to do, was the one thing she wanted more than breathing. She'd woken up this morning happier than she'd ever been in her life. She placed sole responsibility of that happiness at Noah's feet.

The thought that in the future he could find her lacking was more than she could bear. And once the dust settled, he *would* remember just how fucked up she was. Remember how inadequate she was compared to the woman he needed. She couldn't do that to him.

"You *know* she's telling the truth. I saw your face. You haven't seen each other in two years, but you know her. Whatever she's done, you know she's not lying about this."

His face tightened. He nodded even though his eyes held nothing but condemnation. "And what's about to happen to me several months from now is a deal-breaker for you? Is that what you're saying?"

"I'm saying I don't want my presence to confuse the issue. Whatever decision you make, can't...shouldn't include me." She realized how wrong her words sounded the moment she spoke them. "I'm sorry, I meant—"

"It's fine. I get it." His voice held cold, bleak acceptance. Its roughness tore at her bleeding heart. "Things are a little *too* messed up for you."

"No! I mean yes, they are, but I'm doing this for you, Noah."

"Like hell you are!" He gestured indoors to the two people seated out of sight. "He tells you to jump, and you can't wait to ask how high!"

"Warren has nothing to do with this," she shouted. "Credit me with knowing my own damn mind."

He seized her nape, forced her gaze upward to meet his. "If he's got nothing to do with this—with *us*—then stay. God, baby, did last night mean nothing to you?"

Memory slammed into her, making her tremble. "Of course it did. This isn't easy for me."

"But you're doing it anyway. Do you really have so little faith in us?" he demanded gruffly, sliding his thumb back and forth over the short hairs above her ear. She knew he loved that patch of shaved hair. He'd been fascinated with it from the moment they met.

God, had it only been five short days ago that she'd walked into the Indigo Lounge's Ozone Bar and seen him for the first time?

She wasn't ashamed to admit Noah King had become her whole world in a stupidly short time.

And now, she had to walk away.

Tears prickled her eyes. Once she left this place she wouldn't feel his touch ever again. The knowledge slashed her in two. She clung to the wrist that brushed her jaw, treasuring the moment before she had to let him go. When her long nails dug into his flesh, his blue eyes darkened. Unable to speak because everything seemed to come out wrong, she dug in deeper.

His soft hiss was music to her ears. He stepped closer, his fingers tightening.

Just for a moment longer, she wanted to enjoy this, wanted to bask in their unparalleled passion for each other. His thumb caressed the curve of her ear, traced her jaw to the corner of her mouth. Her lips parted, and he slid his thumb in. She sucked him slowly, absorbing his texture and the emotions that flitted over his face. He still looked pale and haggard, but the blood was surging into his cheeks again and his breathing was growing shallow.

His other hand curved over her waist to grip her ass. With a single step they were back against the wall, his body pressing down on hers. She sucked eagerly on his thumb, her diamond tongue stud abrading the pad of his digit the way she knew made him wild. His cock thickened against her stomach, its branding unmistakably possessive as his heartbeat hammered against hers.

He kissed the side of her mouth, his tongue licking at the point where her lips wrapped around his thumb. "I'm not ashamed to beg, Leia," he whispered. "I need you. Don't leave me, baby. Whatever the fuck's going on, we'll work our way through it."

She wavered. Maybe they could work their way through this. Maybe she could even work her mind past the fact that he'd spent time behind bars. That was something else she'd have to deal with. But it didn't compare to the fact that another woman was having his baby.

He pulled his thumb from her mouth and replaced it with his lips. Their kiss was incandescent as Noah mercilessly reminded her of their incredible chemistry. As if she needed reminding. Too soon, he let her up for air.

She tried to gather her scattered thoughts. "Noah..."

"You can have this, sweetheart. So many nights and days of this. Don't you want that? My cock inside your tight, beautiful body?" His hand slid from her ass to wedge between her legs. Subtly applied pressure had her shuddering and suppressing a groan. "I'll take care of you, baby. Worship you day and night. No matter what. You're the most important thing to me. Don't fucking walk away from me now. Please."

The sound of the door sliding back registered at the edge of her consciousness. Half of her was relieved at the intrusion, even as the other half crumbled in inevitable dread.

"Leia."

Warren's voice made Noah freeze. His whole body went rigid beneath the hand she'd clamped around his waist in the heat of their kiss.

She stared into his eyes. The ruthless lover she'd grown to love was very much present. But so was the vulnerable guy who was floundering in the wake of shocking news. She wanted to hold him to her. But that would prolong the agony for them both. Because she wasn't what he needed. He needed a woman who wasn't broken beyond repair. A woman who wasn't at this very moment existing in fear of her life from her stepfather's threats.

"I...I'll be right there, Warren."

Noah's face froze into a mask of pure frost. The mouth that had kissed her so hungrily and reverently moments ago, thinned into a formidable line. His hand slid from between her thighs and the grip on her neck disappeared between one breath and the next. When he spoke his voice was blade-sharp.

"You have exactly one minute. That's as long as I'll hold myself in check. I'm not a violent guy, Leia. Despite your complete lack of faith in me, I hope you know that. But if you're not out of here in the next sixty seconds...the doors get locked, the ropes come out, and you get a taste of how much of a monster I can be. I'll destroy you before I watch you leave with that asshole, Leia. Trust me on that."

Unable to speak in the presence of his arctic-cold anger, Leia jerked out a nod.

He stepped back, stared down at her for another few seconds, then turned away. She knew the threat was real, that she'd wounded him badly. But she couldn't move. Her feet remained caked in heart-wrenching fear and regret.

"Leia."

She turned sharply toward Warren, her nostrils flaring in an effort to stem the hot, scalding tears that surged.

When she finally managed to get her feet moving, Warren held out a hand to her. She ignored it, just as she ignored the sharp reproach in his eyes.

He could go to hell. He, Ashley, her stepfather and the whole fucking world could go to hell. Her heart was hammering itself out of existence because she was choosing to be fucking *noble*. To do the right thing.

She swallowed a hysterical laugh and stumbled into the sun-splashed living room.

Ashley sat exactly where they had left her ten minutes ago, not a single hair out of place. She glanced at Leia and a small triumphant smile played at her lips. Leia's fingers itched to slap the look off her face.

"You think you've won him back? Newsflash, bitch, all you've done is mess up both your lives. Even if he stays with you, it will be out of pity."

"Is that why you're running away? Because you're afraid of competing with a little *pity*? Or are you afraid that it's just a little bit more? Perhaps more than you'll ever be able to handle?" The questions were barely above a conversational murmur, but they raked over Leia's skin like industrial-strength sanders.

Leia heard Warren enter. The sound of the door sliding shut reminded her that Noah was out there, counting down her minute.

Shivering in remembrance of his cold warning, she summoned a smile for Ashley. "Good luck."

About to walk away, she saw the file of Noah's alleged criminal charges. It was open to his NYPD mug shot. Her insides clenched hard. The look in his eyes was truly terrifying. They promised retribution of the worst possible kind - the retribution of a man who believed himself wronged.

"If you did this to him and you're stupid enough to come back for more, trust me you're going to need all the luck in the world."

She had the satisfaction of seeing Ashley's demeanor crumble for a second before that infernal smile returned.

"I'm having his baby. It's as simple and final as that. But if you need it pointed out to you further - baby trumps trollop. It's been nice *not* knowing you." Ashley waved her away.

"That's quite enough," Warren said. She'd forgotten he was behind her and jumped when he touched her arm. "Are you all right, my dear?"

She snatched her arm away. "I'm fine," she responded automatically, unwilling to let anyone see how very much *not fine* she was. "I need...I need to grab my things...I'll be right back."

She glanced at the sliding doors. Her minute had come and gone. Bizarrely, a part of her hoped Noah would storm in just so she could see him one last time. Shaking her head at the pure madness behind that thought, she rushed up the stairs to the bedroom. At the sight of the rumpled bed and the clothes strewn on the floor, she stumbled.

She'd gone on the Indigo Lounge trip to wash away the memories of what her stepfather had done to her, to regain some of the power he'd taken from her. Little did she know she'd be walking away with so much more. An experience of a lifetime. An experience that had been destined to last less than a week.

With an unforgettable man.

Leia trembled as she gathered her things. The top she'd worn all day yesterday was creased and smelled bad. On a selfish whim, she decided to keep Noah's Vassar College T-shirt. Stuffing her top into her purse, she pushed her feet into her heels, grabbed the rest of her belongings and rushed back downstairs.

Warren waited by the front door. Unable to resist, she glanced out to the terrace. Noah was pacing, his phone clamped to his ear.

He started to turn toward her, froze with his glance downward and turned back to the view.

Knowing the move had been a deliberate effort on his part not to look into the living room, clawed at her heart. She inhaled shakily.

What the fuck was she doing? She'd chosen to walk away. Dithering like an idiot only prolonged the pain.

Resolutely, she strode to the front door, her hand clamped around her purse. When Warren sent her one of his calm, barely there smiles, she ignored him. If that was his version of pity, he could stuff it. She didn't need anyone's pity.

Who the fuck's business was it that her insides had turned into a barren wasteland?

THREE

"You heard me correctly. Four, no make that five pregnancy testing kits. I want them within the hour..." Noah gripped the phone through his PA's confused stuttering. "And Maddie? Thank you. I'll make sure you're paid an extra month's salary for doing this...no, it's more than you should have to do for me, especially on a Saturday." He would've gotten the kits himself, except he had no intention of leaving Ashley alone in his condo, and he liked the thought of going to the drug store with her in tow even less.

He hung up and turned toward the sliding doors. His breath punched through his lungs. Realizing his whole body shook with the effort it took just to face the doors, he cursed under his breath. He had to go in there. Had to face the fact that Leia had walked away.

Had to face the fact that if Ashley wasn't totally delusional, he was about to become a father. Through no choice of his own. Bewildering anger flashed through him. He battled through it to think rationally.

He'd think about Leia later. Or maybe not. Maybe he'd pretend the whole goddamn thing had been a fucking dream. Yeah, right. A *dream* was the reason his insides were eviscerated and why his feet refused to move.

But he had to move. His ex-fiancée was spinning dreams he had to nuke before they got even crazier. He took a step and heard his front door slam. The finality of it shook him to the core.

Leia was gone.

God.

He forced himself to walk back into the living room.

Ashley rose with a fluid grace he'd once thought sexy as hell. Now he could see clearly that it was all a studied performance with more polish than allure. For a brief moment, Noah wondered whether it was that allure which had swayed Snyder into staging this morning's confrontation with Ashley. But no, Snyder was just as fixated with Leia as Noah had allowed himself to be.

And now she was gone...

"Noah, darling, I really am sorry I had to break it to you this way," Ashley said.

"No, you're not." He threw his phone on the nearest sofa and circumvented her approach by stalking to the kitchen. Seeing the remnants of the breakfast he'd planned for Leia made his insides congeal. "You had an audience lapping up your performance. An audience you engineered so I couldn't throw you out on your ass. That's exactly how you wanted it. If you want me to entertain any hope of hearing you out, let's cut the bullshit and get to the heart of the matter."

He grabbed the coffee pot and poured himself a cup. Shame it was too early for something stronger. He gulped the first mouthful, winced at the scalding heat, and turned. Ashley lingered near the bar, her wary eyes on him.

"This is your last chance, Ashley. My PA is on her way with a pregnancy kit, several in fact." He reached into the fridge and grabbed a bottle of water. With a grim smile, he slammed it on the counter. "Drink up. You'll be doing a hell of a lot of peeing in the next hour. Unless you're going to come clean and tell me this has been a huge misunderstanding?"

He couldn't stop his gaze from dropping to her stomach. The thought that his child could be growing in there was too much to wrap his head around. Again that earth-shaking bewilderment threatened to engulf him.

A look of challenge in her eyes, she took the bottle. She wrenched the top open but didn't drink.

"I know that's what you want to hear, but I wouldn't lie to you. Not about this."

"So we're agreed that you do lie more than frequently?"

Her mouth pursed in annoyance. "Our situation has forced you to dump your little bit on the side so you're feeling a little annoyed. But I am carrying your child, Noah. Treat me with some respect."

His fingers tightened around his coffee cup. "*Our situation*? How much choice did you give me in this, Ashley? Oh, and by the way don't think I'm not calling my lawyers within the hour to bring charges against you."

A small smile lifted the corners of her mouth. "You're not a monster, Noah. You won't send the mother of your child to jail, no matter what your lawyers recommend."

He froze. "You really had this all planned out, didn't you?" Noah was surprised at how even his voice sounded considering he wanted to roar his anger to the heavens. "The first and last time I mentioned children back when we were together, you didn't even want them. So why this? Why now?"

"I told you. I want you back. And I know you want children eventually."

His gaze strayed to the NYPD file opened on the table. "I haven't changed, Ashley. I'm still the guy who slapped your tits, tied your hands behind your back and forced you on your knees so I could fuck your mouth for as long as I wanted. I'm still the guy who made you pay for snapping his control by tying you to the bed and making you come for eight hours straight. Have you forgotten how I spanked your conniving little ass till you were black and blue? How I left bite marks all over your body? You called the cops on me and had me arrested for assault for that, remember? Remember how much you hated being bound, that you couldn't call the shots, that you couldn't dictate when I could let my nasty little traits come out and play? Is that the sort of father you want for your child?"

She paled a little, then shrugged. "So I thought there was a time and place for...that sort of behavior. So what?"

"So I can't turn it on and off at will! It's part of who I am. It's woven into my fucking DNA! How can you not see that?"

"Is that what your little Leia likes?" Her voice came as close to a sneer as he'd ever heard it.

"I'm hanging on by a thread here, Ashley, so do yourself a favor and don't speak her name." His warning was whisper soft.

She flicked her hair, glanced off to the side then back at him. "Fine. You say you haven't changed. Well, I have. I can accommodate whatever proclivities you insist on indulging in, once our baby is born, of course. After that, between us I'm sure we can work something—"

He slammed his coffee cup down so hard it split in two. "Jesus. There is no fucking *us* or *we*! There will never be. Get that through your thick skull right now, or so help me God..." He stopped and took a breath, his fists clenching so hard his knuckles cracked. "And the only place you'll be after this child is born is in jail so think carefully how you want to spend your last months as a free woman."

Her audacious laugh set his teeth on edge. "I won't be going to jail. Trust me on that."

Her tone reeked with too much confidence for him to put it down to bravado. His eyes narrowed. Before he could ask the question burning on his tongue, his buzzer beeped.

He frowned. Maddie must have dropped everything to get the pregnancy kits.

Even still, that was super quick.

His stomach lurched at the thought of what could change his life in the next half hour.

He answered the concierge and listened with growing incredulity. "What the fuck are you talking about? Hell no, do not send them up. You can throw them out onto the streets for all I care." Replacing the handset, he turned, a stunned laugh escaping his throat. "You really should've been born a man, Ashley. You certainly have the balls to carry it off."

While he'd been speaking to the concierge, she'd fetched herself a glass and was now sipping the water. "What are you talking about?"

"You had your suitcases messengered over here?"

She smiled. "Oh, that. Yes, I thought I could stay here while we sort things out between us. You know how much I hate hotel rooms. The air conditioning messes up my sinuses. And the morning sickness has been a killer. Besides, you have more than enough room here." She looked around, and he could almost see her mentally redecorating.

"Sorry, *sweetheart*, you won't be staying here. If you want to rescue your stuff, you need to hustle yourself downstairs because they're about to be thrown out onto the street. And don't bother trying to talk Miguel into letting you bring them up. He has instructions not to allow the cases anywhere in this building."

Her hand fluttered up to her throat. "I have nowhere to go, Noah."

His jaw clenched. "You should've thought of that before trying to manipulate your way back into my life. And what do you mean you have nowhere to go? If I remember correctly, the lease on the New York apartment isn't up for another three years."

"I've given up my apartment in New York and my job at the art gallery. I gave up everything to be with you. Are you really going to toss me out onto the street?" She pouted.

"You're hardly destitute. My lighter bank account after your damages claim two years ago, bears witness to that fact."

"The money's all gone. Implanting the embryos took a few tries." She gave a little laugh. "I made myself broke trying to have your baby. The least you can do is help me keep a roof over my head."

Noah whirled away and stalked to the French windows. He closed his eyes. He couldn't stand to look at her for another second. Had he really thought he loved this woman once upon a time? Had he asked her to marry him, contemplated spending the rest of his life with her? God, how fucking desperate had he been to have fallen into her poisonous web?

He'd been thinking with his dick and not his head. Fresh out of a series of relationships that had started out great, but had tailed off into vanilla dullness because inevitably each of the women had tried to change him, he'd been ripe for the plucking.

He'd resigned himself to his *Catch, Fuck, Release* program by the time he'd met Ashley. When she hadn't flinched from his attempts to drive her away by testing her boundaries, he'd thought he'd died and gone to heaven.

Noah shook his head. He'd long accepted how well Ashley had played him during their relationship. She'd nearly cost him everything two years ago. Was costing him everything now...

His gaze drifted to the corner of the pool where he'd dragged Leia less than half an hour ago. Yeah, his ex-fiancée continued to cost him dearly, but trying to blame Ashley for Leia walking away was a little too convenient. The truth was Leia wouldn't have walked if they'd been solid enough. If she'd trusted him enough to give him a chance. He turned away from the view outside and faced the woman who made the view inside even less palatable.

Suddenly, he couldn't stand to be in his condo.

The Spartan look of the whole place filled his vision. Was it only a couple of weeks ago that his friends had accused him of using this place just to sleep? The truth of it hit him between the eyes.

Besides his clothes and the work stuff in his home office, there wasn't much here. When he'd left New York, he'd packed everything of emotional value and shipped it to his brother in Chicago. Much of his childhood was locked away in crates in his brother's garage. He'd never made an effort to turn this place into a home. The view he used to love was now soured by memories of standing outside, listening to Leia walk away.

He was an asshole in many ways, but he'd learned, at great expense, that he had to draw a rigid line where Ashley was concerned. She pushed too many buttons for him to risk staying around her for too long. He'd thought himself free of her, but the fury eating away beneath his skin told him otherwise.

Returning to the intercom, he picked up the handset. "Miguel, have Miss Maitland's cases brought up." He hung up and saw her pleased smile.

"I can stay here?"

He retrieved his phone and scrolled through the numbers till he found the one he was looking for. "Until we sort things out, you can stay here, sure. Like you said, if you're carrying my child, I can't turf you out into the street."

"Great, I knew you would see sense and give us a ch—"

"This is Noah King. Put me through to Rex Hartford, please." Noah had the satisfaction of seeing Ashley's face drop when she realized he didn't intend to engage her in conversation. "Hartford...no I'm not calling to check up on you. I wouldn't have invested in your company if I didn't think it was sound. But I do need a favor. Can you send me a list of available properties? Yeah, email is fine. ASAP please. Thanks." He heard Ashley's affronted gasp. When he turned around, she was glaring at him.

"You're leaving me here on my own?" she asked.

"I don't know how else to say this to you so you'll understand. I really, *really* don't want to be with you, Ashley. Ever."

Her face crumpled.

His eyes narrowed. "Don't even think about starting with the fake water works. You created this fucking circus all on your own. For the sake of the child you're supposedly carrying, I'm not going to toss you out. You can use this condo until I verify your lies. But your presence here has tainted this place for me. So congratulations, you got yourself a roof over your head after all."

"You really hate me, don't you?" she asked, her voice curiously hushed.

Noah noticed her trembling hand when she set the glass down. Needing to hammer home his point, he looked into her eyes, to make sure she didn't mistake his next words. "Yes. I really do." Jerking his chin at the half-empty bottle of water, he sent her a grim smile. "Now drink up."

An hour later, Noah dumped his overnight and laptop cases in the suite one floor above his office. He'd only needed the essentials from his condo.

Crossing to the well-stocked bar, he poured himself a shot of whiskey. He downed it in one go, welcoming the temporary warmth that burned its way into his gut.

The glass tumbled from his fingers onto the counter and rolled to a stop.

He was going to be a father...

Despite knowing in his gut that Ashley was telling the truth, a part of him had held out the belief that it was all one huge fucking joke. But five tests - done in his presence because he didn't trust Ashley one iota - had made reality impossible to dismiss.

He was going to be a father.

He clamped shaky fingers in his hair and paced the living room. Walking past the bar, he considered having another drink. But he needed to remain sharp, or as sharp as he could be, considering the punch to his system every time the word *father* rolled through his brain.

Turning away from the temptation to drown himself in alcohol, he went down to his office. At his desk, he dialed the private number.

After a few minutes, an incredulous laugh echoed down the line. "Ah, I know you're not into practical jokes but I have to ask if you're serious. Did you just say—?"

"Yes, I did. Trust me, Sam. I wish I were joking."

Sam Ferranti, his attorney and a partner at one of the most prestigious law firms in Miami, cleared his throat. "I have to look up case law on this, Noah. If you'd been married and then divorced, it wouldn't have been clear-cut, but it would've been easier because there's precedent. This is slightly more uncharted territory."

"Then here's your chance to make history. But make it quickly."

"I understand," Sam responded immediately. The bone-deep bewilderment and anger in Noah's voice had clearly transmitted, "I'm assuming she would've needed you to accompany her to the clinic in order to get the embryos," Sam continued. "Since you didn't, do you know how she acquired the embryos on her own?"

Noah's skin crawled at the memory of Ashley's answer when he'd asked the same question. "She talked her twin brother into posing as me." The scale of Ashley's duplicity chilled Noah's blood.

"Will her brother testify to this?" Sam asked.

"He died of cancer two months ago."

"Christ. Okay, send me everything you have, including the name of the clinic and doctor who took your samples. I'll drop everything and work on it. You'll hear from me as soon as I have something." He paused. "I just need to ask...how hard do you want to go on this considering she's already pregnant?"

It was a question Noah had been avoiding since Ashley had walked out of his bathroom with five blue lines on five sticks sealing his fate. A couple of hours later, he still didn't have an answer.

"Go do your research, Sam. Give me all the options and I'll take it from there."

"And I assume you're going to have a pre-natal DNA test done, just to be sure the baby's yours?"

Noah exhaled. "Yes," he said.

"Good. If you need the name of a clinic, just let me know."

"Yeah, sure. Thanks, Sam."

Noah tossed his phone onto his desk and scrubbed a hand down his face. A million questions crowded his mind, none of them taking enough shape to demand an answer.

When he heard a noise outside his door, he sprang up, for one intensely hot second hoping it was Leia. The ridiculous idea dissolved in the next moment. Even if she knew where his office was, why the hell would she seek him out mere hours after making it abundantly clear they were over?

His gut clenched in disappointment when Maddie knocked and popped her head around the door.

"The movers will be done packing your things from the condo in the next hour."

He nodded. "Thanks, Maddie." After delivering the pregnancy test kits, she'd offered to sort out removing his stuff. He knew she was desperate to make up for being tricked by Ashley into telling her Noah's whereabouts a few days before. He'd welcomed the chance to remove himself from Ashley's presence, ignoring her pleas for him to stay.

"You also have an email from Mr. Hartford with some property details. I'll print them out and make up a file for you." She left after he declined her offer of coffee.

He fired up his computer. Since he was here, he might as well get some work done. Ten minutes later, his cursor was still blinking in anticipation of his password.

The stone, which had lodged itself in his gut when Leia walked away from him, had eased a little. Enough for him to see he'd been slightly irrational about the whole thing. She needed time. He was prepared to give her time. Not long, because the idea of not seeing her again *soon* drove him more than a little nuts. But fuck if he was letting her walk away. He needed her more than he needed to breathe. It was as simple as that. The rest would work itself out.

He was about to reach for his phone to call her, when his cell buzzed to life.

He stared at the number on the screen and cursed. "Hey," he answered.

"Just about to have my third drink. Thought I better check in before I got too hammered to remember your phone number. I can keep going if you're running late?" his PI drawled. From past experience, Noah knew the guy would remain sharp even after several neat bourbons.

"Listen, something's come up. Can we reschedule?"

"Sure, it's your dime. But I thought you'd want to know what I found out sooner rather than later."

Noah's temple throbbed as he pressed the phone closer to his ear. "What did you find?"

"Your girl wasn't his first victim. Also someone dedicated a lot of time and money to cover it up."

Noah stumbled to his feet, his instincts screaming at him. He didn't bother to tell him to elaborate because his PI was paranoid about revealing too much over the phone. "Stay put. I'm on my way."

FOUR

"I've made reservations at Pietro's for eight this evening."

Leia didn't want to pull herself out of the fog surrounding her. The fog numbed her. Made her not have to think about the next second, the next minute. Thinking meant remembering. Remembering brought sharp, blistering pain to her chest. Fog was good. She snuggled in deeper.

"Leia."

That tone again. The one that made her feel like a disobedient subordinate. One he owned through and through and enjoyed controlling.

Snyder looks at you like you're his private possession.

Leia froze, Noah's words clanging through her head. She'd rejected the observation at the time. Now, it imbedded in her consciousness, and she couldn't dismiss the remark. She shivered, despite the sun blazing down on the lounger she'd spread out on in her private solarium, the farthest point from Warren's wing of the mansion. Had someone ramped up the air-conditioning?

She grabbed the remote, lowered the jazz funk she'd been using to drown out her thoughts and faced Warren. Even though it was the weekend, he was dressed in his customary Savile Row suit, complete with waistcoat, pinstriped tie, cufflinks and polished brogues. His hair was combed neatly enough to pass a military dress code test. She looked away and inwardly grimaced at the calm perfection she'd once aspired to.

"I'd rather not go out tonight, Warren."

He took another step forward and she caught a hint of his expensive cologne. It was chilling and impersonal, nowhere near Noah's potent, intoxicating scent.

Noah...

God, it hurt just thinking his name.

"We don't always get to choose life's experiences. I'm hoping the idea of dinner with me isn't one of the less pleasant ones? Especially as it's at your favorite restaurant?"

She turned the music off. "Is this some sort of life lesson?"

"If you want it to be." He strolled forward in that controlled, calculated way of his and paused at the foot of the lounger.

Slowly, his gaze raked over her, and she shivered again. She still wore Noah's college T-shirt but had changed into a pair of dark blue leggings after a hundred-lap swim this morning. She saw Warren's eyes linger on the Vassar logo before they rose to hers.

"If it's any consolation, I think you made the right decision, my dear. Now you need to move on quickly. Excise the wound before the infection sets in." His eyes dropped back to the logo. When she realized they lingered on her breasts, she folded her arms.

"Why did you come to Noah's place with *her*?"

The question had swirled through her mind since yesterday. Once they'd arrived home, all she'd wanted to do was retreat to a dark corner, away from the harrowing reality of what she'd done. Despite knowing she was only prolonging the agony, she'd slept in Noah's shirt. She was nowhere near ready to let it go yet.

But in the clear light of day she had questions. Ones she couldn't shy away from any longer. "Did you know who she was before the airport yesterday?"

"No. She came to see me yesterday morning. When I became aware of the brevity of Miss Maitland's news, I concluded that you shouldn't be left to face it on your own. I came because you needed my protection."

"You mean you didn't trust me to deal with this my own way."

"You dealt with it your way. I just wanted to make sure you were presented with the unsullied facts."

"Well, you certainly did that."

His eyes gleamed. "You know sarcasm isn't a trait I admire, my dear. It's a poor defense mechanism used by the uncouth. If you want me to think you're in control of your emotions, do better."

"Maybe I've discovered that giving my emotions free reign isn't a bad thing after all. Did you stop to think about that?"

"Of course. I factored that in, which is why I gave you twenty-four hours to...wallow. But you need to get yourself together. We have another board meeting early tomorrow. And the unresolved subject of your stepfather still requires our attention. Had you returned home on Friday night, we would have made progress." Again that chiding tone but coupled with something else. A hint of possessiveness. Recognizable now because it was amplified a thousand times with a single glance or word when it came from Noah.

This time her shiver engulfed her whole body. "I haven't forgotten what's at stake."

"Good." He tugged at the expertly pressed cloth of his trousers and sat down beside her. "Besides the...emotional aspects of all this, I wanted to remind you of your corporate responsibility. Nothing can jeopardize what we've spent years building, Leia. We're so close. It would be a shame to do something foolish and risk everything." He gave a single shake of his head. The move was so alien to the Warren she knew that her sharp reply froze in her throat. "I'm beginning to think I shouldn't have allowed you to go on this trip."

She jerked away from him. "*Allowed* me? I'm twenty-three years old, Warren."

He barely blinked at her outburst. "But in some aspects you're still a child, a novice at certain things."

"You really believe that, don't you? Or do you just want me to remain a child? Frozen and helpless at seventeen?"

A look curled through his eyes, but his eyelids descended, shielding it from view. A chill whispered over her. She whipped her legs off the lounger and turned sideways.

"I would never wish you helpless." There was a thread of hurt in his voice that made her feel bad. But it wasn't enough to wash away the anger at what his description of her made her feel.

"Then don't treat me like a child. I'm no longer the broken person you brought home five years ago."

Warren turned toward her, his spine straight and his face somber. "I couldn't be more proud of the progress we've made if I tried. But I wish *you* to not lose sight of that."

"I won't."

"So will you accompany me to dinner? Pietro is holding our usual table."

Leia wanted to refuse. But she didn't want to give Warren the satisfaction of thinking she would be spending another evening wallowing. And if she didn't go out, she knew she would do exactly that. Besides, the idea of not having to think about Noah constantly as she had been the last twenty-four hours, was a welcome thought.

Left on her own, she would wonder if Ashley had managed to talk her way back into his life. If they were, even now, considering names for their child. Another arrow pierced her heart. Over and over that look on Noah's face, when Ashley made her announcement, flashed into her mind.

He may not have planned it, but the idea of a child meant something to him. It was that look on his face, which had gutted her most of all.

He'd been ripped away from her before she'd had time to absorb the fact that she'd fallen in love with him. Drowning in tears in the middle of the night, she'd consoled herself by thinking what she'd done was for the best. She'd never have to face the tough discussion of whether he wanted a family at some distant point in the future. It was better this way. The burn might be too much to bear right now, but eventually she would forget him.

She had to.

"Yes, I'll come to dinner," she replied to Warren.

"Good." About to rise, he paused, leaned in close and pressed his lips against her temple. Again, his chilling scent engulfed her.

Long after he'd left the solarium, she sat, wishing the scent was a different one.

And contemplating the possibility that it was time to move out of Warren's house.

"If we don't leave now, we'll be late for our reservation."

"I'll be right there." She slid her platform heels on and glanced at herself one last time in the hallway mirror. She would need to decide soon whether to shave that patch of hair again or let it grow. She resisted the urge to caress that part of her head the way Noah did, and faced Warren. "I can't find my phone. Have you seen it?"

Warren glanced at his watch. "I haven't. If you need to make a call you can use mine."

She refrained from telling him that wasn't the point and smoothed a hand over her forest green sleeveless dress.

Her firm resolve had wobbled many times before she got dressed. As she stood in the shower, indulging in another crying jag, *wallowing* had seemed a far better alternative to making meaningless conversation with Warren just to prove a point. But she knew her former guardian wouldn't let her off that easily.

In the car, he shrewdly engaged in conversation that would demand more of an effort than monosyllabic answers from her.

All the same, by the time they pulled up to the restaurant in West Palm Beach, she was a heartbeat away from instructing the driver to take her back home. She gritted her teeth and stepped out of the car. The urge to prove she was strong enough not to fall apart from a relationship that had lasted less than a week, battled with the need to bawl her eyes out. Strength won. Her sole aim for indulging in the IL trip had been to have a no-strings-attached fling. She'd fucked that up spectacularly of course, had fallen in love before they'd barely exchanged more than a few pertinent details about each other.

But that didn't mean her life was over.

She sucked in a breath and let Warren walk her into the Michelin-star restaurant.

Pietro's greeting was loud and effusive. Discretion had never been the portly Italian's strong point, but the food here was great enough to make his customers overlook his boisterous mannerisms.

"A bottle of your favorite Grand Cru to start the evening off, *bellissima*?" Pietro asked, once they were seated by the window.

Leia started to shake her head and changed her mind. Getting drunk might be one way to numb the relentless pain. "Sure. Red, please."

She ignored Warren's microscopic frown.

"*Va bene*. And for you, Mr. Snyder? Your usual sparkling water?" Pietro enquired with a slightly more restrained smile.

Warren nodded and the Italian left them, returning moments later with their drinks. She took a healthy sip and saw another frown cross Warren's face.

"I really wish you wouldn't drink, my dear."

"I really wish you would. Maybe then you'd get off my case every once in a while," she snapped before she could stop herself. Not that she wanted to. "Look, you've done your concerned guardian thing. Just...let me deal with what's happening to me in my own way, okay?"

"Drinking is not the answer. Need I remind you of how indulging in alcohol changed your life?"

The stem of the wineglass she'd been slowly twirling trembled and a drop splashed onto the white linen tablecloth. Before she could stop them, tears sprang into her eyes and spilled down her cheeks. Angrily, she wiped them away. "Tough love, Warren? Is that what this is supposed to be?"

"I will not watch you regress into destructive behavior because of him." For the first time in her life she saw animated emotion in Warren's eyes. Emotion that looked very much like anger.

The shock of it held her speechless for several seconds.

"*Him*?" her voice trembled. She clenched her fist on the table. "You can say his name, Warren. And *Noah* isn't the reason I'm drinking," she half-lied and drained half her glass in one hefty gulp.

Warren remained silent for several minutes, his disquieting gaze resting on her. "Forgive me, my dear. It temporarily slipped my mind that there is another subject in this whole misjudged situation that must be painful for—"

"I don't want to talk about that. And the situation wasn't misjudged. I entered it with my eyes wide open. I don't regret anything." The hell she was suffering now might be unbearable, but the four days she'd spent with Noah had been the best of her life.

Warren was stopped from replying when the headwaiter approached. Leia chose a random dish that she had no intention of eating and drank more wine.

Warren turned the conversation to business, and she participated enough to keep him from sending her those narrow-eyed looks. They were at the coffee stage, or rather Warren was, while she finished the bottle, when his phone vibrated. Knowing he was about to ignore it because he never answered his phone at the table, she waved him away. "Answer it. There's hardly anyone left in here. And I'm heading to the ladies' room."

She stood and swayed. Her vision wove in and out, and she flattened her hand on the table to steady herself. When she felt stable enough, she straightened and glanced out the window.

A middle-aged guy stood on the sidewalk, peering at a gadget in his hand. Her vision wove out again. When it cleared, he was gone and only her reflection stared back at her. Her eyes were huge, haunted pools that screamed her pain so clearly, her stomach dropped. Quickly she looked away and glanced at Warren when his phone started vibrating again.

"For God's sake, answer your phone, Warren. It could be important." She grabbed her tiny purse and tucked it under her arm, intent on escape. She'd taken a couple of steps when she heard Warren's answer.

"King, how did you get my number?"

Leia turned around so fast, her head swam. Her purse dropped to the floor. She stumbled back to the table, her breath locked in her lungs.

"No. I will not." Warren's voice was icier than she'd ever heard it. He ended the call and placed his phone back in his pocket.

"Warren?"

"Are you ready to leave?" The modulated tone was firmly in place.

"I know that was Noah. What did he want?" The tremble was back, and she didn't even have the strength to hate herself for it. All she wanted was to know why Noah had called Warren.

"To speak to you."

"And you decided to answer on my behalf?" Anger and the alcohol swirling in her bloodstream made her voice emerge louder than she'd intended.

"Calm down, my dear—"

"No, I will not calm down. Tell me exactly what he said. Right now."

Warren stared down his nose at her, his silence meant to repudiate her for her outburst. She opened her mouth to demand an answer and heard a discreet cough behind her. Balling her fists to keep from letting loose another outburst, she glanced over her shoulder.

Pietro stood behind her, a phone clutched in his hand. "Miss Michaels, a call has come through to you on the restaurant phone from a Mr. King? Do you wish to take—?"

She lunged up and grabbed the phone before he'd finished speaking. "Noah?" She squeezed her eyes shut at the breathless desperation in her voice, then took a deep breath. "What do you want?"

"For you to answer your phone when I call you." His voice was a lethal blade, slicing away any hope that he'd softened since his callous demand for her to get out of his condo yesterday.

She licked her lips and momentarily regretted her free hand with the wine. "I haven't seen my phone since I left your...since yesterday morning. Have...have you seen it?"

"Have I seen your phone?" he asked with a touch of incredulity that made her cringe.

"Yes...I think I may have left it behind."

Silence.

"Noah?"

"No, I don't have your goddamn phone. If I did, I wouldn't be demanding you answer your calls, would I?"

She felt foolish. "Oh, umm, no." Clearing her throat, she tried to focus. "You haven't said why you're trying to reach me."

"I will. As soon as you come outside."

Her gasp drew Warren to his feet. Pietro, who'd been retrieving her purse from the floor, straightened in concern.

"*Outside*? You're *here*?" She hurried to the window, her breath fogging the cool glass as she searched for him.

Dressed in black jeans and a black T-shirt, he leaned against his Maserati. Long legs crossed, Noah stared straight at her. His eyes held none of the heated possessiveness she'd come to crave. Only a chilled glance that was no less domineering.

He held her gaze for a full minute, then he conducted a slow appraisal of her body through the window. When his scrutiny reached her legs, she imagined that his nostrils flared, but she could've been deluding herself. His eyes gave nothing away when they reconnected with hers.

"Come out, Leia. Now."

Heart hammering, she swallowed. "I...okay."

"Oh, and Leia?"

"Yes?"

"Leave your lapdog behind. I didn't come inside specifically because I don't trust myself to be within decking distance without flattening him. If you bring him outside, all bets are off. Are we clear?" The question was soft but filled with a menace that made her shiver.

"Yes, Noah."

FIVE

Noah watched her walk out of the restaurant. The relief he'd felt when he heard her voice after a day and a half of trying to reach her, drowned him all over again. He barely controlled himself from grabbing her and demanding answers. He kept his cool until she stopped several feet away from him.

"Hi," she said.

Hi. Like they were casual acquaintances. Like he hadn't spent four solid days last week branding himself on her. Like he hadn't spent Friday night turning her ass red and her tight little cunt sore enough to make him wonder if she'd ever walk straight again.

Yeah, he'd done all of that. And she'd still walked away from him. To her, he may well be the most casual of acquaintances. The rock-hard stone, which he hadn't managed to shift from his gut since Saturday morning, grew spikes and churned harder into him as he stared at her.

A part of his brain registered that this was the first time he was seeing her without some form of leather on her body. But she didn't look any less incredible in the tight green dress that displayed her stunning legs.

She fidgeted under his stare. He hid a grim smile. Now that he knew she hadn't been avoiding his calls, that she was safe and not in the clutches of her psycho stepfather, he could take his time to deliver the news he'd uncovered.

"Are you going to say something, Noah, or is this going to be a staring contest?"

Ballsy. Fuck, how he loved that about her.

He started to answer and stopped, frowning when her slight slur registered. Straightening, he stepped closer to her. The act of tilting her head to meet his gaze made her sway.

"What the fuck? Are you drunk?" he snapped.

She jumped and nearly dropped the tiny purse she carried. She tried to shake her head and swayed again. Anger roared through his veins. The thought of her in this state, alone with Snyder, dug hot pokers into his gut.

He yanked open his passenger door. "Get in."

"Why? Where are we going?"

"To get some coffee inside you. I'm not having a conversation with you when you're clearly drunk."

"We can get coffee here. I'm...I'm sure Pietro wouldn't mind..."

Looking over her head, he saw Snyder approaching the door, those lizard-cold eyes on them. Noah's palms tingled from the urge to cause harm. "No. We can't. Get in the car, Leia."

Her gaze lurched from him to the bucket seat, and a tiny part of him dared her to refuse him. Right then, nothing would've pleased him more than to bend her to his will, make her feel a fraction of the turmoil going on inside him. But she moved, swayed to him and grabbed the door to steady herself.

He cursed under his breath and slammed the door shut the moment she was seated.

Snyder was approaching as Noah walked round to the driver's seat. The other guy must have sensed that he was on precarious ground. Whatever he'd been about to say died on his lips, and he changed course to the town car parked on the curb.

Noah got in. "Seatbelt," he snapped.

Once she obeyed, he gunned the engine and accelerated away from the restaurant. He breathed in deep to calm his nerves. When her perfume filled every pore in his body, he dragged a hand through his hair.

He knew he was transmitting the vibes his ex-shrink had once jokingly referred to as his Asshole-Alpha mode. And he wasn't in the mood to turn it off. He sped through a yellow light, ignoring the blaring horns of a slow moving car when he overtook it with a few feet to spare.

"I'd like to arrive at wherever it is you're taking me intact. If you want to kill yourself, please do it in your own time."

He didn't ease off the gas until he was forced to at a red light. Gritting his teeth, he glanced at her. She faced forward, her hand white around her purse. He reached over, took the purse from her and threw it on the back seat. When she glared at him, he raised an eyebrow. "What did you say to him?"

"To who?"

"Snyder. Before we left."

She sent him a sideways glance. "Does it matter?"

"Not even a motherfucking little bit." He revved the engine and savored the angry roar of the powerful car beneath him. "I was just making conversation."

"If you want to make conversation, tell me where we're going. And why you've been calling me."

"We're going to the best coffee place I know in West Palm Beach. To sober you up before I attempt *rational* conversation."

She squinted at the dashboard, then blinked his way. "It's nearly midnight, Noah."

"What's your point exactly?" He eased away from the traffic light and turned left onto a street that held a row of trendy bars and coffee shops.

"My point is, I have to be up early to attend a board meeting, so I need to get a good night's sleep."

"A good night's sleep, huh? Tell me, Leia, how did you sleep last night?" he asked softly.

"What? Why are you asking me that?"

He swung the car onto a side street and parked in the employee area behind a one-story building. Killing the engine, he turned to her, sliding a hand behind her headrest.

"Tell me you slept like a fucking baby last night after you walked away from me." His smile felt like it was carved from granite. Moving his hand, he caught a strand of hair between his fingers and caressed its silkiness. "Tell me that so I can congratulate you. Or call you a fucking liar."

"Noah..."

"Or tell me you stayed awake, your gut turning to stone every time you thought you'd never see me again. Tell me *that* so I can accommodate the fact that you're a tiny little bit human."

Her eyes widened and her breath rushed out between shocked, parted lips. "What good would that do either of us?" she whispered.

"It would make me feel a helluva lot better knowing I wasn't crazy. That I didn't spend last week losing my head over a heartless bitch."

A deep tremble shook her body. She looked down and locked her fingers together. Noah waited for her to speak, for her to tell him everything that had happened in the last thirty-six hours had been a mistake.

He stared at her exquisite profile, her perfect creamy skin, and smashed down the need to grab her.

Finally, she sniffed and raised her head. "Are we going to get this coffee? If not, I'd like to go home, please."

The spikes in his gut grew longer, sharper, until his whole body flamed with excruciating pain. He continued to stare at her for another full minute before he yanked his door open and stepped out.

What the hell was he doing trying to rationalize a woman's behavior? He'd needed therapy after being dragged through the fucking quagmire because of one woman. And he was stupid enough to be asking for more pain?

He slammed his door and stalked to the back entrance that led inside *Red's*. Inputting the code, he entered. He heard Leia's heels clicking on the asphalt as she followed him.

Passing two storage rooms and the kitchen area, he walked into the large bistro, which during the day and evening teemed with customers looking for the best lobster bisque and crab club sandwich in Miami.

"I thought that was you."

He turned toward the voice and saw Rita Mancini, or *Red*, as her customers called her because of the short, spiky mane she sported. She nodded at the security camera above the bar that showed the parking lot and other parts of the bistro.

"Hey, Red. You're closing?" he asked when he saw the stacked chairs on top of tables.

She raised an eyebrow. "It's nearly midnight, buddy, I've been shut for over an hour, and I have to be up in four hours to open up again."

Leia entered, and he heard her footsteps slow. Red looked from her to him, a question on her face.

"Can I trouble you for two of your best coffees? If you need to go, I'll make sure the place is locked up tight before we leave."

"Firstly, all of my coffees are my best. And secondly, you own a huge chunk of this place, so you don't have to reassure me that you'll secure it." Again, her shrewd eyes darted to Leia and back to him. "Two coffees, extra-large, coming right up."

"Can you throw in a bottle of water, too? Thanks."

He knew his smile missed its target by a mile. Red nodded anyway and set up a table by the middle set of French doors that led to a wooden deck, which served as an extra seating space during opening hours. Beyond the doors, the waters of the marina glinted under the lights strung up along the walkway.

When Red walked away to get their coffees, he pulled out the nearest chair for Leia and took the seat opposite. "Sit."

She sat, her arms resting on the table between them. Tense silence stretched, broken by the hissing of the industrial-sized coffee machine Red had switched on.

Eventually, Leia cleared her throat. "So, you part own this place?"

Noah nodded.

"I thought your investments were much larger and riskier than a bistro?"

"Red and I...we have a little history," he replied, and shrugged. "But sentiment aside, this is still a good business that earns a healthy profit."

Red had left her birthplace of New York under a cloud, just like him. An ex-attorney with a client base that included senators, media moguls and rock stars, she'd wielded more power than some people deemed wise. A couple of people had done something about it. He wasn't ashamed to admit that his kinship with her past had been the drawing power for him choosing to invest in her business.

"How far back do you two go?" Leia asked.

He watched her fingers playing over the hair above her ear. He gritted his teeth. "You want to make small talk, here's a question for you. I seem to be missing a T-shirt. You know anything about that?"

A guilty blush crept over her face and leaked down her neck. "I...I didn't think you would miss it."

"You thought wrong. I'm aware that we weren't together long enough for you to know that it's more than just a T-shirt to me. Maybe if you'd stuck around, you would've found out. Or maybe I should be counting my lucky stars that I got a clean escape."

Her flinch made his jaw clench harder. "A clean escape?"

"You've proved so far that not only are you a faithless liar, you're also a nifty little thief."

She glared at him. "I'm neither of those things! I realize you're upset—"

He laughed.

She glared harder and raised her chin in cute defiance.

Noah shook his head. "You realize I'm *upset*? Why would I be upset? You had a chance to be mine. You *promised* me you were mine, but you walked away the moment things got a little sticky. Well, now I'm free to fuck any woman I choose. Hu-the-fucking-ray to me." He looked at his watch. "In fact, there's a little club I know not far from here. Once we're done with our little chat, I might swing by, find a willing, *baggage-free,* piece of ass for the night. While you're lying in your cold, faithless bed, you can think about me, pounding my cock into another woman's pussy, making her scream as loud as you did—"

"Stop!"

"Is that too much for you, baby?" he asked softly.

"You don't need to be an asshole, Noah." The plea was laced with anger. Looking down, he saw her nails digging into her palm.

Good.

He smiled. "This was never going to be pretty, baby. I don't play fair and I can't promise that I won't tear chunks out of you every time I see you."

"You can actively choose not to."

"Really? Where's the fun in that? I've never aspired to be the strong, silent type. Pissed and very vocal is more my speed. Now, about my T-shirt."

"Is it worth me saying that I never intended to hurt you?"

"Fuck, no. Intention or not, harm was done. And I'm fucking, hugely pissed. *My T-shirt*?"

"I...I'll have it couriered to your condo tomorrow."

"You could do that, but I don't live there anymore."

"What?"

"You're not deaf, Leia."

Questions flitted over her expressive face as she stared wide-eyed at him. A couple of times she opened her mouth to ask them but then shook her head. Noah knew his caustic behavior had made her wary but perversely, he wanted her to ask. Because asking meant she was still interested in his life. In him.

When she opened her mouth for the third time, he held his breath.

"Two coffees and a bottle of water, on the house." Red set their order down in front of them.

Noah nodded thanks without taking his eyes off Leia, who had better manners and smiled at Red.

"I'll leave you two to it, then."

His friend retreated and a minute later, he heard the back door close and the motorcycle she rode gun to life.

"You have a question, spit it out."

She drank half of the water, then picked up her cup. Her eyes caught his as she took a sip. A new tension drifted across her face. He didn't need a crystal ball to guess where her thoughts had veered.

They were alone. In a place with enough surfaces to accommodate any type of fucking either of them chose to initiate. The thought hadn't escaped him. And as much as he'd wanted her to believe that spiel he'd given a moment ago about finding a willing fuck tonight, there was only one woman his cock was interested in. And she was sitting less than three feet from him.

She drank a few more gulps and cleared her throat. "Umm...where...where are you staying? I mean, where would you like me to send your T-shirt?"

"You don't want to know why I've moved out of my condo?"

"It's really none of my business."

A hurt-laced dart arrowed between his ribs. "Right. Of course not."

She set the cup down with a thump.

"What do you want from me, Noah? You told me she had no hold on you. Turns out you were wrong. She has the *ultimate* hold on you. I'm trying to do the right thing and all you can do is condemn me for it?"

"The right thing by whose standards?"

"By normal human beings'!"

"That's just another fucking excuse! People deal with broken relationships and the fallout from them all the time. So yeah, mine's fucked up beyond description. The bottom line is I thought *we* had an understanding. We accept each other the way we are. The rest is background noise. Or at least it was supposed to be. You were supposed to take me, just me, no one else. I was supposed to take you *as you were*. I was even prepared to tolerate Snyder, as long as he stayed out of my fucking way."

"It's not that simple, Noah."

"Yes. It. Is."

"If you truly believe that, then I'm not sure I even want to contemplate being with you."

His sluggish heart picked up its pace. "Tell me that means you've thought about it? That you haven't written us off?" The hopeful words spilled out before he could stop them.

"I know you think I am, but I'm not a heartless bitch capable of turning my emotions on and off at will. Everything I felt for you when I woke up on Saturday morning is still there. But that doesn't mean I can ignore reality, or my feelings about what's happening here." She paused. "But for the sake of conversation, if you want to tell me why you've moved out, I'd like to know."

He forced himself to release his stranglehold on the cup. Her words swirled through his head and he was sure he was missing something. Something important. But fuck if he could think straight in the midst of hating himself for wanting her as much he did, for barely managing to keep seated when he wanted to bend her over the barstool, bury himself in her wet pussy and let the rest of the world go to hell. He shook his head and forced sanity back.

"Ashley needed a place to stay. I gave her the condo."

Several emotions flitted across her face. "So you confirmed it? She's really pregnant with your baby?" The words were hushed.

"Yes, she's pregnant. Whether it's mine or not is yet to be determined, so you might want to hold off on the congratulations."

Her eyes darkened, but they stayed on his long enough for him to determine that the alcohol was wearing off. Long enough to once again get the sensation that he was missing something when a dart of pain clouded her eyes, right before she lowered them.

She drained her cup and set it down in the middle of the table. "Let's get this over with. Why did you want to see me?"

"My PI found out some things yesterday that I thought you should know."

"*Your PI?* You mean you still went to the appointment?"

"Once he called me with the info he found."

"What info?"

Noah thought about how to play this without alarming her. If his PI's investigation turned up something other than what Noah suspected, he would've alarmed Leia for nothing.

"Something we can possibly use to track Willoughby down." She opened her mouth but he shook his head. "Before I tell you, I need you to tell me about your stepfather. Every single thing you can remember from the moment he walked into your life."

SIX

The moment Noah confirmed Ashley's pregnancy, Leia's heart had dropped to her stomach and stayed there, a heavy ball of steel that refused to beat properly. At the mention of her stepfather, her world greyed further.

Stephen Willoughby was the last person she wanted to talk about. Hell, talking was the last thing she wanted to do, period. Retreating to the numb cocoon she'd been in this afternoon was a much more attractive prospect.

"Leia!"

"Do we have to do this right now?"

"Yes. The quicker I have all the information I need, the better the PI will be able to work."

Right, he expected her to conduct a rational conversation when she was mentally gutting herself for wishing his ex out of existence. "You're forcing me down a road I really don't want to go, Noah."

His mouth curved in a parody of a smile. "It's a good thing I know you're made of much tougher stuff than a quick trip down memory lane. Just give me the bare facts, and you'll be free to go."

She cleared her throat and wished she hadn't finished her coffee so quickly. Her haze hadn't cleared, but she was sobering up enough to feel the sharp knife of loss every time she looked at Noah. To remember that the previous times she'd discussed her father's death, her mother's suicide...her rape, he'd held her, comforted her. He'd made her feel like she wasn't alone, that those strong arms and broad shoulders would be hers to lean on whenever the monsters threatened to suck her under.

Now, he wanted her to relive the tormenting memories while he stared coldly at her from across the table. Her heart wrenched and she shook her head. "I can't," she whispered.

"Leia."

Trembling, she leaned forward, her every sense straining for the warmth she'd walked away from. The warmth she would give anything for now. "Please, Noah, the memories are too painful."

The coldness dissipated, and the man she yearned for appeared. "He needs to be caught. You know that, don't you?"

She nodded. "Yes, Noah."

The two words made him freeze. Slowly, his face closed up again. "Then try."

Anguish biting deep, she fell back into her chair.

With nothing else to focus on in the semi-darkness around them, Noah loomed large, his domineering presence demanding her attention so effortlessly that her gaze shifted back to him against her will.

Her insides twisted as she forced herself to remember.

"My mom kept horses when I was growing up. We had a ranch in Montana. We'd visit in summertime. I liked riding, and my mom...she was different there. Happy." She curled her fingers around the empty coffee mug and sucked in a sustaining breath. "After my dad died, she wanted to spend more time in Montana - I don't think she could face staying in the same house after he was gone. I was out there for a couple of weeks, but I had school. So I came back, and she stayed behind."

Noah frowned. "She left to you here to deal with your father's death on your own?"

She shrugged. "I think Miami was too much for her, but I wanted to come back. I felt closer to my dad here. She understood that, just as I understood that she had to do things her own way. I'd like to say my mom was a strong woman, but she leaned on my dad even more than I did. Anyway...she stayed in Montana for three months. When she returned, she was married to Stephen."

He frowned. "So they knew each other for only a few months before she married him?"

With each second that passed the memories sobered her up. The raw agony of knowing her mother had married a rapist, made her fingers clench around the cup.

Gritting her teeth, she forced herself to reply. "Yes. He bred horses too and owned the ranch next to ours. To be honest, Noah, I didn't really care who he was. At the time he seemed to make my mom happy. When she was happy, she was less problematic, so I was relieved. Selfish, I know. But that was the way it was. Did I think he was a gold digger? It crossed my mind once or twice, when the tension between them started. Some of their fights were about money. But until what happened... happened—" She swallowed, unable to suppress a shiver. "I thought he was more of a pervert than anything else." A sick pervert who would later rip away her chance to have children...a chance to find happiness with Noah.

A rock lodged itself in her throat. She pushed the cup away and grabbed the water. "Are we done with the questions?"

"Almost. Did he ever talk about any family or business in Montana?" Noah's voice was gruff, but the cold look in his eyes remained.

A headache began to pound beneath her skull as her mind and soul rebelled at being forced to relive her bleak past. "He had a distant cousin who showed up one Christmas, I think. Barry or Gary or something like that."

Noah nodded. "Remember anything else?"

One hand rubbed at her temple. "No. Jesus, what the hell does it matter?"

"Because you're most likely not the first person he's assaulted."

Her stomach turned to stone. "What?"

"The PI is chasing down a few allegations, but he's been stonewalled a couple of times."

"Which means what, exactly?"

He shrugged. "It could be nothing, probably a pencil pusher flexing a little muscle, but my guy thinks someone is being paid to keep certain files from being opened."

The room spun as she shook her head. "I don't understand. Stephen has already been in jail for...attacking me. He has no reputation to protect. Why would he pay money he probably doesn't have to keep his sordid past from coming out?"

"I didn't say it was Stephen behind this."

"You're saying someone else is trying to cover this up? Who and why?"

"Someone who has a lot to lose, I suspect."

She clutched the edge of the table. "You're scaring me. This doesn't make any sense."

His raw, incisive gaze slid over her face, making her feel every single heartbeat. He was reading her, gauging her reaction. Latent heat flickered in his eyes, overlaid with a seriousness that made her nape tingle.

"Your company's about to float shares on the stock market in a matter of weeks."

She gasped. "You know this, how?"

He shrugged but the underlying watchfulness didn't abate. "From experience, I know how those with huge financial stakes get jittery before a big deal goes live. Your company is a huge deal. A lot of people will be jittery right about now."

Her heart slammed into her ribs. "What are you saying?"

"I'm saying in a little over a month's time, your company's going to be worth a quarter of a billion dollars. I suspect every single member of your board is living on tenterhooks right about now. Some more than others."

She gasped as the penny dropped. "Warren. You mean Warren."

He nodded. "Besides you, he has the most to lose if anything goes pear-shaped."

"And why would things go pear-shaped? Everything is on track. Once due diligence is completed next week, the SEC will sign off on the paperwork. And what the hell does this have to do with my stepfather?" She shook her head. "I know you don't like Warren," she sucked in a deep breath at his raw snarl, "but you don't know him, not like I do."

"Obviously."

"Noah, don't do this. It's beneath you."

His eyes narrowed into cold ice chips. "What the hell do you see in that guy? How can you not see what I see when he's around you?"

"Please..."

"Fuck, Leia. The guy's a prick with a hard-on pointed at you and your money."

"Even if that were true, does that automatically make him a suspect for fraud? Or accessory to statutory rape? I've known him since I was a child. He's never done anything to hurt me."

His fist bunched. "Not yet."

She lurched to her feet. The sound of the chair scraping the floor filled the silent restaurant. "What you're implying is sick, Noah. You have to know that I won't accept it without any hard evidence. I just can't. I'm sorry." She brushed away tears she hadn't known were forming until they dripped down her cheek.

Noah stood and leaned over the table toward her. "Tell me you're not fucking crying over that asshole?" he snarled.

"Why does this mean so much to you? We broke up. Shouldn't you be more concerned about your relationship with Ashley and your *baby*?" she snapped, her insides twisting all over again at the reminder.

He straightened, his nostrils flaring as he glared down at her. "I thought you'd want to know, seeing as that bastard is still out there with you in his crosshairs. But all you want to do is to keep burying your head in the sand, isn't that right? What? You think ignoring the issue is going to make it disappear?"

She brushed at her wet eyes and glared right back. "Believe it or not, I've been thinking about the situation with my stepfather." Besides losing Noah, her stepfather's threat was her greatest nightmare. "The board thinks the best option is to pay him off."

"Are you fucking kidding me?" he growled.

She raised her chin at his derisive tone. "They think it's the quickest way to get rid of him. Information has a way of coming out, as you've just proved. If you know my company is set to float its shares, then most likely so does he."

"I seriously doubt that he and I move in the same circles."

"I didn't mean it like that. But assuming he's found out about the shares, I need to take action now."

"So you're going to reward a rapist and extortionist with fifty million dollars? Are you out of your fucking mind?"

"The alternative is to leave him to flood the internet with humiliating pictures of me, ruining my company's stock market announcement." She trembled at the thought.

"No fucking way am I going to let that happen."

The brevity in his voice slammed into her. She closed her eyes and basked in that protective heat for a second before she dragged herself out of it. When she opened her eyes, he was staring at her.

She knew it was foolish to ask, that she was leaving herself wide open for hurt, but she couldn't help herself. "Why do you care so much, Noah?"

"Because I'm finding it damned hard to let go of the fact that you belong to me. And no one harms what belongs to me." The censure and icy detachment had drained from his face. Raw possessiveness, which he'd stamped on her the very first moment they met, blazed from his eyes.

Her breath caught. That heavy weight of unhappiness started to lighten as hope teased her heart. But she knew she was fooling herself.

He grabbed her hand, and the plastic bottle crackled. "You will *not* pay that asshole off, do you hear me?" he rasped. "I promised I'd handle this for you and you're going to let me."

Temptation to let him take charge flooded her, but she rejected it. *Stay strong. Stay strong.* "Don't tell me what to do." She tried to snatch her hand away.

His grip tightened until the pressure stroked the edges of pain. "Did any of what I just said get through to you at all?" he rasped.

"Nothing has changed, Noah. Or rather, everything has changed. I thought I was strong enough to be with you, but I'm not."

His brows clamped together. "What the hell does that mean?"

"Don't you see? If I don't leave, all I would be doing is standing in your way."

"Stop speaking in fucking parables and tell me straight."

She forced the question out. "Did you see yourself one day as a father? Before Ashley dropped her bombshell?"

Confusion darkened his eyes. "I guess. Eventually. I'm not fucked up enough to think I wouldn't make an okay dad one day."

Anguish weakened her limbs. "You would be better than okay." She stopped and they stared at each other for an eternity. Then she asked the burning question. "So you want this baby?"

His confusion deepened. "If it's mine, then I don't have a choice but to *be* its father. It's not a responsibility I can walk away from."

"That's not what I'm asking. Do you want a baby? Did you ever want a baby, now or in the future?"

"Yes, I do. But I still don't understand—"

"I have to go, Noah." She fisted numb fingers.

He raked a hand through his hair. "Fuck it, Leia. What am I missing here?"

"Nothing," she tried to keep the bleakness from her voice. "You're not missing anything. I'm going home."

The confusion faded. The brutal Noah, who'd instructed her to leave his presence in sixty seconds yesterday, loomed large in the darkened bistro. She took a step back, then another. Self-preservation kicked in when he started to round the table toward her.

Fear of breaking down and going back on what she'd convinced herself was the best path, forced her feet to move faster.

"Where the hell are you going?" he demanded.

She broke into a run. The kitchen area was dark, but the automatic lights came on as she bolted into the room. Rushing to the door, she slammed on the long exit bar and stumbled into parking lot. Another light came on, throwing a spotlight on Noah's Maserati.

The futility of what she was doing hit her. She couldn't call a cab without her phone. And she wasn't stupid enough to wander unfamiliar streets at midnight.

She whirled as the door slammed, but Noah was already outside, stalking to where she stood, frozen.

One hand clamped around her waist, the other spearing into her hair. The bottle of water fell from her hand and rolled away.

At that hour of night, the warmth of the day had nearly dissipated. Cool air whispered around her legs and back. But her front was on fire, singeing from contact with this hard, angry, male.

"If I didn't know any better, I'd think you're saying you don't want to be with me because I'm about to become a father. Tell me I'm mistaken, Leia."

Her heart turned to stone. Which was curious considering she could've sworn it was bleeding away every drop of blood in her body.

The hand in her hair tightened painfully, twisted until her eyes stung with the pressure. His gaze demanded answers but his body reacted to hers, as inevitably as hers to his. Her temperature shot from zero to a million degrees in a split second, sizzling along every nerve ending and spiking straight between her legs. Her clit pulsed to hungry, demanding life. The reaction was so strong, she gasped.

And that was even before she felt his thickness against her belly. Even before his hands splayed over her ass to press her closer. Her hands skated over his hair-dusted forearms. The sensation of skin against skin made them both shiver. He exhaled harshly, and her eyes dropped to his lips.

God, she wanted to kiss him so badly she could taste it.

The hand in her hair knotted sharply. She winced.

He smiled. "Answer me."

Her fingers froze on his arms. She should push him away, step away from this need searing them both. But her body refused to obey. Not that Noah would let her go. His grip on her was molten steel, fusing her to him.

No. The only way to get him to release her would be to answer his question.

So she told him the truth. "Yes, Noah. I'm afraid your impending fatherhood is going to be a problem for me."

SEVEN

He stared at her as if she'd grown three heads and a forked tail.

"Say that again."

She steeled her spine and raised an eyebrow. "You asked me whether I was deaf earlier. Right backatchya, Mr. King."

His eyes narrowed to tiny slits, his gaze eating into her as he tried to work her out.

She kept her composure, even as Noah's breath turned harsh with anger and disbelief.

"Let me go, Noah." There was only so much bodily contact she could withstand before she broke down and begged for scraps like a pathetic sex-starved groupie.

In answer, he shoved her closer to his car, yanked her head back so her mouth, chin and neck were exposed to him. His teeth bared and her heart thundered. The memory of those white teeth on her neck...her ass...her clit, roared through her bloodstream like a potent narcotic drug. Her pussy flooded.

She knew he smelled her disgraceful need, even as she prayed he'd ignore it.

Please. Please. Oh God, please.

His gaze raked her face, her mouth, the wild pulse beating at her throat. He inhaled her deeply, his nostrils flaring. "Do you know what happens to heartless bitches like you? Bitches who get wet at the thought of tearing a guy to shreds?" he whispered raggedly against her lips.

"I'm not...I don't want to be a—"

"They get their comeuppance from guys like me."

She shuddered hard. He smiled. A smile so deadly, her insides congealed. "Noah don't—"

He shook his head. "Oh no, baby. The time for those pleading, wide eyed *Noahs* has passed. Turn around." He released her so abruptly, she stumbled back and bumped into the hood.

Mouth dropping open, she glanced wildly around her. Beyond the pool of light bathing them, the rest of the lot was dark, silent.

"There's no one here to save you. Turn. *The. Fuck*. Around."

The animalistic authority in his voice had her heeding the command but she didn't move fast enough. He grabbed her waist, whipped her around to face his car, and pushed her forward. Her hands slammed onto the hood to break her forward momentum.

Before she could protest, his fingers were tugging at her hem. He dragged up her dress to her waist and smacked her ass half a dozen times in quick succession. Leia bit her lip through the stinging pain, too shocked to do anything but stay there and take it...and crave more. When he soothed the sting in that infinitely caring way of his that belied his bitterness, tears sprang to her eyes.

The realization that she'd hurt him to breaking point, and yet he still cared for her, made her heartache intensify.

"I'm sorry," she murmured, wanting to soothe him as he soothed her.

"I don't fucking believe you. Not anymore." Another set of smacks rained down on her ass. Her gasp of pleasure at each one seemed to set him off. He released a harsh breath after the last one and petted her longer between her punishments. Laying a hand on her ass, he whispered in her ear, "Do not move your hands from the hood. You're getting punished regardless of what you say or do, but you will get double if you disobey me."

Her arms trembled at the scathing words and she shut her eyes at the shameful need flaring wildly through her bloodstream. She wanted him anyway she could have him, and if punishment for keeping her innermost secrets intact was what it took to have Noah with her like this, then she'd grab it with both hands.

"I didn't hear an answer. It's been barely forty-eight hours, have you forgotten everything I taught you already?"

"I...Yes."

His hand moved from her ass, around her waist to the front of her panties. She held her breath in anticipation, but he stopped at the top line of her panties, his hand covering her belly. "Open your legs," he growled in her ear.

Sluggish with the lust raging through her, she didn't move fast enough. He kicked her legs apart, far wider than comfort allowed. Two fingers breached her panty line, slid through her wet heat and hooked deep inside her.

The hand around her throat tightened until she could barely squeeze oxygen into her lungs. Sensation fired though her, blurring her vision until her eyelids fluttered shut.

"Keep your eyes open. I want you to watch...feel every single thing I do to you."

Her eyes popped open and her gaze collided with his reflection on the windshield. His features were tortured, but he was just as turned on as she was, the blaze between them incandescent and destructive.

"Noah—"

"Do *not* fucking say my name," he snarled thickly.

He hooked his fingers deeper, almost lifting her off her feet. Pain exploded alongside pleasure. Leaving her poised on her tiptoes, he pumped his fingers five times. Then stopped. Her skin tingled with the precursor to release. She flexed her hips, half out of her mind with the need to come.

"You're not trying to fuck yourself into orgasm without my permission, are you?" he asked. "You think you deserve to come, baby? After destroying me like you have tonight?"

The thought that he intended to leave her hanging hadn't even occurred to her. Now it whizzed through her like super-amped electricity. Her mouth dropped open in shock.

His lips twisted in a macabre smile. "Now you're getting the idea." His hand left her throat. She almost begged him to put it back. But when he roughly palmed her breast, her sob died in her throat. He squeezed her tight, tugged painfully on the stiff peak until the pain in her pussy and her nipple connected in a blast of white-hot lightning.

Again he tortured her until she teetered on the brink of release, then stopped.

Pulling his fingers out of her tight wetness, he pressed them against her lips. "Savor your flavors, baby. Describe to me what it tastes like." He shoved two fingers into her mouth.

Biting back a frustrated sob, she sucked greedily, the wet sounds pulsing around the empty parking lot. She licked him clean, the tangy flavors adding to the heady joy of having those strong fingers in her mouth.

"How does it taste?" he crooned in her ear.

She swallowed and tried to speak around a throat clogged with desperation. "Umm...it's okay?"

He pulled his fingers out of her mouth. "Just okay? You sure? Are you certain you don't taste like Slippery Witch? Or Shamelessly Wet Heart-Breaker?"

The bitterness in his voice ripped at her heart. "What do you want from me?" she demanded brokenly. "You won't accept that I'm sorry, that I never meant to hurt you. What do you want?"

"What do I want? Right now, I want you on my tongue. I'm going to eat your faithless little pussy so good, you'll wish you never met me. Because after tonight, you'll never feel my mouth or my hands, or my cock inside you again, so treasure this punishment."

This time the sob broke out, a ragged little sound she tried to bite off but couldn't.

His warmth left her as he straightened, then crouched behind her.

Rough hands reached for her panties. He started to lower them, but with an impatient hiss, he tore them off before they were halfway down her legs. He threw the flimsy fabric on the hood. Her gaze landed on the tattered material, a brazen reminder that she was bare-assed, open to whatever Noah intended to do to her.

"Did you say you had a board meeting in the morning?" His question was deceptively soft as his large hands framed her ass. He parted the globes and her belly spasmed as his warm breath caressed the sodden space between. Her thighs shook with the effort to remain upright.

"Y...yes."

"Good. I'm going to make your ass so fucking sore, you won't be able to move tomorrow without thinking of me. Without knowing what being a bitch has earned you."

He rose.

She heard a distinctive *phlllt* sound of leather sliding through loops.

Her head whipped around, her heart jumping at the unbelievable sound.

At the visual confirmation of what was about to happen, her mouth dropped open in disbelief.

Noah's eyes gleamed with dark relish as he curled his belt in his hand. Hooded blue eyes met hers, hot and unforgiving. "Just so we're clear, do you remember what we talked about the first time we fucked?"

She nodded.

He glared.

"Yes," she enunciated in a shaky voice.

"Repeat it, baby. I want to hear the words," he ordered. He trailed the dangling black leather up her thigh and over her ass. Again and again.

The trembling became relentless, delicious anticipation firing in her bloodstream. "I say stop...you stop."

"Glad to hear you haven't forgotten everything."

She braced herself as he stepped back.

The first lash landed across both cheeks. "Ah! Oh God!" Her arms gave way, and she landed hard on her elbows.

One hand fisted her hair, and he pulled her up. "You better not make dents in my car, sweetheart." He let her go and delivered two lashes, quick and sharp.

Her gasps strangled as the crackle of plastic sounded behind her. A moment later, ice cold water dribbled down her ass and over the back of her thighs, soothing the raw stings. Relief poured through her as his hand spread the wetness over her hot skin.

After a minute, he set the bottle down beside her left hand. "If that falls over, you're getting triple the punishment. Understood?"

"Yes...N—" His name died in her throat as another lash flared across her butt. Her clit swelled, and her pussy clenched hungrily at the roughness ripping her in two. Wetness from her core dripped down her leg, her scent coating the sultry air.

Absently, she started to wonder whether her Ferragamos would be ruined beyond repair. The thought disintegrated under several more lashes. Shame crawled over her, but not enough to dissolve the ferocious need burning through her, or the promise of what was to come if she did as she was told.

Another two lashes and her sticky wetness ran down both thighs.

Noah started to reach for the bottle, stopped and hissed in disbelief. "Jesus, you're fucking dripping."

Her moan was half despair, half a plea for deliverance.

Bottle forgotten, he dropped the belt and crouched behind her. His hands wrapped around her thighs. "You're unbelievable, do you know that? You fucking reject me in one breath and cream like crazy for me in the other. Why, Leia?" he demanded harshly.

"I...I can't help myself," she stammered. "I want you...want this..."

Her essence dripped over his fingers and he trailed it up till he reached her outer lips. His thumbs pressed into the flesh beneath her labia. He groaned. The sound held so much ragged despair, she wanted to tell him to stop. That he should spare them both the agony of this torrid confrontation. But selfishness won over.

She wanted him more than ever, was certain she wouldn't be able to function if Noah didn't make her come soon. Like right now.

He was obviously gripped by the same fever because he gave another groan and replaced his fingers with his tongue. Greedily he lapped up her juices, his fingers biting into her thighs to hold her shuddering body still.

"*Fuck, fuck, fuck*, why do you taste so damn good? You left me, dammit, you're not supposed to taste so fucking incredible."

She tried to grind her pussy into his face, desperate for more than he was giving her. In light of Noah's bitter condemnation for her walking away, she'd never thought they'd end up like this. That she would get to feel his hands or mouth on her ever again. She wasn't about to let this incredible opportunity pass. But he was in no mood to be accommodating. His tongue lapped her clit with slow licks, swirled over the swollen bud before pulling it into his mouth for a meager second.

She growled in frustration.

"You don't like that?"

"Stop talking! Make me come. Please," she gritted, near desperate as her orgasm hovered just out of reach.

A hard slap against her core, brought tears to her eyes and even more wetness to her already dripping sex. Another came quickly on the heels of the first. And another.

Yes!

But as if he knew one more would send her over the edge, Noah stopped.

"You don't call the shots. You never did. What makes you think I'll allow you to order me around now?"

Tears flowed freely down her cheeks. She was a frantic second from rubbing herself to orgasm. "Please..." she whispered, broken.

"That's right. If you want to come, you're gonna have to beg way more than that."

She squeezed her eyes shut and struggled just to breathe. How could she have forgotten how insanely heightened sex with Noah could be?

"*Pleasepleaseplease*," she chanted, the words strung together into an incoherent jumble.

He feasted on her - teeth, mouth, tongue, fingers, dragging every last ounce of surrender from her. When he had her on the brink, he twisted around so his head and shoulders rested on the hood. He dragged her up and spread her over his face.

Splayed on top of his car, she shamelessly ground herself on Noah King's mouth until pleasure exploded through her system.

"Oh God!" She speared a hand through his hair and twisted helplessly against him. Her supporting arm gave way, and she screamed again as she arched out of control, certain she would crack her head on the windshield. But he caught her, steadied her with one hand between her breasts, and the other on her lower back and let her relax. Her forehead touched the cool glass, and her whole body melted against his car.

Still raining kisses on her ravaged core, he drew down her dress, and with one last kiss, covered her up. Rising, he gripped her waist and lifted her from the car. Her head drooped onto his shoulder. In the drowsy aftermath, Leia barely felt it when he deposited her in the seat and fastened her seatbelt.

He returned to the bistro, presumably to finish locking up, and emerged a minute later.

Without speaking, he slid into the car and gunned the engine.

The journey back started in total silence. The air felt thick with acrimony and the heavy scent of sex. Halfway home she glanced at his stony profile. Sensing her gaze, his hand tightened on the steering wheel. The warning made her look away. To his crotch, which bulged with a raging hard-on.

Treacherously, her mouth flooded with saliva and her breath locked in her lungs.

"You hungering for another lesson, baby? I'm happy to oblige. You can take a pick of the lamppost over there, or under the neon sign advertising boob jobs? Or hell, I can lick you to orgasm again on the hood at the next traffic light. But don't stare at my cock because it won't be going anywhere near your pussy ever again."

Face flaming, she averted her gaze. "Don't be vile." Her voice emerged as weak as her whole body felt. And her pussy throbbed with the need to have him fill her, hot and heavy and hard.

"You love me vile. Or you wouldn't be licking your lips right now."

Her hands shook before she clenched them in her lap. "Please don't be like this."

"You *made* it like this. I'm just playing by your rules, sweetheart. And you know what? Right about now, I'm beginning to wonder why I ever abandoned my Catch. Fuck. Release system. Maybe it's time to reactivate it."

"What are you saying, that you intend to fuck faceless strangers again?" The question emerged a jagged whisper.

"Why not? Emotionless fucking has its perks. And it sounds like a great life choice right about now."

"Noah—"

"I told you not to say my fucking name," he snarled.

"But...what about Ashley?"

"What about her?"

"Aren't you going to take her current status into consideration?"

His jaw clenched so hard she feared for his molars. "Her personal feelings matter very little to me."

"God, you're being so..."

"So...what?"

"So cruel."

"You didn't think that when you were begging me to make you come."

She opened her mouth, but no words came out. Her face burned at the smug mockery in his eyes. "I'm going to stop talking to you now."

"Fucking great idea."

He slammed on the gas and the Maserati shot forward.

They arrived at her house fifteen minutes later. The electronic gates swung open, but he stopped the car just inside the gates, his features frozen as he stared at the mansion. The guard who manned the gates started to come out of his cubicle. She waved him away.

When she realized Noah had no intention of driving her to the front door, she reached for the handle.

"Wait," he growled. Pulling a sticky note from the glove compartment, he scribbled on it. "This is my PA's number. Call her early tomorrow and arrange to drop off my T-shirt. She'll also let you know if you left your phone at my place."

She took the note and stared at the information. She'd googled King's Ransom in a moment of weakness and knew exactly where his offices were located. She could probably deliver his T-shirt personally after her meeting—

"Something wrong?" he demanded.

"Umm...no."

"Then get the hell out of my car."

EIGHT

Noah's concentration was shot to hell, and he wasn't even pissed off about it anymore. He'd passed pissed off at around ten this morning when one of his directors had fucked up a business deal and Ashley had left the tenth message for him to call her.

It was now gone midday, and he hadn't heard from Leia. Obviously his instruction for her to call *early* hadn't been explicit enough.

Or maybe she relished goading him to the point where he lost control like he had last night. He hadn't been able to stop himself from giving her the punishment they both craved. And fuck, had she come apart like a firecracker. The denotation still reverberated through him.

God.

His breath shuddered out as the scene replayed in his mind like damned stuck record. The noises she'd made as he'd taken his belt to her, the power and satisfaction that'd surged through him as he welted her ass good. As he dropped to his knees and worshiped her pussy, the sheer, fucking sweetness of her. That look of helpless surrender and ballsy defiance in her eyes when they were done. Images crowded his brain, leaching away any hope of concentration he had left. He could've fucked her hard and fast, right there and then on the hood of his car, and she would've let him.

So, why the hell hadn't he? His cock certainly didn't understand that insufferable decision one little bit - not when he'd been erasing the security tapes of them in Red's office, nor breathing in her incredible scent during the tense ride home.

He'd been rock hard for hours afterward. Rubbing one out hadn't helped. Thinking of Leia just made him harder. He'd eventually taken an ice pack to his groin for a full hour before his erection had abated.

Hell, he'd delayed shaving until the last possible moment this morning because he hadn't wanted to wash the scent of her pussy off his face. Even now, licking his lips, the memory of her taste lingered. One hand stroked his chin and played over his lips as the other passed over his re-energized hard-on. He groaned out loud as another shudder rammed him. Foolishly, he pressed his flesh. Stars exploded behind his eyelids. He was halfway to unzipping his trousers and stroking himself back to sanity when his private phone rang.

For several seconds, he stared blankly at the phone. Then he shook his head.

Jesus, he was losing his mind.

"Yes!"

"Whoa. Down boy. Who the hell pissed in your porridge?"

"I'll give you one guess." There were two but he wasn't about to admit it to his best friend.

Gabriel cursed. "What the hell did Ashley want?"

About to tell him, Noah hesitated. When he'd woken this morning, the first thing he'd felt was raw anger fused with anguish when he thought of Leia. The second emotion had been much more surprising.

Forced to think about having a child of his own, he hadn't been able to stem the mixture of elation and despair. As much as he hated Ashley, she carried a part of him inside of her. She was a bitch through and through, but she was a bitch carrying his child. There were no adequate words to relay that information to his friend.

"Christ, if you can't talk about it, then it must be worse than I thought. She hasn't framed you for murder, has she? Or did she give you a disease before you bailed out of NYC two years ago? Either way, I'll have your back if you want to send a hit squad after her—"

"You back in town?" Noah interrupted him.

"Yeah," Gabe said. "Got back late last night. Minus my possibly-soon-to-be-ex-girlfriend, I might add. And hell no, I don't want to talk about it. Drinks on Wednesday night at The Sphere? I'll round up the guys."

A refusal dangled on the tip of his tongue, then Noah mentally shrugged. He had to tell them soon enough. If not, his friends would snoop and harass until they found out what was going on. "Sure. Usual time."

"So you going to tell me what Ashley wanted?" his friend pressed.

"It can wait till we meet." Noah eyed the clock on his computer, a burning need to find out where the hell Leia was suddenly clawing through him. "I have to go."

He hung up and dialed La Carezza Inc. When he was informed that Miss Michaels was unavailable, his temperature spiked higher. He couldn't reach her by mobile because hers was sitting on his desk.

Slamming down the phone, he called another number.

"Do you have eyes on her?"

"She left her office twenty minutes ago. Looks like she's having one of those powwow lunches with a bunch of suits at a posh restaurant."

Noah stopped himself from asking for the name of the restaurant. The way he was feeling, he needed to *not* be in a public place when he confronted Leia Michaels.

"Have a message delivered to her from me...yeah, I know it's not part of our deal, but do it anyway. Sure, charge me. Yeah, I'll wait for you to find a pen." He stifled a curse, waited, then rattled off the message and ended the call.

Moderately satisfied and his world slightly saner, he pressed the intercom. "Maddie, I'd like to review my schedule for the week. And bring the real estate file from Hartford with you, please?"

He closed two major deals, and was in the middle of shortlisting the condos Hartford had sent, when Maddie buzzed him again at 2pm on the dot.

"If that's Miss Michaels, tell her to come straight in. And hold my calls for the next half hour."

"Er...Yes, Mr. King."

The door to his office swung open.

Leia entered and kicked the door shut. Noah realized he'd been holding his breath and released it.

Holy hell, she was so fucking beautiful. The memory of her grinding her sweet cunt into his face, plastered itself across his vision. His body revved up, forcing him to remain seated.

Let her come to him.

His gaze swept greedily over her, then conducted a slower journey. Her skirt suit would've been boring had it not been for its short length and the two-inch panels of leather running down both sides. Underneath her leather-trimmed jacket, she wore another one of those semi see-through tops. His fingers itched to undress her, spread her on the floor and pound his frustration into her.

Chunky jewelry draped her neck. On closer examination, he noticed faint finger marks on her throat. He'd done that. Left his imprint on her skin. The guilt he'd expected to feel never materialized as satisfaction tipped his lips. He may be as pissed as hell with her, but the idea of Snyder seeing those marks on her filled him with childish glee.

She slammed the piece of paper in her hand on his desk. "'*Be in my office at 2pm sharp or what I did to you with my mouth last night will feel like a Disney sing-along compared to what I'll do to you this time?'* Do you have any idea how I felt having this delivered to me during my lunch meeting?"

"I wanted to make sure you didn't mistake my intentions. I take it you read it out loud to your lunch companions?"

She gasped. "Are you insane? Of course I didn't!"

"Then I fail to see what you have to be embarrassed about."

"That's not the point. I was in a public place. Your note could've fallen into anyone's hands. Hell, the waiter smirked as he gave it to me so he most likely read it. And who was that guy who delivered the note? He wore a disgusting smirk too, by the way."

"A friend of mine."

Her fingers closed over the note and scrunched it into an angry ball before tossing it back onto his desk. "Oh, and he just happened to be in the neighborhood where I was having lunch?"

"Sure, let's go with that," he answered.

Her eyes narrowed. "You're having me followed, aren't you? That's how you knew where I was last night."

"Let's go with that too."

"I want it to stop."

"No fucking chance in hell."

"The deadline for delivering the blackmail money isn't till the end of the week. I hardly think Stephen's going to do anything stupid before then to jeopardize things."

Noah laughed. "Are you seriously trying to rationalize how a psychotic rapist's mind works? What do you think he's going to do when the deadline comes and goes and he doesn't get his money?"

A trace of apprehension slid over her face. "I can protect myself."

"Wake up and face reality, Leia. He's been in prison. And people like him, they don't get rehabilitated. He proved that by coming after you the second he was free. Finding that bastard

ASAP and putting him back behind bars is the only option here. Until he is, I won't be telling my man to stand down. End of subject."

She looked ready to argue the point. He short-circuited it by picking up her phone and holding it out to her. "You left that on my bedroom floor, apparently."

"Apparently?" Her hand brushed his, and a tiny gasp escaped her as electricity zapped at the point of contact.

"Maddie found it when she was packing up my stuff."

Dark grey eyes met his for a second before they skated over him to the view beyond his window. "You never did tell me where you're staying."

He relaxed in his seat. "Upstairs, for now. I had some of the offices converted into a corporate suite when I leased the place."

Her gaze snapped upward and stayed there, as if she had x-ray vision that could see his current sleeping quarters.

He suppressed a smile. "You have something for me?"

Nodding reluctantly, she reached into her large handbag and passed out the neatly folded T-shirt. Her movements were slow when she handed it over. "What's so special about this T-shirt anyway?"

He took it and tossed it onto his desk. "You forfeited the right to know about 11 a.m. on Saturday morning. Did your board meeting go okay this morning?"

"As well as can be expected," she said vaguely, her gaze sliding from him to flit around the room.

Irritation snapped through him. He got up, rounded his desk and perched on the edge. "Focus, Leia. What's going on?"

She looked at him and frowned. "What do you mean?"

"I mean you haven't looked at me for longer than two seconds since you walked into my office."

She cleared her throat and fidgeted some more. "What we did last night—"

He chuckled. "You mean, me turning your ass red and eating your pussy, and you loving every second of it?"

Her face flamed bright red.

Noah barely stopped a smile from splitting his face. Good to know some things hadn't changed. He tucked a stray hair behind her ear and had the satisfaction of feeling her shiver.

"What about it, baby?"

"I don't want it to happen again."

His almost-smile evaporated, and he grabbed her arm. "Come again?"

A cute grimace crawled over her face. "That's the problem. I don't want to. Not with you."

He straightened. "Then who the hell with?"

"No, I didn't mean that," she said in a rush, then shook her head. "You...this...it's messing with my head. I don't want to see you again, not if..."

"Not if what?" he grated.

"Not if we can't be friends."

Blind anger surged high. "Are you fucking kidding me? You break up with me less than three days ago and you want to be *friends*?"

She flinched. "You don't want to be friends, but you have people watching me and you think you can summon me to your office whenever you please?"

"I never claimed to be a rational human being."

"God, how can you not see how fucked up all this is?"

He shrugged. "I know how we can make everything sane again." And it didn't involve him being fucking friend-zoned.

She stared at him with a mixture of sadness and determination. "I'm not changing my mind about us, N..." she pressed her lips together to stop his name spilling out.

"I'm not going to beg you to come back if you that's what you think. I was going to suggest a straight-up fuck."

She choked. "Excuse me?"

"You. Bent over the back of my couch. Me. Pounding into you. One time only offer. No muss. No fuss. We never really got a chance for a proper goodbye."

NINE

"Did you not hear what I just said? There's no chance in hell of that happening. Ever," Leia snapped, but her pupils dilated before she stalked to the window. After a handful of seconds, she turned. "Besides, didn't you tell me last night I'd never feel your cock inside me again?"

He smiled grimly. "Yeah, I was kinda hoping you'd forget that part. My cock certainly chewed me out for laying down that insane gauntlet."

"I told you I don't do angry sex. I especially don't do angry sex with exes. So if you don't want to part friends, I...I hope at least you don't hate me forever." Bruised eyes connected with his and held.

Shit. She really fucking meant it.

Noah sagged back onto the edge of his desk, his thoughts roiling.

"You really want me to leave you alone?" His voice didn't sound normal. And his hands were growing numb from gripping his desk.

She bit her lip and remained silent for so long, Noah's heart soared.

"Yes, I do," she said.

The words dropped like acid onto his skin. He swallowed and nodded. "Do two things for me before you leave, would you?"

"W...what?"

"First all of, promise me you won't pay the fifty million until you hear from me. And don't worry, I'll only contact you by phone if that's what you want."

"Umm...okay. I promise," she said softly, puzzlement in her eyes.

"Good."

"And the second thing?"

"I want you to turn around and lift up your skirt."

"What? Noah..." she bit her lip, eyeing him warily at her slip.

But while the sound of his name on her lips sent a bolt of longing through him, it didn't stop him from demanding what he needed. "Those are my terms. Do it, and you'll be free to go."

She shook her head in bewilderment.

He stared back at her.

Dropping her bag on the floor, she slowly turned around, faced the door and grabbed the hem of her skirt. The moment her lace-topped stockings ended and her naked flesh was exposed, he stopped breathing.

The garter belt was the same dark leather as the belt he'd branded her with last night. "Is that one of your creations?" he croaked.

She shook her head. "N...no."

"Keep going," he instructed hoarsely.

The skirt crept all the way up, and he bolted upright. "Tell me you haven't been walking around attending meetings with no fucking panties on?"

The look she sent him held a mixture of defiance and embarrassment. "I couldn't. The welts were too painful even with a thong."

His gaze dropped to her ass. He let out a groan. Long red welts covered her from lower back to the top of her thighs. He'd been excruciatingly careful not to break her gorgeous skin, but some of the streaks were raw enough to make him uncomfortable. Fuck, he hadn't been careful enough. Regret coated his mouth. He was about to apologize when he caught the look in her eyes.

Raw, filthy, hunger.

"Jesus, you love being fucking sore, don't you?"

She stared back unapologetically. "You woke something inside of me. I don't see the point in denying what this does to me."

He released his grip on the edge of his desk, reached blindly behind him until his fingers closed over what he wanted. He fumbled with his phone until he found the right app. At the sound of the camera clicking, she spun around, shock widening her eyes.

"Oh God, you took a photo of me?"

"Specifically of your ass, yes." He turned the camera and showed it to her.

She stumbled toward him. "Noah, please delete it."

"It doesn't show your face. No one would know it was—" His insides froze. "Tell me you don't think I'd ever violate your privacy like that asshole did."

Her eyes squeezed shut for a second and shook her head. "The way you feel about me right now, I don't know what you'll do next. That's my honest answer."

Noah forced himself to keep breathing until he had himself under control. "Come here."

He made space between his legs, and she stopped a few inches from him. Having her this close, her skirt around her waist and her sweet pussy within touching distance, was fucking torture. But he resisted the urge to slide his fingers between her thighs.

Shifting his position, he adjusted the pressure on his cock and angled his phone toward her. "For the last six months, I've been working with a couple of grad students from MIT with a view to King's Ransom backing them. Without going into technical and confidential detail, they've developed hack-proof software that can be used to store sensitive data."

"No software is hack-proof."

"It is if it's developed by two of the world's best hackers. It's triple-password protected and encrypted. No one will see this picture but me. But let me ask you this - if you had a compromising picture of me, would I be able to trust you with it?"

She bit her lip. "Yes."

He nodded, then gave up trying to resist touching her. He slid his thumb over her lips and nearly groaned when she parted them. "Do you want me to delete it?"

"Not if you're sure...no."

He stared at her, saw the unadulterated need in her face and quickly made up his mind. Jesus, if she wanted him even half as much as he wanted her, surely they could find a way? He slid one hand into her hair and the other gently over her ass. "Does it hurt when I touch you?"

"A little but...Noah—"

"Shhh, just let me soothe you for a minute." For reasons he hadn't yet been able to fathom, she wanted him but was denying herself the chance to be with him. He wasn't ashamed to use sex to sway her. What they had was too powerful, too potent, to let it go.

Sexy, mewling sounds purred from her throat as he petted her. Her eyelids drooped and she stepped closer.

He leaned forward to kiss her...and cursed when a loud noise buzzed from his desk.

Letting her go, he stabbed the intercom.

"Maddie, I told you I didn't want to be disturbed."

"I know, Mr. King, and I'm sorry, but your private line has been flashing for a while and I answered it. It's...it's the specialist, confirming that he's able to see you and Miss Maitland first thing tomorrow for the DNA test? Shall I tell him it's okay?"

Jaw clenching, he looked up and saw the pale horror on Leia's face. He half expected her to clamp her hands over her ears to block out the conversation.

Any hope he'd been harboring about how she felt about him died a painful death.

Jerking away from her, he spoke into the intercom. "Yes, confirm it."

He hung up and faced Leia. Her skirt was back in place, her handbag on her shoulder. "Do you hate kids? Is that it?" he asked.

"Excuse me?"

"I'm trying hard to understand what's going on in your head. You say you can't be with me, but less than a minute ago you were purring in my arms, a millimeter away from being fucked. So it can't be the sex. And I know it's not Ashley because you know damn well how I feel about her. So the game changer has to be the kid."

Her mouth worked for several seconds. "No, I don't hate kids."

"Then what the fuck is it?"

She glanced past him to that damn window again. Collected herself and gave a shrug so fake, he wanted to shake it off her.

"I'm twenty-three years old. Is it so wrong to believe that I don't want to be saddled with a kid by proxy just yet?"

He called himself ten kinds of fool for allowing the words to rip into him. When the hell was he going to learn his lesson? Give up on her and move on?

Right fucking now was good.

"Understood. Goodbye, Leia."

Bunching his fists, he shoved them into his pockets and strode to the window. She barely made a sound, but he knew the moment she left.

Ragged breaths chased through his chest as he collapsed into his chair. Almost against his will, he reached for the T-shirt and brought the cotton to his nose. He caught the faint scent of her perfume and crushed the material into his face.

With an angry curse, he yanked open his desk drawer but still he couldn't let go. Not until her words crashed into his head one more time...

I don't want to be saddled with a kid by proxy...

Promoting his status to three dozen kinds of fool, he tossed the T-shirt in the drawer and kicked it shut.

TEN

Right up until he walked through the doors of The Sphere in South Beach, three nights later, Noah contemplated cancelling on the guys. He would have, if he didn't hate the thought of being alone even more.

He detested not being able to get Leia's words out of his head. The worst thing was - he didn't believe her. But the more he tried to unravel what she wasn't saying, the crazier he got running circles around himself. His world had descended into hell minutes after she'd walked out, starting with the realization that all she seemed to be doing since they'd landed in Miami was walk away from him.

His seriously grey mood had turned pitch black this afternoon when Sam Ferranti had called to deliver the good news. Ashley could be charged and prospectively sent to jail for a long time.

Except for the minor issue of her carrying Noah's first born and therefore remaining untouchable...

He'd snapped Maddie's head off for interrupting him midthought. He'd calmed down enough to apologize and send her home early. Then he'd toyed with calling it a day. But the idea of locking himself away in the minimalistic, soulless suite upstairs had made his head throb. So he'd called Hartford and arranged to meet him at the condos he'd shortlisted.

All three were top of the line, with enough space, privacy and security to suit his needs. But unable to settle on the one he wanted, he'd dismissed a puzzled Hartford, returned to his office and indulged in a stiff whiskey.

When Gabe's reminder had popped up on his phone with an intuitive addendum that he wasn't allowed to cancel, he'd growled and knocked back another stiff drink. Then endured a trip at the back of a cab with nothing but his thoughts to occupy him.

Fucking. Hell.

Walking into the bar, he immediately spotted Mike waving him over.

Damon had discovered The Sphere a couple of years ago by accident, when he'd stumbled into the place after a disastrous night with a blind date who'd turned out to be a call girl. He'd literally jumped out of a moving limo to avoid the hooker, and called Mike. Mike had ribbed him mercilessly, then taken pity on him and rescued him from a back booth in The Sphere hours later.

That booth had become their personal drinking oasis ever since, reserved for their exclusive use come rain or shine.

Noah sprawled into the nearest seat, nodding thanks when their waitress set a chilled beer in front of him.

Gabe twirled his JD on rocks and eyed him. "You look like shit rolled up in crap, my friend."

Noah raised his bottle to him. "Thanks. You look fresh as a fucking daisy."

Gabe cracked a haggard-faced smile and sipped his drink. Damon took a bite of the huge club sandwich in front of him, his glance swinging between them.

"I know you ladies like to play hard to get, but would you just fucking spit out what the hell is going on with you two already? It's getting to the point where I think I'll need a code breaker just to have a conversation with you."

Gabe shrugged. "Sure, princess. Just so you don't hurt your pretty little head, I'll break it down for you. My sex life is going to hell in a shit basket. I haven't fucked my girlfriend in three long, excruciating weeks, and I'm pathetic enough to admit I don't want to fuck anyone else but her. Has she got me wrapped around her pinky like some spineless fool? Fuck yes. Do I like it? Fuck no, I detest it enough to contemplate hopping back on a plane to Bora Bora and strangling the bitch. I've given myself more hand jobs than a milkmaid in Texas, and I'm terrified one more jerking off will literally *jerk* my dick off. So tonight, I intend to get triple shit-faced so I can forget I have a dick, or a girlfriend. Is that succinct enough for you?"

Damon had started choking halfway through Gabe's diatribe and held out his hand in a *please stop* sign when Mike went to thump him on the back a tenth time.

Gabe downed his drink and held up his hand for another round. "Your turn," he said to Noah.

He tried to find the right words to break the news. But two whiskeys and a quickly downed beer, not to mention the brainpower he'd wasted trying to decipher Leia's words, had worn him down. He drained the dregs of his beer and slammed the bottle on the table.

"Ashley Maitland is pregnant. She claims the baby is mine."

Silence.

Damon made a dogged effort to chew and swallow the food in his mouth without choking again. Mike stared at him as if he wasn't sure whether to perform an exorcism or hunt down a Hazmat suit.

As for Gabriel...he just looked intensely disappointed. "All this time, you were claiming not to know why she was trying to reach you..." he shook his head. "And you were fucking her?" he condemned in a flat tone.

"What the hell?" Noah frowned.

"Wait a minute—"

They both ignored Damon. "What did you just say to me?" Noah demanded from Gabe.

Gabe pointed an accusing finger at him. "You claimed you had no idea why she was in Miami. If you were stupid enough to fuck that psycho bitch, I'd have thought you'd be man enough to admit it."

"You need to stop right now, before my fist says hello to that pretty boy jaw that Playboy photographer's been wanting to memorialize for over a decade."

The table lapsed into silence as their drinks were delivered. It didn't stop his best friends from glaring their anger and confusion at him though. Seeing as they'd spent the better part of two years worrying that Ashley had fucked him up for all eternity, he couldn't blame them.

He raked a hand through his hair and grabbed his second beer the moment it was placed before him. The waitress looked around the table, rolled her eyes and muttered, "I'm not even gonna ask," and walked away.

Noah gulped down half his beer before he glared at Gabe. "If you'd have let me finish, I would've told you the *psycho bitch* didn't conceive my child by conventional means, asshole."

Gabe's glass froze halfway to his mouth and his eyebrows hit his hairline.

Mike frowned. "Fuck, I'm beyond confused."

Damon just kept shaking his head.

Noah relayed the story of the sperm and egg harvesting two years ago. "I never hid the fact that I wanted a kid eventually. When she got ill, and the doctors thought it might affect her ability to have kids, we thought what the hell, might as well freeze mine too…just in case."

"So she used your soldiers to knock herself up without telling you?" Damon's face clenched in anger. "Jesus. Fuck."

"You win the whole fucking world, my friend," Mike muttered, his face frozen in shell-shock mode.

Gabriel's mouth compressed into a white line, but his chest rose and fell in silent rage as his eyes met Noah's. Seeing the clear apology in his friend's gaze, Noah nodded his acceptance.

They clinked glasses and sucked down more booze.

"How far along is she?" Gabe asked, his tone calm but ice cold.

"She claims two months. DNA tests happened yesterday. I get the results tomorrow."

Gabe nodded. "Lawyers involved? She can't get away with this."

"Ferranti's on the case. He has a list as long as my arm to charge her with. But..." Noah stopped talking as a wave of helpless rage washed over him.

Gabe's glass hit the table. He shook his head as a few more pennies fell into place. "*But,* if the kid's yours, then you can't really touch her, can you? At least not while she's pregnant. Shit!"

"Yeah, I can sue the pants off the clinic and everyone else involved in this, but I can't send Ashley to jail unless I want my first child to be born in prison. Fucking ironic, isn't it?"

"Seriously. What. The. Fuck?" Damon's ex had tried to trap him into early fatherhood a while back so he was taking the news badly. "What is wrong with these gold-digging whores?"

"We don't have eternity, buddy, so ask a simpler question," Mike suggested.

"Where is she now?" Gabe asked.

"She's living in my condo. I moved out. No, I'm not going to explain. Next question."

Damon rolled his shoulders and made a visible effort to get off the volatile subject of Ashley's pregnancy. "How did the Indigo Lounge trip go?"

Noah's jaw tightened. He remained quiet for so long another deathly silence descended on the table. The waitress, Katie, if he remembered her name correctly, walked past and kissed her teeth in irritation.

"Hell, was it that bad?" Mike asked. "Because Sonja came across a clip on YouTube the other day. She swears it was you playing the guitar and some hot chick groupie-ing on you like she wanted to have your babies." He paled immediately and then howled, probably from a kick under the table from one of the guys. "Sorry, unfortunate choice of words. But seriously, I'd hate to think I spent 250k to send you on a shitty trip..."

Noah knew they would blame themselves if he didn't answer. "No, your girlfriend was right. That was me...us in Vienna. As for the trip, it was that good." The residue of beer turned bitter in his mouth. "Until it wasn't."

Gabe raised an eyebrow. "*Us*? We need details, man."

Noah gave them the lowdown without going into details as to why he had to cut the trip short. Again his friends stared at him, dumbfounded, then at each other.

"What's her name?" Damon asked eventually.

Noah swallowed. "Leia Michaels."

Mike's eyes narrowed. "That name rings a bell. Why?" His fingers drummed on the table.

"She was in the news a while back. About five years ago," Noah volunteered. It was no use keeping that a secret. They were resourceful enough to acquire the info in minutes.

Mike blinked rapidly, then his mouth dropped open. "Holy shit. The murder/suicide?"

A knife twisted in Noah's gut. "Yeah."

"So you cut your trip short because she needed to come back to Miami, and you came back with her?" Gabe asked, eyeing him in that incisive way that said his friend was reading between the lines.

"Yeah."

"But?"

Noah shrugged. "But nothing. We met. We...got together. She...we went our separate ways."

Mike shook his head. "Nah, from what I saw on that clip, she was seriously into you. And you looked like..." he stopped and cleared his throat.

"Like what?" Noah growled.

He shrugged. "You looked like you'd died and fucking gone to heaven."

The memory of Leia in the parking lot last night flashed through his mind. He gritted his teeth. "What's your point? Friday night, she went to sleep clinging to me like I was the last raft in her fucking tsunami. Saturday morning, she changed her mind. Fuck if I'm going to lose any more sleep over that shit."

"Women aren't that complicated—"

"Says the guy who's mainlining Jack D because he doesn't know *why* he's being dumped."

"Shut the fuck up, Mike," Gabe growled. "All I'm saying is there has to be a reason for her doing a one-eighty on you." He stopped and cursed. "Ashley? The baby?"

Acid eroded his gut. "Yeah, she says doesn't want to be saddled with a kid."

"And do you believe she means that?"

"What the hell does it matter?"

"Maybe nothing. But women - at least the ones who don't set out to fuck with your head - use excuses to stop themselves from getting hurt. Your girl might mean what she says about not wanting to be saddled. Or there may be another reason why. I've spent four ball-strangling days learning to read between the fucking lines when it comes to women. No reason why you shouldn't endure that torture for the sake of getting that someone-just-killed-my-puppy look off your face."

Noah raised his beer in a mocking salute. "Crazy good pep talk, buddy. Thanks."

Gabriel slapped him on the shoulder, and turned to rile Damon about his cowardice during the phone call to Noah the week before when he'd failed to mention Ashley was in Miami. Damon hunched his shoulders and cursed under his breath. The table erupted in laughter.

Noah was about to raise his beer and drain it when the ten-ton clanger dropped.

Groupie-ing on you like she wanted to have your babies...

"Jesus! Oh, fuck." His head swam at the depths of his own stupidity.

His friends exchanged looks. Mike rubbed his jaw. "You okay there, buddy?"

Noah vaulted to his feet. "I need to go." Grabbing his wallet, he dropped a stack on the table.

"Care to fill us in on what just happened?"

"No. I don't." He looked at Mike. "But thanks."

Mike frowned, then shrugged. "Gentlemen, I think he's just found his personal woman-deciphering holy grail."

Noah paced his suite after he left his sixth message, debating whether to storm that Palm Beach monstrosity of a mansion where Leia lived.

Two things stopped him. One, it was past midnight and he didn't want to come across like a desperate, stalking creep, even though he could probably talk his way round that. Two, he was drunk enough to make good on the temptation to do bodily harm to Snyder should the other guy get in his way, a scenario that was highly likely to unfold if he attempted to reach Leia at...he peered at his watch...1.23 a.m.

Gritting his teeth, he pressed the button on his phone again.

"Dammit, Leia, you have your fucking phone back now. Use it and call me back. Making me wait to hear from you isn't doing my disposition any good. And you sure as hell don't want to keep doing it." He stabbed the end button, then immediately redialed. Voicemail.

"Oh, and I know why you ended us. But I need you to have the balls to tell me to my face. After which, I'll tie you to my bed and make you pay for the shit you've put us both through. Good fucking night."

ELEVEN

I know why you ended us.

Leia's hands shook as she replayed the message for the twentieth time on her way to the office. Part of her felt relief that Noah had finally remembered she couldn't have children.

But elation had turned to despair very quickly. He'd called her a faithless little liar long before she'd told him the lie in his office about not wanting to be saddled with a kid. A brief moment after she'd uttered the words, he'd looked highly skeptical. She wasn't sure what had changed his mind but it didn't matter anyway.

Why would he want anything to do with her when she remained a broken body and soul he would tire of eventually?

Or maybe that was the problem. Maybe he just wanted a fuck toy to play with until the more serious business of becoming a father kicked in for him. Lying in bed, pondering everything his message meant, she'd veered toward the temptation of being just that – his fuck toy for the next seven months. A few months of Noah was better than an eternity of nothing, right?

But could she walk away after that time?

It had nearly killed her to walk away after a few days of meeting him. Months would rip her soul to pieces.

Because being with Noah would only deepen her feelings for him. Look at what had happened in the parking lot on Sunday night? Even at his most icily domineering and condemning, he'd made her want him to the point of insanity.

She'd craved his merciless hand and his wicked tongue so badly, she would've given her life for a taste of his brand of pleasure. She'd goaded him into letting him leave his marks on her, marks she still treasured because she was that pathetic.

Hell, she'd briefly panicked this morning when she'd noticed the finger marks around her neck were beginning to fade.

Prolonging contact with him was asking for trouble. He'd become so ingrained into her sexual psyche that she'd been unable to get herself off in the shower this morning. Despite the residual pain and pleasure of a frenzied masturbation, her body had held back on her, wishing for Noah's hand, his mouth, instead.

Dear God, she was in serious trouble—

Her phone vibrated, making her jump.

Noah. The ringtone pierced through her consciousness and her heart stopped. He must have tracked down the session he'd done with *Fused Realms* because her ringtone for his number was now the five-second piece of the jam. When exactly had he tracked it down? And when had he put it in her phone—?

She cursed when the phone went silent. A second later it flashed to life again.

Forcing herself to remain calm, she answered it, despite her pulse beginning to race. "You know, you can't keep summoning me to your presence like I'm your personal lapdog."

"I wouldn't have to summon you if you answered your phone like a normal person," he gritted.

"I was doing what normal people do at one a.m. Sleeping."

"And you sleep with your phone turned off?"

"When I don't want to be disturbed, yes."

She didn't want to admit that she'd had her headphones on with the music turned high to drown out her thoughts. The lie she'd told Noah just to get away from him on Monday had eaten at her until she'd been a whisker away from calling him to confess why she couldn't be with him.

Well, now he knew.

Her palms dampened at his silence. Was he going to say something, or was he going to let her twist in the wind?

"I...I was going to call you back," she ventured.

"Yeah? When?" he demanded.

"After my meeting this morning."

"You didn't think what I had to say was important enough to schedule me in before your meetings?"

She bit her lip. "I'm meeting with retailers from across the country. I couldn't afford to have you—"

"Fuck with your head? Or fuck you sore once we'd dispensed of this bullshit?"

Her pulse skipped so hard her hands shook. "It's not bullshit."

"I beg to differ. You decided *how I feel* without waiting to hear my side of things. What's that if not fucking bullshit?" His voice was growing colder, a sign that he was getting angrier with her. "I made the mistake of forgetting what you told me in Switzerland. I remember now, Leia. I know you can't have kids. Isn't that what this is all about? You bowing out of this relationship because you think that affects how I feel about you?"

"Doesn't it?" She held her breath.

"You get your answer to that face to face. Not over the phone."

She exhaled. "Noah..."

"Are you interested in having a conversation?"

She closed her eyes and laid her head back against the seat. Bargaining furiously with herself that this would be the last time, that she wouldn't let Noah sway her *no matter what*, she answered, "Yes." She'd hear him out and explain to him why they were better off without each other. And this time, when she walked away, she would stay away.

But maybe she could walk away with another reminder of how incredible Noah could make her feel?

"Good."

Opening her eyes, she noticed her driver had pulled up in front of her office. She had six of the major retailers from all over the country flying in for a meeting about stocking La Carezza's latest lingerie in their stores. She needed her head in the game, not dreaming of Noah's belt. Or his hand. Or his tongue. Or, please God, his cock.

"...did you hear what I said?" he growled in her ear.

"Umm...sorry no. I spaced out for a minute," she confessed.

"I said we'll talk tonight," he repeated. "My place. Come straight up when you get there. The code is 77493. Repeat it." She recited it. "Six-thirty on the button, Leia. Don't be late." He hung up.

She squeezed her eyes shut again as weakness engulfed her. Whatever happened tonight, she knew she was going to fuck Noah again. For the last time, she assured herself.

But she was going to fuck him.

Hard.

"That went well, don't you think?"

Leia gathered the papers in front of her, placed them in the crook of her arm, and glanced at Warren. "Yes. Far better than I expected, although the rep from Saks was a little too snooty for my liking. I had to bite my tongue several times not to snap his head off when he kept asking me how old I was."

A rare smile crossed Warren's face as he stopped before her. Impeccably dressed as always, he adjusted his silver monogrammed cufflinks. Leia tried not to read anything into the fact that he was blocking her way to the door of the conference room.

Her meeting had gone on for an hour longer than she'd anticipated. With her schedule now crammed together tighter than she wanted, she'd be lucky to get out of the office by six to make it to Noah's place in time.

Would her lateness mean punishment? A feverish shudder of anticipation raked through her. She tightened her grip on the folder to keep her shaking under control.

"Yes, I noticed," Warren said. "But you held your own admirably. You sent them all away with the firm impression that your intelligence far eclipses your age when it comes to business savvy. I'm proud of you, my dear." He reached up and traced his hand down her cheek, another caress in a growing number that he'd been initiating for the last few days.

Although the backhanded compliment irritated her and the caress made her feel uneasy, she didn't react to either. But neither did she welcome it. The suspicion that Warren felt something for her beyond their former ward/guardian relationship had grown into a solid fact she couldn't hide from. A fact that would need addressing sooner rather than later.

Aside from the times when she couldn't read him properly, he'd been there for at her lowest moments and seen her through the worst time of her life.

But...

Remembering Noah's allegations, she stared back at him, trying to see beneath the unruffled exterior Warren always presented. But it was as if she was looking into a bottomless lake at midnight. She turned her head from his cool fingers. His hand dropped, but he didn't step away from her. Instead he joined her as she headed for the door.

Entering the elevator, he pressed the button for the floor above, where both their offices were located. "Are you all set for Saturday?"

She frowned for a moment, and then remembered. "Yes. My gowns arrived this morning. I'm not sure I went with the right couturier though. I might have to resort to Plan B."

"I'm having a tuxedo fitting this afternoon. I can pick something up from Oscar de la Renta's collection, if you wish?"

The thought of Warren picking out a dress for her to wear sent a heavy bolt of discomfort down her spine. Smiling to take the sting out of her words, she replied, "No need. I have my favorite designer on speed dial. I wanted to try something different this time." She laughed. "Goes to show that different doesn't always mean better."

He didn't return her smile as they exited the elevator and headed down the corridor. "Not always. But a calculated leap of faith can reap rewards."

"Isn't that a contradiction in terms? How can a leap of faith be calc—?"

She stopped as her secretary, Celia, emerged from her office with a flustered look. "I'm sorry, Miss Michaels. I just returned from the copier room and she was here. Reception let her up without letting me know..."

About to ask her what she was talking about, Leia looked past Celia and froze.

Ashley was poised in the doorway to Leia's office.

Her choice of ensemble today was just as impeccable as every single time Leia had seen her. Despite the Miami heat, she managed to look cool and composed, with a Hermès scarf around her neck and her straight black hair tied in a chic bun at her nape. For a hysterical second, Leia thought how perfect Ashley and Warren were for each other.

"It's okay, Celia. I'll deal with this."

Celia nodded and darted back into her office. Leia caught the wary look Warren sent the other woman before he glanced at her. "Would you like me to stay, my dear?"

Ashley's brows rose at the endearment. Leia bristled and shook her head. She would have to talk to Warren about that. The possessiveness in those two words was beginning to grate.

"No, thanks. I'll see you later."

He nodded and left.

Turning, Leia brushed past Ashley and her cloud of Chanel No.19 and entered her office, very much aware that the other woman was following closely behind.

Leia reached her desk and resisted tossing her folder across it. Showing Bitch Face that she was rattled wasn't an option. Why the hell was she here? Had Noah sent her?

"How the hell did you get up here without an appointment?" she asked in what she hoped was a disinterested voice.

Ashley smiled faintly and dropped her cream Balenciaga purse, which matched her stylish dress, on the chair facing Leia's desk. "We haven't been acquainted long enough for you to find out for yourself, so I'll let you in on a secret. I always get what I want. Always." The last word was wrapped in steel and spat with venom.

Leia resisted the urge to unsheathe her own claws and remained in front of her desk, her arms crossed. "I don't have time to entertain your whimsical illusions. So spit it out. What the hell do you want? I have a business to run here."

Ashley looked around the office and nodded. "I was quite impressed to find out that you're involved in all this. It was probably why Noah was taken with you too, for a while. I ran a very successful art gallery in New York when I met Noah." She smiled. "Isn't it adorable that he likes ambitious women? But only to a point though. I found that out the hard way—"

"Are you approaching anywhere near a point here, or shall I build a fire so we can braid each other's hair and exchange boy stories?" She faintly recalled Warren's view on sarcasm and sent the thought the middle finger. Sarcasm at the right time, such as times like these, when her heart was being pulverized, was hugely bolstering.

"We got the results of the DNA test back today."

Leia's heart took a dive at the *we* and plummeted at the rest. Keeping her expression blank, she studied Ashley's smug smile, already knowing but dreading the answer before the question left her lips. "Why would I be interested in that?"

"Oh please. I know you two are still sniffing around each other like teenage fuck-buddies. I just thought you'd like to know - woman to woman - that the results are conclusive. The baby is his. And you know what else?"

"I'm sure you're dying to tell me so please, knock yourself out."

"Noah asked for an ultrasound. Then he got all choked up when he heard the heartbeat and saw our little blob of joy. Afterward, he asked for a copy of the scan to keep in his wallet. Does that sound like a man who hates the idea of his impending fatherhood?"

The shaking got too much. Leia propped herself against her desk before her legs gave way. Pretending to arrange the papers on her desk, she said, "I'm sorry, you lost me somewhere in the middle of that mumbo jumbo spewing out of your mouth. Again, this concerns me how?"

Her expression hardening a touch, but not enough to ruin her perfectly made up face, Ashley leaned in close. "Make no mistake, Noah will commit to me and to this baby sooner or later. You seem like a nice girl—"

"And you seem like the words *Condescending Ho-Bag* should be your call sign before you barge into people's offices. Since we're clearly finished here, would you like to leave under your own steam or shall I get security to carry your skinny ass out?"

Ashley picked up her bag and tucked it into the crook of her elbow in a poised move that would've made any Stepford Wife weep with jealousy. "I won't warn you again, Little Pixie. Stay out of my way."

By the time Celia approached to shut the door Ashley had left wide open on her exit, Leia was shaking so much her teeth were chattering.

"Can I get you any—?"

Leia shook her head and waved her secretary away with a stiff smile. "No, thanks Celia. I'm...I'm good."

Unfortunately, she was so far from good, she'd need a rocket to get back. She stared blankly into space for interminable minutes, aware that she had two options. She could either call Noah and verify everything Ashley had said. Which would make it glaringly obvious to him that despite her stating she didn't want anything to with him or his child, she cared way more than she should. Which would in turn mean that if Noah had any plans to make her his fuck toy until he cast her aside for the sake of his impending fatherhood, she would be playing right into his ruthless and clever hands.

Or she could pretend Ashley's visit hadn't happened. Go to Noah tonight and have that talk he wanted, all the while pretending she wasn't aware he was carrying in his wallet an ultrasound scan of a baby he hadn't planned for but seemed to want with every fiber of his being. Could she do it? Could she truly bury her head in the sand just for the sake of one last fuck from the only man capable of delivering the kind of pleasure she needed?

Her phone rang.

Forcing herself to reach for it, she pulled herself back into her business day.

She didn't allow herself to contemplate a third option until five thirty. Knowing Noah's man would be watching her, she riffled through the emergency sets of clothes she kept in her office. Pulling on her jeans and a nondescript top, she slid her feet into black runners and stuffed her hair under a baseball cap.

Luckily, the corridor and elevator were empty. Arriving at the underground parking, she walked past her car and through the security door. Two minutes later, she blended into evening pedestrian traffic until she was a block away, then hailed a cab.

"The Mandarin Hotel, please."

Twenty-minutes later, she checked into the double room. If Noah looked hard enough, he would probably find her, but if she was lucky, she would have a night to come to terms with her decision.

Fetching her phone from her bag, she dialed his number. He answered immediately.

"It's six thirty-one. I'll let your tardiness pass if you're in the building. Did you forget the code?" he sighed. "Don't sweat it, I can override the elevator from here. I'll let you—"

"Noah, I'm not coming."

Silence. Then his breath whistled out, like he was finding breathing difficult. "You're not coming." A flat statement.

"N—no. I didn't want you think I'd stood you up—"

His derisive snort shattered her composure for a minute, but she forced the words out. "For a while there, I was forgetting my life and my choices are my own. And I'm ashamed to admit that part of my reasoning was to do with sex. I can so very easily let it blind me to the things that should be important to me. But I don't want to be blind. You're having a baby with another woman. I can't handle that, Noah. I really can't. I don't want to suppress how I feel about that with sex. I'm sorry."

"Leia!"

She hung up, turned the phone off and ejected the battery as an extra safety precaution in case Noah's guy could track her.

Undressing, she slid into the cold, lonely hotel bed and pulled the covers over her head.

TWELVE

"What the fuck do you mean you lost her? What the hell am I paying you for?" Noah shouted into the phone less than thirty seconds after Leia hung up on him. "Yes, she just called me. No, I don't know where the hell from or I wouldn't be asking you!" Exasperated beyond belief and seriously fearing for his blood pressure, he pulled the phone away from his ear and rubbed at the throbbing in his temple.

A full minute later, he pulled in a breath and spoke to his PI. "When did you last have eyes on her?"

"My guy on the roof on the building opposite her office said she spent a couple of hours in a meeting. Then she went to her office at about three. That was when your other girl showed up."

Noah's temperature spiked. "My other girl?"

"Yeah, you know, Snow White's stepmom?"

He stopped dead in the middle of his suite. "Ashley?"

His PI snorted. "That's her."

"I'll call you back. You'd better have located Leia by the time I do."

"If she's deliberately covering her tracks—"

"No excuses!" Noah hung up and dialed his condo. Ashley picked up on the third ring.

"What the fuck did you do?"

"I'm assuming we're talking about your little pixie?" Noah could almost hear the shrug in her voice. "I paid her a little visit. Don't tell me she's upset? Seriously, I don't know what you see in her if she runs to you with every—"

"She didn't run to me, you fucking bitch. She ran away." He regretted the words the moment they were out of his mouth.

"Well then, that kind of proves my point, don't you think?" Ashley crowed in triumph.

His vision blurred, and he worried if he would pass out just from the rage coursing through his veins. "For the sake of all things holy, I'm going to give you five seconds to tell me what you said to her. Starting now."

"I thought she needed to be aware of the DNA test results and act accordingly, that's all."

"What did she say?"

A long-suffering sigh. "Noah, you won't believe me if I told you so perhaps you should ask her."

"Tell me what she said, dammit!"

"She said she didn't care. About the baby...or about you. I think she found the whole subject boring, to be honest. She had the nerve to threaten to throw me out of her office." She sniffed.

A ball of lead settled in his stomach. Even as he warned himself that he knew better than to believe a word Ashley said, he couldn't shift the glaring truth. He may have remembered that Leia couldn't have kids and imagined that it altered the facts enough for it to matter what happened between the two of them, but what if he'd been grasping at straws?

Was he trying to force an issue with Leia that he would be better off letting go? He was damn certain her dig about not wanting to be burdened with kids had been a protective mechanism. But had it held a grain of truth, a truth he was willfully turning a blind eye to?

"Noah, are you there? Aren't you going to say something?"

"Yeah. I'm sorry she didn't throw you out on your ass. Stay away from her, Ashley. Don't make me tell you again."

He shoved his phone in his pocket and rubbed a hand down his face. Encountering his stubble, he cursed.

He'd deliberately stopped himself from shaving this morning because he knew he would be seeing Leia. Looking around the suite, he cursed louder.

Fused Realms' album, the one Leia had told him in Vienna was her favorite, played softly in the background. He'd stopped himself from cooking, had reckoned if they got to the stage of being hungry, he could always call up the gourmet take-out service he used. But he'd put a bottle of her favorite wine on ice. Two large bouquets of flowers, courtesy of Maddie's mad skills, had turned the suite from a clinical, soulless place into a passably comfortable space with some strategic lighting.

And all for what? To sway a woman who didn't give a shit about him or the child he was expecting to change his life?

He staggered to the nearest sofa, slowly pulled his wallet out of his pocket and stared at the grey blob on the plastic film.

Christ, he hadn't expected to experience such overwhelming feelings the moment the machine had picked up the heartbeat. But the rush of warmth and protectiveness had been beyond description.

The only fly in the ointment had been the woman carrying his child. Even then, Noah hadn't let it spoil the moment. Hell, he'd even allowed the psycho bitch to hold his hand. But he'd thought of Leia in that moment, had wished it was her lying on that table with his child growing inside of her. Jesus, his eyes had even misted at the powerful need for that alternate reality.

His fingers trembled, and he blinked back into focus.

God, he was a fucking idiot. An idiot who was perhaps better off back in therapy.

He let out a grim laugh. Hell no. Never again. He knew exactly what was wrong with him.

He couldn't stop himself from making the same fucking mistakes over and over.

It was high time he got his shit together.

His phone's vibrations roused him to a darkened room and the discomfort of a severely sore neck. Digging it out, he eyed the Private Caller ID displayed and answered. "You better have good news for me."

"We've found her."

Noah's breath shuddered out. "Is she safe?"

"The only thing she needs to worry about right now is whether the mini-bar in her hotel room is up to scratch." He heard the thinly veiled question and closed his eyes against the need to ask.

Get your shit together. Starting now.

"Keep an eye on her. Tomorrow is the deadline for the blackmail demand. Hire extra men if you need to. I don't want that bastard anywhere near her once he finds out he's not getting a dime."

"I know. We're working on that too. You sure you don't want to know where she is?"

Noah grimaced and rubbed his jaw. Temptation burned through him, but he gritted his teeth. "No. I don't."

"You know where I am if you change your mind."

Noah disconnected the call and clenched his fist around the phone. He'd taken the first step into regaining his sanity. His ex-therapist would be thrilled enough to drop her panties for him right now.

Shame he felt like going ten rounds with a punching bag instead.

The moment Leia turned her phone on, it began to ping. Several missed calls from Noah and two from Warren. Tugging on her jeans and T-shirt after a quick shower, she took the time to get herself together before checking them properly. Part of the weaning-herself-off-Noah process demanded she not jump at the sight of his name or the promise of hearing his voice.

He was probably pissed that she'd disappeared from his radar, but she needed to be able to stand on her own two feet from now on.

A shaft of fear lanced down her spine as she thought of what she'd decided in the middle of the night. Noah was right. Stephen Willoughby was the reason her life had descended into hell five years ago. Her mother had killed herself because of him. Rewarding him with fifty million dollars, even to stop him from exposing the photos he had of her, would be spitting on her mother's grave and her memory.

A sharp twinge of shame pierced her. She'd forgotten that in the midst of trying to save herself from the pain of losing Noah. But last night, she'd remembered why she needed to remain strong. Slipping her feet into her runners, she paused as another message came through. A quick glance showed an attachment with a play button.

The message at the top of the screen was simple and bone-chilling.

Today's the day. In case you need a reminder...

The video was a five-second clip. It showed her in her bedroom just over five years ago. On her back, her eyes wide with fear and her mouth bruised and bloody from the blow he'd dealt her when she'd dared to struggle. Her nightshirt was ripped, exposing her right breast, which he was palming roughly as he pushed himself inside her. It ended with her head coming off the pillow, screaming as her gaze veered to the door.

It was the moment her mother had walked in with the gun...

Shaking, she dropped the phone and rushed to the bathroom, barely making it to the toilet before she vomited the meager contents of her stomach. She heaved over and over until there was nothing left.

As she sagged against the cold porcelain, too weak to get up and wash her mouth, her anger grew.

Fuck Stephen Willoughby. Fuck him all the way to a hell where men like him were fucked in the ass with spikes just for entertainment. He wouldn't get a cent from her. If she needed to, she would spend every dollar of that fifty million bringing the man who'd made her life hell to justice.

Getting up, she finished dressing and went downstairs. The doorman held the door open. About to order a cab, she paused when a tall, middle-aged man with greying hair approached her.

"Hey there, Miss. I'm the car service you ordered."

She shook her head. "I didn't order a car service."

"I'm sure you did. You're headed to the office, right? I can have you there in less than twenty."

He attempted a smile, but her instinct told her this guy wasn't used to that particular social grace. And although he looked nondescript enough to be dismissed by most people, there was an air of ruthlessness about him. Plus, he seemed familiar somehow. Her eyes widened as her mind connected the dots. "You were the guy outside the restaurant on Sunday night. You work for Noah."

He raised an eyebrow and shrugged. "I cannot confirm nor deny that."

"What's your name?"

"Call me Paddy."

She eyed him and the luxury town car door he held open for her. "That's not your real name, is it? And that's not your car." This guy would be more comfortable in a blacked out van, not one that screamed high profile billionaire.

"Doesn't matter one way or the other. I doubt we'll be seeing each other again after today. Get in the car, Miss. We're beginning to attract an audience."

She looked around. The only person interested in them was the doorman. About to refuse, she stopped when her phone pinged. Heart hammering, she glanced warily at her phone.

Get in the car. N.

Relief weakened her limbs. Sliding into the back, she put on her seatbelt and waited for Paddy to get behind the wheel. "What can I do for you, Paddy?"

"My employer wants to know if you've heard anything from our mutual friend."

The fact that Noah hadn't called to ask her himself sent a shaft of pain through her, despite the very sane argument that this was exactly what she'd been striving for.

"Would he believe me if I said no?"

Shrewd eyes met hers in the rearview mirror. "Depends if that's the truth or not."

Leia's eyes slid away at the memory of the video. "I received something this morning."

Paddy nodded and stopped at a traffic light. He passed her a grey rectangular gadget about the size of a small smart phone.

"Hold this against your phone for ten seconds. It'll give me what I need."

Leia blinked and shook her head. The idea of the video falling into a stranger's hands made nausea rise. "I'd rather not do that."

The lights changed. Paddy's gaze returned to the road. "The gizmo's already capturing everything on your phone, Miss. Holding it closer will make it work faster." His eyes connected with hers again. "I assume you want your stepfather found?"

Swallowing thickly, she nodded.

"I already know almost everything he did to you. The bastard needs to be put down, fast." Hard, unapologetic words.

Suppressing a shiver, she pulled her phone out of her purse and did as she was told. Several minutes later, he pulled up in front of her office. "One last thing. We can't protect you if you insist on wearing disguises and leaving via back entrances. You're giving him the power that way. Same as you will be if you pay him off."

"I don't intend to pay him off, but I'd like to pay for *your* services to help catch him—"

He shook his head. "It's already taken care of."

She pursed her lips. "I'd rather pay for my own protection."

"I'll run it past my employer, and we'll get back to you."

Gritting her teeth, she snatched up her purse.

"Oh, and my employer and I would like to remind you that the next few days will be hairy. If you could restrict your movements to your office or your home, that would be great."

"I can't. I have a charity thing tomorrow night."

"Details in your diary?" he asked.

"Yes."

"Then security will be taken care of."

Deciding that asking him how would only gain her even more cryptic responses, she passed back the gizmo and alighted.

Watching him drive away, she experienced another pang. It was clear Noah had finally written her off in everything except his promise to keep her safe. She could tell him to back down and let her take care of herself, but she'd already tried that to no avail. Short of confronting him again, a prospect she didn't think was a good idea considering how she'd left things, her only option was to let him carry on with his course of action and ask him to send her a bill afterwards.

Her lips pursed. She was one hundred percent sure that wouldn't go down well with Noah.

She'd just have to convince him when the time came.

After a quick change of clothes, Leia did a few breathing exercises and tried to immerse herself in her business day. But with each hour that passed her nerves grew colder and tighter with apprehension.

She jumped as a text message came through at four.

Stay strong. No excuses. N.

Her breath punched out of her lungs and her eyes prickled. Unbidden, his words from Friday night in his bathroom flashed through her mind.

You're mine. Even when I threaten to kick your ass, you will still be mine. Mine to take care of. Mine to fuck. Mine to cherish.

A tear slid out. She brushed it away. What the hell was wrong with her? And why the hell did love have to hurt so much?

Grabbing her phone, she texted: *Thanks. For everything.*

She regretted her words the moment she hit send.

Groaning at her stupidity, she squeezed her eyes shut.

Thanks for everything? Really?

She was staring at her phone, wondering whether he would reply when Warren walked in carrying a cup of tea. She remained seated behind her desk, hoping he'd stay on the other side. He set the steaming cup down in front of her and sat down.

"I thought you might need company." He steepled his fingers and watched her over them. They'd had a tense conversation this morning when he'd demanded to know where she'd been last night. Her reply that it was none of his business had not gone down well, even though he'd merely inclined his head and returned to his office.

"Thanks, but I was hoping to get through these projections before the end of the day." The scent of the chamomile hit her nostrils and her empty stomach heaved. "And you seem to have forgotten that I prefer jasmine to chamomile." Was it deliberate? Because Warren wasn't a man who forgot things like that.

"On this occasion, I thought chamomile would be better. It's a special blend."

Her gaze returned to the cup. She picked it up, took a tiny sip and set it back down. "There. We happy now?"

He rose and leaned over her desk. She sat back, unease stirring inside her at the gleam in his eyes. "Happy would be a false description of my present state, my dear. But I am counting on that state returning once we're over this...hurdle."

She was sure he meant more than the situation with her stepfather. About to reply, she stopped when her phone pinged.

Her phone was upside down so she couldn't see the display, but every nerve in her body thrummed with the knowledge that it was from Noah.

"I really have to get back to work."

Silence greeted her pointed remark. Then with a stiff nod, Warren left.

She pounced on her phone and pressed the button to read her message. Her heart plummeted at Noah's reply.

I'd say it's been a pleasure but I'm not a faithless, fucking liar.

THIRTEEN

In a way, she was thankful for Noah's text leaving her in a frozen state when the next message arrived. Numb and in shock from unbelievable pain was the correct state to be in when you receive a link to a sex auction website featuring your violent rape.

The blood drained from her face as she replayed at the video. Her face had been blurred out (for the moment) but the auction was already growing frenzied, aided by the caption: *Famous CEO In Teen Rape Tape.*

The tape had pinged into her inbox at 5:15 p.m. The group of lawyers, who'd arrived at 5:00 p.m. to deal with the fallout of Stephen releasing the pictures, were huddled with Warren at the end of the conference table. So far their best advice had been *wait and see.*

She swallowed and re-read the last of her stepfather's message.

Are you really willing to call my bluff, little whore? Check the auction closing time and reassess your priorities. You have until one minute before the auction ends.

The auction was set to finish at midday on Monday, but the bidding had been going for just over an hour and was already at three million.

A cold shiver spilled more ice into her veins.

Her phone rang. Breath stalling, she rose from her seat at the conference table and moved to the window.

"Yes?"

"This is Paddy. My employer wants you to know we've seen the auction tape. We're working on it. Don't do anything rash." He hung up before she could answer.

The breath she was holding shuddered out. Great. The man who thought her a faithless fucking liar was in charge of her fate, along with a bunch of lawyers who wanted her to *wait and see*.

Hysterical laughter curdled up her throat. Turning on her heel, she stalked to the door.

"What are you doing?" Warren asked.

"I'm leaving. This is going to go one of two ways. Either we catch the bastard before Monday, or the video goes viral. I'm not going to spend any more time discussing the issue."

She walked out before he could respond. Entering her office, she snatched up her bag, walked back out and nearly bumped into Warren. He caught her by the arms and steadied her. When he didn't let go immediately, she pulled away.

His mouth compressed for a split second. "Are you going home?"

"Maybe. Maybe not. I'm growing tired of answering to you, Warren. For the last damn time, I'm a big girl. Let me be."

Again, a minuscule display of his displeasure in the tightening of his jaw. "My dear—"

"That reminds me. I hate that term. Use my name. Or not. But I'm tired of being addressed like I'm some wilting English rose. And you're not Mr. Darcy. So stop it!"

Noah stared at the phone app he'd had his tech guys build for him, his anger growing by the minute. When he couldn't contain his frustration anymore, he swiped it closed and dialed the number he'd sworn never to call again.

She answered after four rings.

"What the fuck do you think you're doing wandering the streets at this time of night? And where the hell is your driver?"

Leia laughed, but the sound was so hollow and ragged, his chest tightened. "I sent my driver home because, right now, I'm shopping. In about fifteen minutes, I'll be stopping to grab some dinner at Pietro's. Didn't you see the video? I have three whole days' reprieve before the world is one-click away from watching my rape in full Technicolor. So before then, I intend to party like it's 2099. Care to join me?" Her voice turned soft, inviting.

"What about your life choices? Remember those? The ones that don't feature me?" He called himself an asshole for mentioning it. But it was out there. And the silence that greeted him killed him.

"I'm willing to make an exception...for one night only." Husky and drenched with an emotion he refused to let touch him, the words emerged haltingly.

Something crushed inside of him as he stepped back from the edge of temptation. "No, thanks. The offer to be used and abused sounds fantastic, but I turn fuck-toy only if a woman deserves it."

A muffled sound, like a strangled sob was quickly smothered. "Fine. Maybe I'll find someone more accommodating."

A growl bubbled up his throat. He managed to swallow it down before he could speak. "You do that only if you want me to hunt you both down and break every fucking bone in that unfortunate guy's body. Then I'll teach you a lesson you won't soon forget."

Again a laugh that screamed the edge of endurance. "Wow. Macho, Ruthless Noah. Teacher of Lessons. I still have your marks on my ass, you know that?" A hollow giggle.

He gripped the phone tighter. "Jesus, Leia. Are you drunk?"

"Sadly, not. I'm stone-cold sober. No wait, that's not true. I'm sober, but my brain is spinning at the speed of light, like I'm high or something."

He frowned. "What the hell does that mean?"

"I don't know… Noah, I can't stop playing the video in my mind. It's making my heart race, but I can't really feel my fingers…God," she whispered brokenly, "please, make it stop…"

"You're still in shock. Dammit, Leia, you shouldn't be out on your own. I'm going to put you on hold. Don't you dare hang up, you hear me?" Cursing, he reactivated the app, reached for his office phone and dialed. Issuing instructions, he hung up and paced along the west wall of his office. "A car will be pulling up to you in two minutes. Get in."

"Is he…is he bringing me to where you are?"

"No. But the driver's an ex-army medic. You do exactly as he says."

"Yes, Noah."

He banged his head against the wall, hoping the pain would stop him from reacting to those two words.

"What happens after that?"

"You wanted to go to Pietro's? He'll take you there, then to Palm Beach."

He hung up before he could do something stupid, like ask her to wait for him. He stared down at the app and judged how long it'd take the Maserati to reach her. Too fucking long. Stalking back to his desk, he woke up the laptop screen and stared into the small box at the bottom right hand corner. "Any luck?"

Two sets of faces stared back at him. The spectacled one in an MIT sweatshirt had the nerve to roll his eyes. "Damn, you super-rich dudes all want everything like yesterday. Chill, man. Hacking is like seducing a woman, surely you know that? Come on too strong and she gives you the finger, and you have to go home alone with killer blue balls." He nudged his friend and they dissolved into high school cackles.

Noah suppressed a smile and glared at them. "I can't believe I'm thinking of investing fifteen mil in a company to be fronted by fools. Maybe I need to rethink our business venture?"

The boys sobered. "Jeez, chill. We'll have something for you soon."

"Make it sooner." He exited and reactivated the app tracking Leia. He frowned and managed to resist for all of ten seconds before he redialed her number.

"You're headed in the wrong direction for Pietro's."

A soft hum. "I'm not hungry anymore. Your guy checked me over. He claims I just need rest. I'll grab something when I get to Warren's house."

Razors slashed his gut. "You mean home?"

She hesitated. "It doesn't feel like home anymore."

He jackknifed in his chair, his breathing non-existent. "Then fucking do something about it."

"I will. I intend to...if I get through this nightmare."

"*When*. When you get through it," he insisted through gritted teeth.

She sighed. He heard the sound of soft leather creaking as if she was relaxing against the seat and bedding in for the long ride. At this time on a Friday night, the traffic at her part of town was horrendous. It'd take at least half an hour to get onto the highway leading to Palm Beach. "Are you still there?" she whispered.

Hang up. She's safe and secure. Hang up now. "Yes."

"I need something to take my mind off of my shitty life, Noah." Her voice sounded so small. His fist clenched on his thigh.

"Your life isn't shitty.

"We'll agree to disagree. Tell me about the T-shirt. What it means to you?"

"No. You don't deserve to know."

She inhaled sharply. He steeled himself against the wounded sound. "Noah, I'm sorry if I...I didn't mean to hurt you..."

"Do me a favor? Let's agree to leave our feelings out of any future discussions we have, okay?" She didn't reply and Noah could almost see her grey eyes darken with hurt. He turned his chair to face the window and relaxed. "What are you wearing?"

"What?" Her confusion almost made him smile. Almost.

"You want something to distract you, tell me what you're wearing."

Her breath hitched. "I'm wearing a red and black block leather dress."

"Go on," he said.

"Umm...it's sleeveless, with a long zipper at the back—"

"So it opens all the way down to your ass?"

"Y...yes."

"How short is it?" he asked gruffly.

"It comes down to mid-thigh and it has a couple slits up the sides."

"And pantyhose. Are you wearing pantyhose, Leia?" Fuck, what the hell was he doing?

"No, I'm wearing black stockings with a red garter and four-inch black heels."

Her husky voice poured over his senses like the smoothest, most expensive whiskey. His fist unclenched and hovered over his crotch. Leaning his head back further against his chair, his eyelids drooped as his blood pounded.

"So you power dressed and then decided to end the day by feeling sorry for yourself?"

"I never claimed to be invincible, Noah. I do what I can to survive."

Her words struck a deep chord within him. He closed his eyes. Taking a deep breath, he proceeded with the game. "You're only weak if you think yourself to be weak. Now...panties. Tell me you're wearing panties underneath that short dress."

"Yes, I'm wearing a black thong."

He swallowed hard. "One of yours?"

"Yes."

"Describe the design to me." His voice sounded so thick he wondered if she had understood him.

She cleared her throat and he heard the sound of leather creaking again. "There's a cluster of silver studs centered just over where my...umm..."

"Your clit?"

"Hmm...it sends a small pulse of heat if I rub my hand over it."

The image of her sitting at her desk, her fingers sneaking beneath her dress to touch herself every now and then, attacked his brain to the point where he pulled the phone away from his ear and bit down hard on his knuckle.

When he could breathe without feeling as if he would explode, he brought the phone back.

"Why did you wear it today?" He wasn't sure why he asked, but the words spilled out anyway.

"I guess I didn't want to feel completely helpless. Wearing the panties reminded me that I wasn't useless, that I was worth something. It also reminded me that I had ultimate control over my...my sexuality."

"Does that sound like a shitty life to you, Leia?"

Her breathing changed. A sigh. An acceptance of truth. "No."

"Good. Is the partition up in the car?" He was skidding on dangerous ground, but he already knew he was too far gone to turn back.

The faint whine of the partition sliding up answered his question. She was just as up for it as he was. He hadn't wanted to discuss feelings. So, sex it was. Phone. Fucking. Sex.

"Switch to video, Leia."

Her breath caught. "What?"

He suppressed a smile. "You thought what's about to happen would take place in dark anonymity? Wrong. Turn on the video link. Now."

He heard her fumble for a few seconds, then her face flashed into view. She'd had the good sense to turn on the interior light at the side rather than overhead, which meant the driver would only catch a faint glow through the dark partition. But Noah could see her just fine. Her face was lightly flushed, and her eyes were wide with anticipation and arousal.

"Hi," she murmured, her raspy voice a touch shy.

"There are two coat hooks just above you to the right. See it?" She glanced up and nodded. "Slide your phone in there."

He turned back to his desk. Thanks to his tech prodigies, he'd learned a few new neat tricks. He grabbed the phone on his desk, issued a new set of instructions to his driver and connected his mobile to his laptop. He hit the full screen button and her image flared into wide view.

Somewhere in the madness of his helpless rage and frustration at the chaos ruling his life, he'd forgotten just how incredibly beautiful she was. The angled view of her looking up into the camera, eyes wide, mouth full, parted and trembling, stopped his heart for a terrifying few seconds before it slammed into his ribs.

Christ...

Her tongue slid out to lick her lips nervously before she pouted. "Noah, I can't see you."

His gaze darted to the small box and saw that her view was of his throat not his face. Giving in to the insane urge, he drifted his fingers over the image of her cheek, her throat and lingered on her lips, his heart still racing. Then he schooled his features and angled his phone. "Release your seatbelt."

She frowned. "I'm in a moving car, Noah. It's not safe."

Had he not been aroused to the point of pain, he'd have laughed. And reminded her how she'd crawled onto his lap on the way back from the jazz funk gig in Vienna. "You're no longer moving."

FOURTEEN

Leia glanced around her in surprise. "Where am I? And where's the driver?" she whispered with a touch of embarrassment.

"You're in a safe place and he's close by. Release the seatbelt and take off your dress, Leia."

Her gaze lowered, and she complied albeit with excruciating slowness. Watching her lift her hips to wriggle out of her dress was pure torture. But the sight of her bare breasts and the filthy decadence of the stockings and garter was even worse. Or better. Hell, he didn't know anymore. He was going insane. Because if he'd had any brain cells left, he'd have ended this call the moment she was safe.

She dropped the dress, settled her red-tipped fingers on her thighs and glanced up into the camera. That look of submission sent fire through his veins.

"You are so fucking beautiful," the words tripped out of his mouth before he could stop them.

A slow stretch lengthened her body, as if in direct reaction to his words. He clawed a hand through his hair and pulled hard, hoping the pain would focus him. All it did was make him yearn for a different pain. The pain he wanted to deliver to those tight nipples. His mouth flooded with saliva as the urge to bite, suck and feast on her charged through his body.

"What next, Noah?" she asked. Her head tipped back against the seat in supplication, her body slowly opening wider to his gaze. Awaiting his command.

"Slide your right hand over your stomach. Slowly. Now use your nails. I want to see the blood surge under your skin." She gasped and her nipples tightened into stiffer peaks. "Again," he growled.

Over and over she scoured her flesh, until her stomach showed four lines of red.

"Slide your panties down to your knees. No, keep your knees together." He couldn't handle seeing her pussy. Not just yet.

Without raising her gaze, she hooked her fingers into the sides and did as he commanded, leaving the flimsy thong caught at her knees. That picture of utter perfection made the hand caught in his hair tremble. Noah didn't dare touch himself. Not yet. Or he'd explode into a million useless pieces.

Taking a deep breath, he concentrated on staying on the right side of coherent. "Pull on your nipples for me. Show me how tight they are. Look at me when you do that," he growled.

Letting go of her panties, she slid her hands over her body, lightly cupped her breasts, catching the rock hard nubs between finger and thumb. Even through the screen, he saw how tightly she pinched. His groan drowned her gasp and her eyes grew hazy with desire. But he wanted...*needed* more. "Harder, Leia. Make it hurt."

"Yes, Noah." She caught her lip between her teeth, pulled and let out a helpless cry as her back arched off the seat.

Holy hell...

Again and again she tugged at her nubs until her thighs quivered under the sensations rolling through her.

"Tell me how you feel," he ordered. His breath fogged the screen and he realized he'd leaned so close to the laptop, he was in danger of unseating himself. He relaxed a touch and groaned when his erection brushed against the edge of his desk.

"My skin's on fire and...and I feel like I'll go crazy if I don't touch myself."

"But you are touching yourself, baby. You're fondling your pretty little nipples. Is that not enough?" he taunted.

Her eyes met his, sultry and alluring, wide and imploring. She shook her head.

"*Vocalize.*"

"I need to touch my pussy." She tugged harder on her nipples, and her mouth dropped open as she gasped in frantic breaths. "Please." Her knees started to part.

"Not yet!"

Her legs slammed shut again.

He sucked in a satisfied breath. "There's a folded blanket behind you. Grab it." He gave her time to gather herself and do as instructed. When she had the cashmere cloth in her hand, he said, "Fold it over again, lie back on the seat and use it as a pillow. Do it without opening your legs."

The haste with which she complied spoke of her frenzied need for release. She swept her hair out behind her, swung her legs onto the leather seat and stretched out. Without him asking again, her eyes rose to his, her gaze fully compliant.

"How badly do you want to come, baby?" he rasped.

Her hips rolled once before she settled, but her hands fluttered over her stomach, as if magnets pulled them toward where she burned hot and urgent. "I'll do anything for it."

He stilled as a spike of anger pierced his arousal. "Don't you fucking make promises you can't keep. We both know you won't do *anything*, so use different words. How badly, Leia?"

Fear entered her eyes. "Badly enough that I'm willing to do whatever you ask me to."

"That's better." His gaze dropped to where her fingers had crept lower to her mound. "Hands down by your side, now." The boom of his voice made her jump.

A touch of rebellion narrowed her eyes, but she was caught up in their connection enough to know she would pay dearly for non-compliance.

Her hands settled beside her hips. She swallowed. And waited.

Noah finally gave in and gripped his hard on. Electricity jolted from his fingers, through his cock and into his body. The rush was so powerful, he closed his eyes and cursed. His heartbeat thundered loudly in his ears. With his free hand, he tore at his tie, loosening it before he passed out from lack of oxygen.

When he'd freed a few buttons, he sucked in steadying breaths and opened his eyes. She was staring at him, her mouth parted. That hint of her tongue stud had him rubbing at his agitated cock all over again. He needed to bring this to an end. Right fucking now.

"Take off your panties. I want to see how wet you are."

Exhaling, she folded her knees against her chest and Noah caught a glimpse of her sweet, glorious, glistening pussy. He fumbled for his fly, pulled down the zipper and curled one hand inside his boxer briefs to release his desperate cock. It jumped in his hand, screaming for satisfaction. Gripping the base to keep from prematurely blowing his load, he stared at the breathtaking woman filling his screen.

Her panties were dangling from her finger and her spiky heels were crossed against her ass. His tongue thickened in his mouth.

"Brace your feet on the roof, baby," he croaked as a bead of sweat trickled down his temple. "And then...then do what you need to do."

She wasn't expecting that. Her head rose off the blanket and her eyes clouded. "Noah?"

He heard her confusion. The knowledge that she was wary of accepting the control he was giving her should've thrilled him no end. Had their situation not been so fucked up, it would've meant she trusted him to be the sole provider of her pleasure, to withhold or reward as he saw fit. But they were fucked up. And he was hanging by a frayed thread, which he suspected would snap before the minute was up.

"It's okay, baby. Do it."

Slowly, her head sagged back onto the blanket. Her heels planted several feet apart on the car's roof and her eager fingers slid alongside her clit. Eagerly, he stroked himself in rhythm. Pre-cum dripped over his thumb. He groaned at the sight of the rough treatment she was giving her beautiful pussy.

She caught her swollen clit between two fingers and squeezed just the way he'd done to her before. She whimpered at the sensation and rolled her head from side to side.

Releasing the engorged bud, she slid two fingers inside her tight sheath. The sound of wet suction filled his ears, and Noah's cock jerked. As if the sound had triggered her hunger beyond endurance, she went to town, fucking herself with fast deep strokes. Her stomach quivered as she writhed and drowned in pleasure. In another time, another place he'd have told her to slow down so he could savor the experience.

But not tonight. Letting out a deep moan, her head rose drowsily off the blanket. "I want to see you, Noah. All of you." A quick, desperate swirl of her tongue over her upper lip. "Please."

He was too far gone to deny her. Rising, he kicked his chair away and leaned against the wall, his cock still wrapped in his fist. "Is this what you want?"

Her gaze dropped to his engorged staff, and she made a guttural sound of need.

"Yes. Oh God!"

Her stomach muscles quivered. That physical evidence of her hunger for him set the last of his brain cells on fire.

"Now, Leia!"

Nodding eagerly, she plunged in and out. Her skin flushed. Her moans grew louder as she neared her peak. "I can't hold on any longer," she gasped.

Noah pumped his fist and grunted, unable to speak. Leia's movements turned frantic. When he realized she was holding her breath, his mouth dropped open in shock. Then she totally blew his mind by slapping her pussy hard.

Again and again she delivered firm, stinging smacks to her sex. His heart pounded as he watched, completely entranced. Her face grew pinker with the need for oxygen and the pleasure churning through her. But she locked her gaze on him. Seeking permission. Even now.

Jesus.

"Let go, baby. Come for me."

With a breathless scream, she climaxed. Her legs dropped to the seat, her stunning body convulsing in the grip of feverish pleasure.

A roar ripped through his throat as he came hard and helplessly. Resting his head against the wall, he forced his eyes open. He didn't want to miss a single moment of her pleasure. After several minutes, she stilled, her eyelids drifting closed.

Staggering back to his desk, he collapsed into his chair. Another five minutes went by. "Leia, get up. It's time to put your dress back on."

"Hmmm, do I have to?"

"My driver's a good man with a young family. I'd hate to have to kill him for seeing you naked, so yes, dress on now. You'll find a hand towel in the compartment to your right. Use it to clean yourself up."

She rose slowly, her body sleek, her hair sexily disheveled and stunning as hell. But her brows were bunched in a frown. "You seem to have come prepared. Have you done this before?"

He opened his drawer, grabbed a white handkerchief and cleaned himself up. "Do you care?" Now that his brain cells were regenerating, the feelings he'd pushed to the side were resurrecting too.

Her nostrils flared and she bit her lip. "Yes. I care."

That stupid lance of pain again. "No, I haven't video called a woman in the back of my car and watched her make herself come for me before. I prefer to be an active participant in my sex games."

She slid a hand through her hair. "Oh. Okay...good."

He laughed, the sound coated in rough pain. If she heard it, she didn't show it. Maybe she was still caught in a hazy aftermath. She found the towel and slowly swiped it between her legs. His cock twitched, and he forced himself to breathe. The moment she folded it one side and pulled her dress on, her eyelids began to droop. "Seatbelt, Leia. Now."

With another pout, she wriggled into place and snapped the belt on.

"Noah?" Her voice was little above a whisper.

His cock twitched with a weak spurt of semen. "Yes?"

"It was good to...talk to you." Her eyes were almost shut. She sighed and settled back with her head turned toward the camera.

His throat tightened. "Yeah...sure. Lie back for a minute."

A weak smile. "Okay."

And because he really was a weak, pathetic fool, who had just come in his hand from watching the sexiest woman on earth finger-fuck herself to orgasm...because every single cell in his body regretted not being right there with her, holding her, Noah watched her sleep.

FIFTEEN

After getting slammed on her back with enough force to jar her teeth for the fifth time in a row, Leia growled. "If you're trying to say something, can you use words rather than actions, please? I'd prefer not to attend tonight's event covered in bruises."

Warren straightened and slicked his hair back into place. The previously pristine bandages wrapped around his knuckles were spotted with blood, making Leia wonder just how long he'd been in the gym before she'd arrived half an hour ago for their weekly sparring match.

"Very well. Either you concentrate, or concede the fight. I won't have my time wasted with paltry attempts."

"What the fuck are you talking about?" she snarled through the pain in her right shoulder. "I was doing okay before you decided to go into Terminator Mode."

"If you seek clarification using such coarse language, then perhaps we need to end this session."

She hadn't wanted to spar today, but the alternative had been to lie in bed, thinking about Noah and what happened last night. Wanting to repeat it again and again. And again.

In the end, the need for some other form of pain to mask the one gouging itself endlessly through her heart had won out. "No, I'm fine," she said and pulled herself up. "Consider me concentrated. Let's go!"

Loosening her knees into the desired bartitsu stance, she rolled her shoulders and brought her fists up. Warren took his time centering himself, long enough that her concentration slipped again.

He attacked without warning.

She managed to block him a few times before he caught her in the ribs with a merciless chop. Her breath knocked out of her and unable to move fast enough, he swept her feet from underneath her with a vicious kick. She landed painfully on her left hip.

"Dammit! What the hell are you trying to prove?" she shouted.

"That you're useless to me unless you're as committed to this as I am."

She blinked at the cryptic warning. "For heaven's sake, say whatever the hell it is you mean, Warren. I'm too fucking tired to decipher your codes today."

"You're tired? It's only seven-thirty in the morning," he delivered icily. "You didn't come home on Thursday and you were out of touch until past midnight last night. Your behavior this past week has been quite disappointing. Can I presume to ask where you were? Or should I hazard a guess? You were with King?"

"No, I wasn't with King." She didn't feel bad at the technical half-truth. "I haven't been with him since..." She stopped as her stupid emotions painfully counted the days. "I checked into a hotel on Thursday night because—" She paused again. Knowing about Noah's suspicions where Warren was concerned, did she want to tell him that Noah had people watching her? "Because I wanted to be alone. And I stayed there because I didn't have any pressing appointments in the office yesterday morning. As for last night..." She shrugged. "I went for a drive." Also technically true, but it had been a drive like no other. Her stomach still quivered at how the hot and steamy drive had ended with her so wrung dry, she'd fallen asleep in the back of Noah's car and woken up two hours later to find Noah watching over her.

Her heart had tripped over itself at the look on his face. But before she could speak, he'd sent her a crooked smile, wished her good night and hung up.

"I find that hard to believe since your driver returned without you at nine o'clock."

She refocused reluctantly on Warren and admitted with a sinking heart that their relationship had indeed changed beyond recognition. And not for the better. What she'd suspected before she'd taken the Indigo Lounge trip had come to fruition. She couldn't avoid it anymore. "Are you calling me a liar?"

"I find myself unable to trust you as readily as I used to...but I'm willing to make allowances for the sake of your present circumstances."

She laughed and shook her head. "So because I'm a little stressed, it's okay that I'm a liar? Hmm, I wonder what else I can get away with."

She lunged at his unguarded flank, but he was too quick for her.

He countered her attack with another hard chop to her side. She crumpled onto her knees and wheezed. When he held out a hand to her, she struck hard at his midriff.

He doubled over but delivered another flat kick with his foot that sprawled her out on the mat. He landed on top of her. His arms imprisoned hers and his strong legs trapped hers between the steel of his.

Dark brown eyes gleamed displeasure, mixed with other emotions. Focused on setting herself free, Leia didn't feel the full impact of his body until he shifted. Then the truth of his feelings became unmistakable.

Hell. She didn't want to admit what his body was blatantly stating to hers but the truth of it was pressed against her belly.

She shook her head, unease tightening her body as her conversation with Noah in the bistro rolled through her mind. "No, Warren...no."

His expression hardened. "If you pretend you didn't know this was coming, I will be very disappointed in you." The words were breathed softly against her cheek.

Turning her head a fraction, she concentrated on the ceiling, struggling to remain calm as he kept her pinned. "I knew it was coming."

He remained silent for so long, she reluctantly brought her gaze back to his. Satisfaction flared in his eyes. "So it's not foolish of me to deduce that you're here, with me, because the idea isn't repugnant to you."

"It'll never work. We don't want the same things, Warren."

A cool chill replaced the satisfaction. "Explain."

She thought about Noah, about how being with him made her heart, hell her very soul, lift, race toward danger with sheer abandon.

"You crave being controlled," Warren said. "But you wish to have free will as to who you let control you. I've known that about you since you were a child. Have I not given you that, nurtured that in you?"

"Yes, but I also crave warmth. Passion. And a little loss of control every now and then isn't a bad thing." It showed that she was human. That the man who commanded raw, gut-wrenching emotion from her was human too.

"You haven't been ready for what I can give you. Now you are."

"What you don't get is that I don't want it with you, Warren."

For several seconds he said nothing. Then he vaulted off her and held out his hand. "We will revisit this another time. When you're in a better frame of mind."

The Leia of a few weeks ago would've acquiesced immediately. Avoiding confrontation had kept her safe for five years. But, for good or ill, she was no longer that person. She rose without his help and went to the cooler to grab a bottle of water. "Don't hold out hope of me changing my mind."

He half circled the room, his fists clenching and unclenching once. "You won't afford me the courtesy of a discussion?"

"There's no point in discussing it. I won't change my mind. Once Stephen is caught, I'm moving out."

He tensed. The atmosphere grew icier. When he faced her fully, she accepted once and for all that the cool, unflappable Warren, whose strength she'd leaned on, was gone forever. A flash of malice blazed in his eyes before he banked it.

"You are not strong enough to leave me."

"You're wrong. I'm more than strong enough to stand on my own two feet."

The curling of his lips was so evanescent, she thought she'd imagined it. "Did King put you up to this?"

"You used to think me capable of making sound decisions before I met Noah. Have I suddenly changed so much that you can't accept that the decisions I make are my own?"

"Countless errors of judgment in the space of a week beggars that belief."

Her shoulder, ribs and hips ached. She wanted to walk away but she knew this conversation needed to happen. "You're welcome to make any conclusions you want. But I'm doing this, Warren. I'm moving out. I'll always be grateful for everything you've done for me. Please, know that. Without you, my life would've turned out a hell of a lot differently. But I don't owe you the rest of my life."

She headed for the door of the gym. She was one step from it when she heard him behind her.

"Wait."

Suppressing a grimace, she turned.

He stood in the middle of the room, cool, lean, his hair slicked back in place. "This sparring session isn't over. You've never given up mid-lesson. Are you going to start now?"

The challenge was a blatant test, a taunt for her to prove to him that she hadn't abandoned everything he'd taught her. She was tempted to say to hell with it and walk away. But walking away would mean he'd won. She needed to stand her ground. To fight. She headed back to the center of the mat. "Okay, let's get this over with."

A whirling series of kicks and blocks followed that made her grunt in pain, but Leia didn't give up. She even managed to get in a hit or two of her own. A few minutes before the fifteen minute session was over, he increased the strength of his strikes.

"Warren, that's enough..." She tried to block another one, but he came at her. "Warren!"

"You think you're strong enough? Then fight harder!" Another lethal strike.

She cried out as he caught and twisted her arm up her back. "Warren, stop. Shit, that hurts!"

He pushed her to the floor and slammed his body onto hers. "Show me how strong you are, my dear. Once I deem you worthy enough to stand on your own two feet, I'll let you go."

"Fuck you! Who the hell do you think you are?"

"I am the man who wants what's best for you." A soft kiss landed on her cheek. She shuddered and closed her eyes. "The *only man* who knows what's best for you. Why do you fight me?" Another kiss caressed her jaw before it trailed down the side of her neck.

"Warren, get off me." She tried her best to emulate calm even though her heart was racing loud enough to drown every other sound.

"I'd never hurt you. Not the way he did." He brushed her hair off her temple and trailed his fingers over the shaven patch above her ear.

That touch...right there in that exact spot, felt like the worst violation. She relaxed her body long enough to distract him, then launched herself up. The back of her head caught his nose.

He grunted in pain. She scrambled to her feet, but his grip on her arm tightened. Using the advantage of his superior strength and height, he yanked her closer. Her wrist exploded in agony, but she didn't have time to acknowledge it before he lifted and propelled her back against the wall. Once he had her caged in, he let go of her arm.

"I'm sorry, Leia. I didn't mean to frighten you. Please don't think badly of me."

Fear and shock held her rigid long enough for his head to descend toward hers again.

Oh God.

She started to turn her head but couldn't avoid him quick enough. His mouth crashed onto hers. Cool and moist, he explored her with a clinical expertise that left her cold. And angry.

She lifted her hands to his shoulder, ignoring the painful throb in her left wrist, and locked her fingers behind his neck. He made a sound, perhaps of satisfaction. Or arousal. She didn't waste time examining it. With his thighs braced on either side of hers to trap her, he'd left himself wide open.

She brought her knee up hard and fast. Bone connected with soft tissue. An angry howl accompanied her freedom.

Leia stood over Warren's bent form, her heart thumping in pain and disappointment. "You taught me to defend myself, Warren. Did you think I wouldn't defend myself against you?"

He wheezed in answer, his impeccable hair hanging around his face in disarray. Weirdly, Leia pondered how that made him seem a little bit human.

She backed away, keeping an eye on him as she neared the door. "Come near me again, and it'll be more than just your crushed balls on fire."

Noah checked his watch and cursed himself for the hundredth time for not taking his Maserati. Why the hell was he stuck in the back of a limo? Oh yeah, that's right. He didn't plan on getting through this evening sober. But then he should've ordered a different car or taken a goddamn helicopter to the event.

Because sitting in the same spot as Leia had done last night, surrounded by her exquisite perfume and the lingering smell of her arousal, was beyond stupid. Not to mention the enclosed space and the images smashing through his mind, were giving him the boner to end all boners. He would be lucky if he arrived at his destination alive.

He lowered his window and let in fresh air he hoped would cleanse his mind. Feeling marginally better, he passed a finger beneath the collar of his studded shirt. As the key speaker at the Silver Spoon Charity Ball, he hadn't been able to back out as he'd wanted to when Maddie had sent him the reminder yesterday.

King's Ransom had given a lot to the charity, which rehabilitated young offenders and victims of abuse. He'd agreed to give this speech because Gabe was also on the board of the charity and had talked him into it.

Gritting his teeth, he re-read the text message he'd received ten minutes ago - *Must pass on wing-man duties. Angie's back. She wants to talk. My dick may not fall off after all. Don't wait up.*

Fucking Gabe. A spike of jealousy shamed him. He would've given his right arm for an uncomplicated life right now. Leaning back, he rested his head against the seat then immediately swung his gaze upward. Sure enough, there were the two indents in the felt roof where Leia had planted her feet before ravaging herself to orgasm.

His cock hardened so fast his vision blurred. Holy fuck. Would he ever be able to sit in this car again without those hot memories torturing him?

"We're here, Mr. King," his driver informed him.

With a stiff nod, Noah threw open the door and strode past the group of paparazzi crowded at the stunning entrance to the five star hotel.

He greeted business acquaintances, drank champagne and schmoozed for fifteen minutes then breathed a sigh of relief when the announcement was made for guests to take their seats in the main gala room.

As he passed the easel that held the seat allocations, he paused. Irritation snapped through him when he realized who else was on his table. Shannon Gleeson, his ex-therapist.

This should be fun...

About to turn away, he froze when a name caught his eye.

Snyder. And seated right next to him...Leia.

SIXTEEN

Leia's wrist throbbed like a son of a bitch.

In a hurry to leave after the hotel doctor had examined her, she'd forgotten to take the painkillers he'd provided.

Sitting at her table in the stunning gala ballroom, she gingerly massaged the tensor bandage. Despite her injury being ruled a mild sprain rather than a break, it ached badly. She bit her lip as a dart of pain shot up her arm.

God, it hurt...

But the pain didn't compare to the absolute emotional devastation she'd experienced when she'd walked into the room and seen Noah with his arm around a statuesque redhead.

They'd been so absorbed in each other that he hadn't noticed Leia frozen beside his table for a good half minute.

Only a blind fool would've missed the *familiarity* between him and his buxom friend. Even then, Leia had been unwilling to accept it. Until the redhead had leaned in and whispered in his ear. Leia had watched her red lips mouth the word *fuck* and a dagger had speared deep into Leia's heart.

Perhaps sensing her agony, Noah had finally raised his head from the no doubt scintillating conversation, but only to grace Leia with a dismissive glance, before doing that half smile thing.

Then his gaze had dropped to her bandaged wrist. He'd vaulted upright in his seat, his face transformed into a furious mask.

The head usher, whispering urgently that Leia really needed to take her seat, had been the prompt her feet needed to carry her away from Noah.

The last hour had passed in an excruciating cauldron of hell. Although her seat was out of his direct eye line, she could feel Noah's gaze boring mercilessly into her from his executive table. She'd barely touched her food, nor been able to force down more than a mouthful of water.

They were ten minutes away from the *Krug & Regroup* interval. From past experience, she knew it was the power half-hour when deals were struck over more booze and expensive cigars. Once that was over, the keynote speaker, Noah King—oh God—would give his speech.

She risked a glance over her shoulder. His blue eyes hooked into hers, furious and demanding. The redhead leaned closer and whispered in his ear again. He gave another lip twitch but his eyes didn't release Leia's.

Beside her, a masculine throat cleared. "Did my flowers arrive?"

Leia pried her gaze from Noah's, past the redhead's fingers, which now caressed his neck, and faced forward.

"You cannot ignore me for the whole evening," Warren pressed. "My actions were...unfortunate. You set me straight in no uncertain terms. I'd like to think we can draw a line under it and move on?"

She finally deigned to look at him, her stomach roiling in sickening remembrance. "I asked to be moved from this seat. Unfortunately, the doctor who was called to attend my *sprained wrist* was unavoidably delayed. The charity hostess thought I wasn't coming, so they didn't bother to move me. *That* is the only reason I'm sitting next to you. Do yourself a favor and pretend I'm not here because I intend to do likewise." She turned and smiled at the guest to her right, cradling her wounded wrist in her lap to avoid anyone noticing how badly she was shaking.

The moment the MC announced the interval, she excused herself and jumped up. From the corner of her eye, she saw Noah rise too. She made it to the ladies room and collapsed into an empty stall. Half expecting him to storm in after her, she sat on the toilet, her heart in her throat. It took several minutes for her heart rate to drop from runaway-freight-train to speedhound pace. And for her to wonder whether she'd blown the whole thing out of proportion. Had Noah really been that interested in her, or had he been getting up to attend to someone else, like the redhead?

Her stomach churned with acid jealousy as she shakily rose and flushed the toilet she hadn't used. Opening the stall door, she went to the sink as three women walked in—including the redhead.

Fucking A.

Socialite Number One, the blonde in the group, checked herself out in the mirror, before leaning forward to tidy up her re-applied lipstick with the corner of a tissue.

"Brandon's getting on my last fucking nerve with this threesome bullshit. It's his birthday next week. I think I'll just do it, get it over and done with."

"Hmm, make sure you set the rules before anything goes down. Mine got a little awkward when Stanley tried to make it an ongoing thing. He claims I said he could have one whenever he pleased," Socialite Number Two huffed. "As if I'd want some skank rolling around in my Sferra Milos sheets every other night of the week."

They dissolved into giggles fuelled by too many glasses of champagne. Socialite Number Two turned to the redhead.

"So what's going on with you and the yummy Mr. King? We saw you two cozying up earlier." She smacked her lips together in rapid succession. "God, if I didn't love my Stanley, I'd hit that with everything I've got and then some."

Redhead swept her fiery curls over one bare shoulder and gave a sultry smile. "My lips are firmly sealed. But I can guarantee they won't be later." She winked and more giggles ensued.

Leia stood frozen at the sink, her face drained white enough to give Marilyn Manson a run for his money, as the trio trailed past her and out the door.

The adrenaline, which had coursed through her system when she thought of Noah, suddenly drained out of her. Nausea churned in her belly. Taking several deep breaths, she forced herself to straighten her spine.

Raise her chin.

Move.

Fuck Noah.

Fuck Warren.

Fuck every last man on earth—

Firm, merciless hands grabbed her waist the moment she stepped out of the washroom. Before she could blink, she was dragged through a dim archway and into an empty, smaller ballroom.

Instantly, the adrenaline shot back into her system.

"What the hell do you think you're doing?" she demanded.

Noah didn't stop. He slammed his hand against a door that opened onto a wraparound balcony on the south side of the sprawling hotel. Converted from a pseudo French Chateau, the clever design of the building allowed them to see into the gala ballroom but offered privacy unless anyone stepped out onto the balcony.

To one side, a set of wide stairs led down to the private driveway and beyond it to extensive gardens complete with intricate mazes and manicured lawns.

He trapped her against a stone pillar, hands braced on either side of her head.

She'd forgotten just how utterly devastating he looked in formal attire. Now, towering over her, with his shoulders blocking out the world and those eyes fixed squarely on her, her breath caught all over again. Her nipples hardened into tight, painful nubs and her sex throbbed to life.

She shouldn't be feeling this way about him. Not when he planned to fuck someone else tonight—

"What the fuck happened to your wrist?"

She'd seen Noah angry, but the furious intensity in his eyes was unlike anything she'd experienced before.

"Do you care?" She couldn't resist throwing his words from last night in his face.

Some desperately anguished part of her wanted him to remember last night. To remind him of how incredibly soul-shaking their mutual self-pleasuring had been. How primitive and visceral he'd been, leaning against that wall, stroking his cock. God yes. He had to remember because no amount of bravado could disguise the knowledge that she couldn't bear him moving on so quickly.

"Tell me how you hurt your wrist, Leia."

"Who is that woman?" she blurted.

He frowned. "What woman?"

"The redhead."

His hand slashed through the air in arrogant dismissal. "She's nobody. Your fucking wrist, Leia."

"I was sparring with Warren this morning...he grabbed me..."

His mouth worked for several seconds without any sound emerging. Then he crouched until he was eye level with her. His cobalt blue gaze bored into her. "*Snyder did this to you?*"

Pulse racing, she pressed her lips together.

He cupped his left ear and leaned closer. "I didn't catch that, sweetheart. Did. Snyder. Do. This. To. You?" His voice dripped lethal ice.

"Yes."

He straightened slowly and rocked back on his heels. One corner of his mouth lifted and Leia's heart stopped. He took several steps into the ballroom before she realized his intention. Pushing away from the pillar, she grabbed his arm.

"Noah, wait."

He stared down at her. "Take your hand off me, baby," he advised softly.

Fear spiked through her. "No. Where are you going?" The picture of his NYPD mug shot flashed through her mind. She knew how badly he'd hated himself for losing control two years ago. "Please, don't do anything..."

She caught a glimpse of Warren walking toward them at the same moment Noah did.

Dislodging her hand, Noah lunged through the French doors, grabbed Warren by his lapels and dragged him to the balcony.

Noah's first punch landed with a sickening crunch on Warren's jaw. With the element of surprise on his side, he got another punch in before Warren started to recover.

Years of bartitsu and Wing Chun had rewarded Warren with quick reflexes.

He kicked out with his foot, but Noah's reacted quicker. Sidestepping the other man, he delivered a powerful jab to Warren's ribcage.

Warren coughed once and went down. When Noah started to reach for him, Leia caught his arm.

"Noah, stop! Oh God, stop. Please!"

He planted his foot on Warren's throat, exerting enough force to keep him down. Then his eyes sought hers, a puzzled look in them. "Excuse me?"

An usher, heading their way bearing a tray of drinks, braked to a stop when he witnessed the spectacle unfolding. Leia shook her head frantically at him, and he beat a hasty retreat. "Please, Noah. Let him go."

Warren gripped Noah's ankle and started to struggle.

Noah pressed harder, exerting all of his lean muscle strength into blocking Warren's windpipe. "You want me to stop? You sure about that?"

Her breath shuddered out, her fear for him making her heart stutter. "Yes."

"Think about this carefully." Despite his easy stance, she couldn't mistake the deadly threat behind the words. "I let him go, everything changes for us. Are you ready for that?"

Her heart hammered. "Noah—"

"Those are my terms. You want me to spare this piece of shit despite him putting his hands on you, I will. But there will be consequences."

He didn't have to spell them out. His eyes blazed with an all-encompassing dominance that told her once she stepped into his orbit there would be no going back.

A shiver drenched her from temple to toes. "Let him go. Please."

His gaze raked her face slowly, imprinted the force of his will on her until she feared she'd drown in the sheer magnitude of it. Coolly, he stepped back, straightened his bow tie and cuffs.

Warren rolled over to his side, coughing and sucking in desperate breaths. One corner of his mouth trickled blood, and his jaw and throat were red and swelling.

Reaching into his pocket, Noah extracted his phone. "I have some trash that needs taking out. South side entrance." Icy blue eyes met hers. "Discretion preferred but not completely necessary."

Two men appeared minutes later, one she recognized as the driver from the night before. They lifted Warren like a sack of potatoes and headed down the stairs to where a dark grey SUV idled on the driveway. Still caught up in how fast everything had gone down, she stood dazed as Noah followed them down. Hands on his lean hips, he watched them push Warren into the back.

The SUV executed a tight turn and accelerated down the driveway.

Noah stormed up the stairs toward her. "We're leaving."

She shook her head. "We can't. You're the keynote speaker. You're due to give your speech in ten minutes."

"Fuck the speech. Look at me, Leia." He held his hands out to her. They were trembling. His rapid pants soughed in and out as if he couldn't catch his breath. "How the hell am I supposed to stand up and talk about giving juvenile offenders a break, when I'm feeling *fucking homicidal*?"

"But...you can't just leave..."

"Watch me."

Tugging his phone out again, he spoke into it. An usher hurried out and Noah passed him a note from his pocket, presumably his speech.

The limo she'd used yesterday pulled up. He led her to it, yanked open the door and rasped, "Get in."

Every nerve in her body jangled in warning of imminent...*exciting* danger. Her mouth dried as she looked up at him. Despite his ferocious expression, her heart squeezed for him.

He stared down at her, his teeth bared in complete, emotionless savagery. "Would you like me to repeat the request?"

Leia slid inside the car, wincing when she inadvertently leaned on her injured wrist. Noah slammed the door and reached over to secure her seatbelt.

For several minutes, he stared down at her damaged wrist in silence. Then he lifted it gently and turned it over, examined every inch of the bandage. His jaw clenched, and the corners of his mouth quivered with rage. "It is broken?" His words were so gruff, they were barely coherent.

She shook her head. "No, just a sprain."

"Did you have it checked out?"

"The doctor at the hotel examined me earlier this evening."

His gaze sharpened. "Hotel?"

"I'm staying at The Celestial. I...moved out of the Palm Beach house this morning."

He inhaled and exhaled, his eyes never leaving her face. "In an hour or so, when the urge to kill isn't riding me so high, you and I will have a very long talk." He started to rest her wrist on his thigh, then cursed when she winced again. Carefully setting it down, he pressed a button. A compartment slid out from beneath the seat. He grabbed a packet of pills, popped out two tablets and poured a glass of water.

"They'll help with the pain."

She swallowed them.

After putting the glass away, he cradled her hand on his thigh and yanked his bow tie free. Tossing it aside, he opened the first two buttons of his tuxedo shirt and rested his head against the seat.

Silence reigned for almost twenty minutes before she realized he didn't plan on speaking.

Leia couldn't keep quiet, not when one question burned holes into her. "You didn't answer me before."

He slid her a glance, which still held an unhealthy amount of fury. "Sorry, I must have been off my head with rage. Ask away."

Beneath the waves of volatile energy flowing from him, she nearly faltered. "That...that redhead..." She licked lips gone dry and tried in vain to calm her nerves.

"What about her?"

"Did you fuck her? Not tonight, I mean. In the past. And before you think of denying it, let me remind you that two people who've fucked have a way of looking at each other that makes it un-fucking-deniable," she spat the words out.

His jaw flexed. "I wasn't going to deny it. Yes. I fucked her. Back when she was my shrink."

"Were...were you going to fuck her tonight?" Why the hell was she doing this, driving poisoned knives between her own ribs?

"Frankly? Yeah, the thought did cross my mind."

By the savage satisfaction in his eyes, she knew her raw, anguished reaction to that news was plain to see on her face. She tried to snatch her wrist away. He imprisoned it against his thigh, the other curling around her nape.

"You can't handle seeing me with someone I fucked long before I met you? I've watched you take that ass-wipe's side over and over again. I've spent every night this past week drinking myself into oblivion because I didn't want to think that might be the night he finally crawled into your bed. So don't you fucking dare look at me with that broken look in your eyes."

SEVENTEEN

Noah watched her lips quiver and resisted the urge to smash his fist through the window.

He raised her arm until her delicate, bandaged wrist dangled between their faces. "He did this to you this morning, and you didn't call me. For that, you will pay. For now, you will reassure me thoroughly and repeatedly until I'm satisfied, that you'll never be alone with Snyder again."

"I wasn't planning on it, but not seeing him at all...that'll be hard to do since we work together."

"Not fucking good enough. I want your word, or we do things my way. And don't think I won't know, because I will."

Her hand trembled in his. "I won't be alone with him. I promise."

He wanted to ask her whether she was hurt anywhere else, but Noah didn't think he could handle an answer in the affirmative.

Despite knowing she would be attending the charity event, a bolt of shock had rocked him when he'd seen her standing in front of him. Especially after Snyder had arrived alone.

One look at her injured wrist and everything had ceased to register in his brain.

He suppressed a grim smile. When Shannon had reminded him tonight of the detrimental effects of repressing his emotions, he was sure she hadn't meant him to smash another guy's jaw. Her wandering fingers had told him exactly how she expected him to unleash his emotions...

Leia's hand moved beneath his.

He turned his head and captured her gaze.

Fear. Excitement. Hunger. He tracked the emotions across her face, and a different monster took hold of him. One that wanted to consume her until there was nothing left.

He cupped her cheek with his free hand. "You belong to me now, Leia. No inhibitions. No excuses. You scarified yourself for him. I accepted your sacrifice. Now, you're completely and irrevocably mine."

He rubbed his thumb along her lower lip. Her mouth dropped open. He breached the soft tissue, took control of her mouth and explored. His nail scraped her stud, triggering a bolt of electricity up his spine.

"If I want to fuck this mouth for a solid hour, you'll let me. If I feel like eating your ass until you drown in your own juices, that's what I'll do. But remember this - the second you say *stop*, all bets are off and I bury that motherfucker in the deepest, darkest hole. Understand?"

Her eyelids fluttered down, and she mumbled around his thumb. He slowly withdrew his digit and smeared her saliva over her pink mouth. "Speak."

Wide eyes threatened to drown him. "Yes, Noah."

A savage part of him regretted her easy acquiescence. The dark part, which craved to punish her for allowing herself to be hurt, wanted an excuse to go after the bastard.

When the car stopped in front of his building, he was almost relieved. Alighting, he looked up at the steel and glass structure and acknowledged he couldn't continue living in this soulless place anymore.

First thing tomorrow, he'd rectify that.

For now...

Tucking her right side into him so he wouldn't aggravate her injury, he walked them to the elevator and pressed the button for his floor. In her heels, she came up to his jaw. The scent of her shampoo tickled his nostrils as he breathed her in.

Their eyes met...meshed in the mirror opposite.

He positioned her in front of him and slowly circled her tiny waist with his hands.

"If this wasn't an office building, I'd commence your punishment right now. I'd bend you over and fuck you raw right here," he growled in her ear. He pressed himself forward and delighted in her shameless shiver when his rigid cock jumped against her ass.

The elevator stopped, and he guided her forward. He only bothered with the lights he needed to get them to the bedroom. Stopping before his bed, he shrugged out of his tuxedo jacket and flung it over the dresser before facing her.

"First you shower. Then we'll talk. Then I fuck you."

He started to walk away, but stopped when he noticed she wasn't moving. "Problem?"

She held up her wrist. "I can't undress myself. The chambermaid at the hotel helped me get dressed earlier."

Struggling to preserve the last of his endurance, he closed his eyes. If she couldn't undress herself, she couldn't take a shower on her own either. Inhaling deeply, he retraced his steps.

First, he removed her jewelry and placed them on the night stand. Then he steadied her, so she could kick her shoes off. He caught hold of her jacket, started to pull it off. She tensed.

"Noah..." A trace of apprehension darted over her face.

He saw why a second later. A large, purpling bruise covered her right shoulder.

"*What the fuck?*" He pulled the jacket off her shoulder, remembering in time to take care with her wrist. Smaller bruises covered her upper back.

Fingers shaking, he pulled down her zipper. With every inch of skin exposed, the blood thrummed in his ears until all he could hear was the sound of his rage.

"Jesus, Leia! He did this to you, and you asked me to spare him?" His voice trembled badly. Feeling his eyes itch, he rubbed them. His hands came away wet.

The hell...?

Turning away sharply, he strode to the window, one hand spiking into his hair. He tugged hard, making his scalp scream and his eyes sting even more. Reassuring himself that the wetness came from the pain, rather than any other stupid emotion, he slammed his hand against the window.

He wasn't sure how long he stood there, the urge to howl in pain and frustration building inside him.

When her hand settled on his back, he stiffened.

"I didn't just take it, Noah. I fought back. His face was already aching before you punched him tonight. And he'll need an icepack for his balls for the next month."

Bitterness churned his stomach. "If you're saying that to make me feel better, save it."

"I'm not. I promise."

His breath shuddered out. "Go to the bathroom, Leia. I'll be there in a minute." He didn't want her to see the state he was in.

She walked away without argument.

He pressed his forehead against the glass and closed his eyes.

What the fuck was wrong with him? Why couldn't he walk away from her? From the very first moment they'd met, he'd known she had the power to turn him inside out. Hell, she'd proved that over and over since then. He'd believed he was a masochist only when it came to sex.

Now, he was starting to believe he was defective enough to like having his heart ripped out and shredded repeatedly. To his knowledge only foolish assholes who made the mistake of falling in love—

Hell no...

He'd made the mistake of thinking himself in love with Ashley and had ended up in an NYPD cell for his troubles. And even if he was prepared to make room in his life for the possibility of love, Leia had made it clear she wanted nothing like that from him. Sex was what she wanted.

Well, sex was what she would get.

Gritting his teeth and forcing the absurd trembling in his body to cease, he toed off his shoes, removed his shirt and crossed the room to the bathroom.

She was reaching behind her with her uninjured hand, squirming to grasp her zipper. Her hair had lost its fight to stay up and tumbled down her back, hiding most of the bruises.

"I told you to wait for me," he snapped.

"No, you *ordered* me to go to the bathroom."

That little hint of fire sparked a flame in his belly, eating through the icy rage engulfing him.

Moving her hand away, he took over, lowered her zipper and let her dress drop. She stepped out of it, clad in only white, lace-topped stockings and a matching thong.

He crouched and came eye to eye with the bruise on her hip. The sound that escaped his throat didn't seem human.

She glanced warily at him. "It looks worse than it feels."

"Is that supposed to appease me? Because it's not working." He pulled off her thong and rolled down her stockings. Her hand steadied on his shoulder as she lifted each foot. Her fingers slid over his nape and curled into his hair, caressing gently.

"Tell me what will work and I'll do it," she murmured.

Pulling her fingers free, he stood, pushed her into the shower stall and turned on the jets, making sure to keep her bandaged wrist out of the spray. He didn't want to spend time drying her hair, so he twisted it up in a bun on top of her head. Then grabbing a cloth, he washed her.

"Your...your trousers are getting wet."

Noah ignored her, focused on getting the job done before he lost it. Each bruise he washed made rage thicken his blood. Every inch of smooth skin made him crave her with a wildness that reminded him he'd been helpless against their insane chemistry from the very start.

When he was done, he dried her, wrapped her in a towel and swung her into his arms.

She stared up at him with a mixture of wariness and worry.

"Noah, please talk to me."

In the bedroom, he pulled the towel free and slowly circled her, allowing himself to finally study her properly. The worst bruised places were her shoulder and hip. A few faint ones dotted her back and ribs, but those would fade within a day or two.

Returning to the bathroom, he took a tube and brought it back. Uncapping it, he applied the balm on the affected areas, swallowing a growl of rage every time she winced. Done, he tossed the tube aside and cupped her face.

She must have witnessed the true depths of his fury, because her eyes widened.

"Noah—"

"Shut the fuck up and listen to me, Leia. From now, until I set you free, I'm the only one allowed to bruise this skin. Not even you are allowed to mar it. I don't give a shit if you hurt yourself by accident. I see a mark or a scratch on you that I didn't put there, the monster comes out. Are we clear?"

She nodded. He let her get away with not vocalizing. There was no way she could've misinterpreted his words.

Slowly, he stepped back and pulled down the covers. He picked her up and placed her in the middle of the bed.

"Before we start, are you hungry? Do you want a drink?"

A small shake of her head, her beautiful eyes wary. "No."

Nodding, he walked into his closet and opened the large box he hadn't yet bothered to unpack. Locating the items he needed, he returned to the bedroom.

Her breath hitched the moment she saw what he held. Eyes wide, she shivered and her thighs clenched together. He laid the items on the bed and sat down.

"Tell me exactly what happened with Snyder."

He listened, eyes fixed on the headboard so he wouldn't lose his shit. When she was done, he forced an exhale and looked into her eyes. "What do you feel for him, Leia?" He needed to absolutely sure.

"Before this morning, I was grateful for what he did for me. But now, I can't help but think he was..."

"*Grooming* you?"

Her eyes clouded. "I know what you thought when you first met him but I couldn't...I didn't want to believe..."

Noah rose to his feet. Grabbing the items, he held them up.

"I need to erase what he's done to you. I need you to feel my hand, not his. So which is it to be? The ropes. Or the bull whip?"

Her mouth opened, but no words emerged. Her eyes, totally devoid of her earlier apprehension, darted between the two choices, her nipples slowly peaking. "I can't...I don't know..."

"Fine. The ropes it is." He tossed the whip away and picked up the three white silk ropes. Passing them between his hands, his blood began to thrum to a different beat.

Her nipples furled tighter, her nails digging into her thighs.

"Place your wrists up on the pillow beside your head. Because of your injury, I'll have to tie your elbows." He waited for her to obey before he moved lower on the bed. "Draw your knees up. Open them wide." Again, he forced himself not to become absorbed in her body. The ferocious hunger running rampant through him dueled with the rage. The second emotion needed to be dealt with before he did anything to put her at risk.

Working quickly, he looped the rope twice around her waist, placed the knots where he needed them, then hooked two loops on either side of her thighs and bound her ankles before securing them to the special hooks set into his bed. He stretched the ropes so she was wide open to him. Once he'd secured her elbows with knots that restrained her in a perpendicular hold, he stood back and looked down at her. "Does it hurt anywhere?" he asked.

Her tongue darted out, wetting her lower lip. "It's a little...uncomfortable but no, it doesn't hurt."

He bent down and gently kissed her forehead. "Your comfort is a non-issue here. This is supposed to be punishment, remember?"

"Yes, Noah."

Unable to resist, he traced a hand between her breasts, down to the rope securing her waist. Fighting his instincts, he drew back. "I can't take you when I feel like this. You're not the only one who deplores angry sex. So I'm going to take a minute."

He left while he still had use of his legs, leaving the bedroom door ajar so he could hear her if she needed him. Striding to the bar, he poured a neat whiskey and tossed it back. Then another. The third, he sipped, shutting his eyes as the liquid followed the same burning path.

Whirling away from the bar, he crossed to the living room and dropped into a sofa, desperately trying to blank his mind of what had happened to Leia this morning. How badly things could've gone.

He didn't think for one moment Snyder was incapable of rape. He was a little gratified that Leia had fought back, but hell...

He started as his phone rang. Frowning, he dug through his tuxedo jacket and stared, incredulous, at the number.

"Did you forget I'm no longer your patient?" he snarled into the phone.

Shannon laughed and did that pausing thing that had always irritated him. She was waiting for him to fill the silence, to volunteer information. He'd never fallen for the ploy during their therapy sessions. He sure as hell wasn't going to fall for it now.

He waited her out until she cleared her throat. "It was great to see you again last night. I thought we reconnected, but you left without saying goodbye."

"I didn't realize I was obligated to."

"Well, a goodbye would've been nice, Noah. I thought we were getting along—"

"You mean you thought I'd be crazy enough to return for seconds after I told you it'll never happen? I distinctly remember telling you to lose my number. Or do you want the ethics board to be apprised of the fact that you banged a patient?"

A husky laugh. "You're no longer my patient and that wasn't what I called for."

"Then get to the fucking point." He knew he was being an asshole. But he couldn't help himself. Leia had shredded every bit of his control and left him exposed...bleeding. Shannon had picked the worst possible time to call.

"Earlier this evening when we were talking, I thought you'd made progress. But now I'm convinced you haven't. I think you need to talk to someone."

"You mean you?"

"No, I can never be your therapist again, but I care about you....and I was hoping—"

He sighed. "It's never going to happen. We may no longer be patient and shrink, but we did fuck when I was your patient, so you need to decide if you want to let one fuck ruin your career, or if you wanna stop debasing yourself and walk away with some dignity. If I were you, I'd choose option two.

She went silent again. Noah waited her out. "In that case, I have a few highly reputable colleagues who—"

"No."

"Noah..."

"I said no. Believe it or not I know exactly what my problem is, Shannon."

"You do?" Surprise made her voice squeak.

He leaned forward and held the glass against his forehead. He shivered, his body suddenly terrifyingly cold, drowning him in the truth that drenched his soul.

"This time my problem isn't holding back. My problem is letting go."

EIGHTEEN

The harsh rasp of Noah's voice ceased, followed almost a minute later by the sound of glass smashing against a wall.

Leia's heart stuttered. Her mind raced with the possibilities of who could be calling him at this time of night, unable to dismiss the idea that it was the redhead making a reverse booty call.

She jerked the ropes, which tied her elbows to the bed, then forced herself to calm down.

Noah was hers.

If there was one thing she knew with unshakeable certainty, it was that he would never cheat on her while they were together...while he'd put his absolute claim on her. As warped as their situation was, that was one thing she didn't need to worry about.

That didn't ease the fear spiking her heart however.

Until I set you free...

She'd tried to drown out those five words since he'd spoken them. Heck, she had a lot of things to worry about between now and whenever Noah deemed it right to toss her aside.

But the threat grew in her mind until she whimpered with the pain of it.

Fuck. She was trussed up like a chicken, her sex bared to her primitive and possessive lover, and all she could think about was some point in the future when he would throw her away like a used rag.

The minutes ticked by, slow and excruciating. Her wrist began to throb as the painkillers Noah had given her earlier wore off. She wanted to call out to him but knew that he needed to take time.

At last, footsteps approached, and her mind gratefully emptied of everything except the man stalking toward the bedroom.

He entered, and her lungs ceased to work.

He'd said he needed a minute. He'd taken close to half an hour. And yet that look of a feral predator clung to him. His beautifully sculpted chest rose and fell in heaves, and his jaw clenched hard enough to rival granite.

A glass containing amber liquid on ice hung from his fingers. He raised it to his mouth and sipped before shutting the bedroom door. Either he'd replaced his drink, or he'd smashed something else earlier. The memory of that violence sent a shiver racing over her body.

Strolling to the bed, he slid a hand under her head and held the glass to her lips. The scent of whiskey hit her nostrils. She took a sip and felt it burn down her throat.

Lazily, he tested the ropes then stopped at the bottom of the bed.

Sculpted so beautifully it hurt to look at him, nevertheless Leia couldn't take her eyes off his golden perfection.

Despite his damp trousers and the air-conditioning blasting into the room, the enormous hard on Noah sported was unmistakable. Her racing heart sprinted faster. Instinctively, she tried to pull her knees together, to savor that sweet ache between her thighs. But the ropes wouldn't give more than an inch or two.

Mesmerizing blue eyes gleamed as he watched her struggle. Lifting his glass to his lips every few minutes, he stared at her, claiming her from head to toe with a ruthlessly possessive look, which promised complete annihilation.

Tilting his head back to finish his drink, Noah walked round and placed the glass on the nightstand. Reaching in, he caught a cube of ice between his fingers, then sat down on the bed.

He started at her forehead, a delicate touch that sent a judder slamming to her core. Her nipples tightened and goose bumps broke out all over her body. Next, he touched the ice to the pulse racing at her throat, then to the crook of her elbows above where the ropes held her down.

"Ah," she groaned, her knees jerking together again as the ache between her legs intensified.

Drops of moisture trailed the swiftly melting ice down the inside of her arm, over her collarbone and up her opposite arm. The size of the cube had reduced to half when he trailed it between her breasts. He left it there and just stared at her.

A muscle jumped in his cheek, and his breathing grew long and deep as if in a trance.

"Noah..." she stopped, unable to find the words to release him from the strange head space he was lost in.

He cupped her jaw and lowered his face to hers. "If I decided to keep you here, tied in my bed forever, would you hate me?" he whispered fiercely.

Her heart hammered. "Noah?"

"You've *completely* fucked with my head. I can't think straight when you're out of my sight. So, now you're mine, I'm thinking the best way forward is to keep you here like this for eternity."

Licking her lips, she attempted to pull him out of his weird funk. "You could, but the maid would find me like this, and she'd call the authorities. Some idiot will put me in a museum display case labelled The Woman Who Died From Coming Too Much. I'd be ruined forever."

One corner of his mouth twitched, but any trace of mirth quickly disappeared again. He traced his fingers over her collarbone and watched two rivulets of water roll beneath her breasts. She shivered again as the last of the ice melted. He took another cube from the glass and traced it around her navel, down to the top of her mound. Leaving it there, he stood and removed his trousers and briefs.

Dear God...

Thick veins curled over his engorged cock, its broad and beautiful head touching his belly button. His balls hung heavy and tight and her mouth watered with the need to taste him.

A bead of melted ice rolled onto her clit. "Oh!" Her hips bucked hard enough to rock the bed. He calmly picked up the dislodged ice and placed it back on her mound.

"Dislodge it again, and you don't get fucked until morning."

She stilled immediately, her mouth dropping open on a shocked breath. There was no way she'd last if he carried out the threat. Swallowing, she watched him watch her. The intensity of his gaze seared her as he traced his hands up and down her inner thighs. Another bead of water touched her throbbing nub and she shuddered. Never in her wildest dreams would she have guessed how insane a cube of ice could drive her.

But she knew it was the man more than anything else.

Noah heightened her every emotion, drew out and expanded each reaction into a unique experience.

The trickles were coming faster now, her body heat turning the ice into a puddle. It chilled her clit and pooled into her opening before spilling over her sphincter. Leia gasped and squeezed her eyes shut at the burst of sensation.

A stinging slap to her right breast drew a cry from her clogged throat.

"Same rule applies. Eyes open. I want to see your every emotion."

Another slap on her twin breast, before he soothed the sting with soft touches. Finally lying down on the bed next to her, he scoured his blunt nails down her stomach and over the rope around her waist to rest his hand on her wet pussy.

Her legs strained against the ropes, but he'd tied them expertly, maintaining a careful balance between the knots to keep her from chafing.

"You're on fire, baby. Are you dying for my cock?" he crooned against her cheek.

"God, yes! Please..." She turned her head, eager for his kiss, but he moved away before their lips touched. Frustration burst underneath her skin. She was seconds away from coming, but she knew Noah wouldn't let her until he was ready.

One hand fisted in her hair, tightened until her scalp burned. "How many times did you finger-fuck yourself to orgasm this week?" he demanded roughly.

"Just once, in the limo...with you."

"You mean this hungry little cunt didn't scream for satisfaction at any other point in the last seven days?"

A wave of heat rushed up her face. "I tried. I couldn't...couldn't stand my touch. It didn't feel the same..."

He leaned in and bit the sensitive spot beneath her ear. Hard. "But now you're straining against your bonds, eager to be set free. To do what? Touch yourself, make yourself come?"

"No. I want to touch you. Please."

His mouth drifted over her throat, grazed his teeth over her armpit before biting the side of her breast. She yelped. "Request denied."

He rose and plucked another cube from the glass. Then he straddled her body, his thick thighs braced against her rib cage. Leia's mouth dried at the sheer magnificence poised above her.

"It's time to cool you down a little. I can't have you coming from those greedy little hip rolls you think I haven't noticed."

Without warning, he pressed the ice cube into her sex. She screamed at the insane sensation. Head slamming against the pillow, her whole body shook as chilled pleasure shot up her spine. But the effect of the ice soon took hold, applying the brakes on her headlong spiral into ecstasy.

Panting desperately, she groaned as he pushed the ice in further with his middle finger. His other hand grabbed his cock, caressed it from root to tip and slowly rose to lean over her face.

NINETEEN

"Open," he instructed.

She obeyed without question. Her eagerness to taste him overwhelmed her every other sense. Her tongue stud brushed his balls and Leia watched him shudder above her.

His finger withdrew from her pussy. "Keep that in there."

She heard his silent warning loud and clear. If the ice slipped out, she wouldn't get fucked.

Swallowing a whimper, she clenched herself tight. Her walls turned numb around the ice. The sensation was so incredible, she lost her train of thought for a moment.

"Leia," he growled another warning.

She flicked her tongue eagerly against his balls, making sure her stud grazed his perineum. A hiss escaped his throat, and his cock jumped in his fist. Greedily, she licked and sucked, absorbing his hoarse sounds of pleasure and the waves of arousal replacing the angry void from minutes ago.

Her pussy clenched harder around the ice. Her hips rolled again, her juices dripping from her pussy to trickle around her tight hole. Every nerve in her body felt alive, aroused like she'd never been before. When Noah leaned forward and cupped the back of her head, she read his intention and immediately wet her lips.

Taking the broad head of his cock in her mouth, she sucked hard. His thighs juddered against her. With an animalistic growl, he pushed himself in until his broad head hit the back of her throat. She curled her tongue so her stud pushed up into the underside of his cock. The hands fisting her hair trembled. Watching his breathtaking face, she moved her head up and down, silently indicating how much of him she could take.

He established a rhythm, pushing himself deep, withdrawing before her gag reflexes kicked in. She felt the last of the ice melt and gush out of her. Within seconds the hunger built, her pussy clenching and unclenching. Desperate for him, she opened her throat and flattened her tongue, greedy for the only part of him available to her. The short hairs on his thighs tickled her nipples as he rode her. When a trail of pre-cum coated her tongue, she groaned, barely able to stop her eyes from rolling at the potent taste.

"Jesus. Even tied up, you fucking destroy me," he groaned with a desperate lunge. Unbelievably, he thickened, stretching her mouth as he threw his head back and cursed.

"Shit, I'm gonna come." He shuddered hard.

Her mouth clamped around him, begging him not to deny her. Eyes dark as a midnight sky, he stared down at her.

"You want me to blow my load in your mouth, baby?" he rasped. "Is that what you're begging for?"

"Hmmm," she pleaded.

Still keeping the rhythm, he released her hair and cradled her skull. One thumb absently brushed back and forth over the short hairs above her left ear. Lost in the carnal sensation, Noah groaned over and over again as he neared his peak.

"Damn! Fuck, are you ready, baby?" he growled.

Her head bobbed up and down.

He pulled back a couple of inches to give her room, then flooded her mouth with a thick gush of semen. She couldn't swallow fast enough. A drop dribbled down her chin and landed on her chest. Noah made another guttural sound, threw his head back and spurted another load on a soul-deep groan. His chest expanded as he struggled to inhale.

Leia had never seen a more magnificent sight.

When he was spent, he withdrew. Almost reverently, he laid her head against the pillow, caught up the drop of cum on his finger and held it against her lip. She licked his finger clean then kept his digit trapped between her teeth.

That lopsided smile made a lightning fast appearance and he got off her. Leia stopped herself from begging him to stay put. But she had other, more desperate needs.

Stretching out beside her, Noah lazily sucked on each nipple, the back of his hand caressing down her body.

"Now, what to do about this." He pressed the pad of his fingers between her legs. She was shamefully slippery and her clit was so engorged, Leia was sure it would pop in a second.

"Fuck me." Her voice broke between the words.

"Repeat that, baby."

"Fuck me hard. Punish me, Noah. Please—"

Two fingers plunged inside her as he bit her nearest nipple. Leia screamed as her orgasm exploded from her core. The force of it sent her hips off the bed but her ropes gave little room for movement. With her legs wide open and her body restrained, her pleasure took its time to roll through her, catching every nerve in electric fire and prolonging her climax.

"Oh God!"

Every time she started to come down, Noah would bite harder, curl his fingers so he hit the spot in her pelvis that sent her into orbit again. Or he'd remove his fingers and bring his hand down hard on her pussy, delivering a piercing mixture of pleasure and pain that unraveled another orgasm.

She was babbling her way through her fourth climax, when he shifted positions and dropped his head between her legs. On a thick groan, he lapped up her juices, his tongue curling into her core as convulsions raked her. Catching the two ropes framing her sex, he pushed them together, plumping her up even further. Opening his mouth wide, Noah sucked her into his mouth. The sight of him gorging on her was so erotic, Leia blinked back helpless tears.

God, she loved him. Not because of what he did to her in bed. But hell, that counted for a lot of her feelings. Even incandescent with her, he was delivering pleasure where other men would have taken what they wanted and left her high and dry.

His thumb probed her second hole. Gasping, she tensed. He continued with the caress, his eyes holding hers. Slowly she began to relax. The pressure increased until he breached her.

The pleasure/pain synergy escalated, the sensations different but oh so incredible. Just when she abandoned herself to another epic release, he pulled away.

"No, please! Oh God, please don't stop."

"I have no intention of going insane tonight, baby. And not fucking you right now is guaranteed to land me in a straitjacket."

She squeezed her eyes shut on a prayer of thanks, only to pop them open when he slid one hand beneath her ass and plunged his middle finger where his thumb had been a second ago.

"Noah!"

With a grunt, he thrust his cock inside her. The world ceased to make sense from then on.

He fucked her like she was his worst enemy and his best friend.

Rough and tender, hard and soft, he kept her balanced on the brink until dawn lightened the bedroom blinds.

Finally, with both their bodies covered in sweat, he gripped the rope around her waist, and used it to yank her onto his cock. He was full enough and hard enough to hit her edge of her womb. Pain chased up her spine, quickly overtaken and drowned out by pleasure so deep, her heart quivered.

"God, that feels so good! Don't stop, Noah...please..." she whispered, her voice hoarse from screams.

He paused and looked at her. Something shifted in his eyes and he sucked in a huge breath. "Holy fuck, you're breathtaking.

And so goddamn beautiful open to me like this, abandoning your control and helplessly drowning in your pleasure. Do you have any idea how much I crave this?"

She clenched around him in answer and he groaned.

He resumed the pounding, his eyes absorbing her every reaction. "Step over the edge with me, baby. Come. Now."

She shattered into a million pieces. He followed closely behind, his beautiful body collapsing onto hers.

His head dropped between her breasts, and he made a choked, wounded sound. She curbed the sound of distress, clenched and unclenched her fists uselessly as the need to comfort him rushed through her.

When they'd caught their breaths, she whispered his name. "Noah?"

Slowly he raised his head. "Yeah?"

"Kiss me. Please, kiss me."

His eyes dropped to her mouth, and a corner of his lips tilted in a sad smile. "No. I'll kiss you only when you've earned it."

TWENTY

She woke up alone in bed. Jackknifing, she threw her legs over the side and stood.

Her legs wobbled, the byproduct of being tied up and fucked by Noah for the last twenty-four hours. Parts of her body were so sore she couldn't think about them without wincing, and she had rope burns in places that made her face flame.

When she determined she could walk, she rushed out of the room before her brain had fully deciphered why panic was flooding through her veins. Halfway down the hall, she heard voices. Déjà vu froze her in place. Then, shaking her head, she crept closer. Peeking into the room closest to the living room, she saw Noah seated behind his desk, the light from a laptop bathing his bare chest.

Relief weakened her. Feeling foolish for her bare-assed dash from the bedroom, she considered silently retreating. But as usual, the sight of him arrested her and reduced her willpower to nil.

He looked up, saw her and hit a button. The voices from the computer stopped.

Blue eyes narrowed. "You walk in here naked and I'll paddle your ass so hard you'll wear an ice pack for a month," he growled.

She started to backtrack. Now she was assured Ashley and Warren were nowhere in sight, and that there wasn't going to be a reenactment of last week, she could return to bed. Or...

She glanced back at Noah and found him staring at her.

One eyebrow quirked. "What?"

"I don't have any clothes besides my gown."

His gaze shifted to the screen and he held up a finger at whoever was on the other side. He rolled his leather chair to the side and his sizzling gaze travelled over her nude body again. She wasn't ashamed to bask in the thrill of watching his eyes darken with lust. "Dressing room to your left in the bedroom. Find something to wear and come back here when you're dressed."

Not stopping to question why her heart was bouncing around her chest in joy, she rushed back into the bedroom. There was enough daylight to see where she was going without stopping to work out how to open the blinds. She bypassed his formal stuff and headed for the stack of T-shirts and jeans. Since there was no way she'd fit into any of his pants, she stuck to riffling through his tops. Her breath caught when she saw the Vassar T-shirt.

Questioning herself over the wisdom of her actions, she gave a mental shrug and pulled the slightly worn T-shirt over her head. The burning need to know what the item of clothing meant to him ate at her as she smoothed a hand over her hair. She could ask, but she had a feeling her queries would remain unanswered.

Noah may have cradled her close after untying her and rained kisses on her temple and cheeks before they dropped off to sleep in the early hours of the morning, but there was still a barrier between them. A Warren-shaped barrier which only time and trust would smash through. And they were very much in the early stages of that journey.

She entered the study and Noah's head snapped up. Electric blue eyes raked her, then narrowed when he saw what she was wearing. She waited for him to tell her to go take it off.

After a moment, he beckoned to her. "Hold on a second, boys."

She rounded his desk and stopped. He scrutinized her some more before he pulled her into his lap, tugging the hem of the T-shirt down over her knees.

Two faces stared at her from the screen. The boys couldn't have been older than seventeen or eighteen.

She glanced at Noah and back to them. "Hello, I'm Leia," she said.

They eyed each other, then gaped at her.

Noah growled. "The lady said hello. Have you drowned your manners along with your brains cells in all those battery acid energy drinks you guzzle by the gallon?"

"Uhhh...hi—"

"Yeah...hey—" They spoke in unison.

"These two knuckleheads are Tim Savarino and Harry Johnson. Believe it or not, they're grad students at MIT."

"I'm the youngest in my class," Harry piped up.

"Yeah, only by 2.35 days," Tim countered with a punch to his friend's arm. They proceeded to tussle.

Noah pinched the bridge of his nose. "Jesus. Stay on point or I swear to God..."

Leia curbed a smile and glanced back at him. "Are these the guys who designed the app?" she whispered.

Capturing her gaze, he nodded. His hand crept up her back and around her waist and tucked her body into his. Leia tried to contain the jumping of her pulse.

Tim cleared his throat and flipped his black and orange-tipped bangs. "Okay, umm, like we were saying...we shut it down."

"And like I said, I need proof. The deadline is in just over five hours. I need to know there's no way it can be brought back on line."

Leia tensed. Noah sent her a loaded, piercing glance.

Swallowing, she returned her gaze to the screen.

The boys exchanged hurt glances and stared back at him. "You don't trust us?"

Noah's hand tightened around Leia's waist. Her nerves were making her squirm her ass crack right against his hardening cock.

And she was wearing his T-shirt again. That and the knowledge that she was naked and warm threatened to scramble his brain.

He wrestled his concentration back. "I trust you. But I still want proof. This is to do with her." He cocked his head at Leia and slid one hand over her nape. Her purr of acceptance of his ownership was for his ears alone. His cock grew stiffer, which considering the amount of action it'd seen in the last day and night, was nothing short of a miracle. He cleared his throat.

"That means there can be no room for error. Error means I hunt you two down and deprive you of your genitals. And as young men who're about to get richer than your wildest dreams, I guarantee you'll need your genitals. So talk me through what you've done. And use words I'll understand so I don't—"

"Come over here and castrate us. Yes, we get it," Harry griped. They exchanged glances again and Noah wondered whether they'd devised a way to communicate telepathically.

Tim pursed his lips. "In the simplest terms, we infested their website with a self-replicating trojan. But the beauty of it is that while they were bouncing the auction site through about a hundred proxy servers, we're bouncing our trojans through just under a thousand servers across the world. So they can't send their virus after ours. And our trojan is also designed to find and destroy theirs whenever and wherever it pops up." Harry grinned. "And we installed a message for anyone who tries to log on. Go on, try the link," he urged excitedly.

Leia stiffened. Noah smoothed a hand down her thigh, kissing her cheek in reassurance. "It's okay baby. They may not look it but these two are quite good at what they do."

"Umm...you know we can hear you, right?" Harry grumbled.

Noah ignored them, staring at Leia until she swallowed and nodded. The flash of pain in her eyes gnawed at his insides, but he forced himself to access the file he'd kept under specially encrypted code and clicked on the link.

His screen flared to life with a picture of two yellow and blue goggled cartoon characters frantically fondling each other and giggling.

Leia burst out laughing. Noah reluctantly chuckled.

He tried to access it half a dozen more times before finally shutting down the site. "Okay, you get to keep your little peckers for now. But keep an eye on the sites. Anything happens, let me know straight away. Understood?"

They nodded.

Leia leaned forward. "Wait, crashing the site doesn't stop the auction, though, does it?" She chewed on her lip.

Harry smile disappeared, and his face turned serious in a way that reminded Noah why investing in these two brilliant minds had excited him in the first place. "No, but finding the top bidders' website as per Mr. King's request, and infesting them with a worm so they can't broadcast any material at all, sent them the message. The...umm...porn industry is worth billions." He blushed at the word *porn* and Tim smirked. "Shutting down a website, even for a few hours, is seriously bad for business. Four of the bidders dropped out before we crashed the site. We've taken care of the rest."

Leia's head whipped round to him, her eyes wide with delighted surprise. "You did that?"

He nodded. "I did that. For you."

She blinked and a sheen misted her eyes. Turning to the screen, she gave a little wave. "Thank you, boys," she said with a smile.

They openly gaped at her. Tim recovered first. "Umm...you're welcome. And it was nice to meet you, Leia."

When his gaze dropped to her breasts, Noah growled and terminated the link.

"They're sweet," she said.

He slammed down the lid of the laptop. "They're horny teenagers whose only saving graces are that they're blessed with some cool skills."

She took his head in her hands and pressed her mouth to his jaw. "So...I said thank you to the boys..." Her fingers trailed down his throat and her nails scoured his chest.

He hissed as his heartbeat escalated. "Yeah?"

"Now I want to find a way to thank you."

Mentally inspecting the box of toys he'd had delivered from storage, he said, "I'm sure I can come up with a few sug..." He stopped when she shook her head.

"I have one in mind." Her face reddened. Her eyes darted to his and slid away.

He captured her jaw. "Spit it out."

"I want you to...umm, fuck me in the ass."

His fingers tightened and his senses caught fire. The need to grant her wish screamed through him, but he forced himself to shake his head. "Baby, I'm too big for you. You cried last night when I tried, remember?"

"I was overwhelmed by...everything. I can't guarantee I won't be overwhelmed this time too, but I really want you to take me there. I want you to hurt me like that, Noah," she whispered huskily.

Blood roared in his ears until he thought he'd burst. He stared long enough to make sure she meant it. Then he picked her up and rearranged her so she straddled him, her legs thrown over the arms of his chair. His hands teased the bottom of the T-shirt, every sinew in his body tightening in anticipation of the treasure beneath. "We'll try again...soon," he added when she opened her mouth to protest, "but not right now."

He smiled at her adorable pout. Placing a hand on her stomach, he pushed her back until she leaned her elbows on his desk. Then he lifted the T-shirt and bared her to him.

God. Fuck. No matter how many times he ate, fucked and fingered her, his hunger only grew wilder, stronger.

Addicted. That was the word he'd applied to her the first time they'd fucked.

That addiction had survived all the shit of the last week and had puzzlingly multiplied a thousand fold.

"Noah..." she murmured.

And the way she said his name... He gritted his teeth.

Lifting his head, he looked into her breathtaking face as he flicked a thumb over her swelling clitoris. "Tell me you did the sensible thing and didn't schedule any meetings for today?"

Her eyes were darkening with arousal, but she shook her head. "Nothing that I can't handle over the phone or with a l...laptop," she groaned the last word, and her head fell back, her mouth dropping open to gasp her pleasure.

"Good girl." Noah quickly unbuttoned the jeans he'd pulled on to call the boys. His cock sprang free, immediately seeking her core like a fucking guided missile.

Leia made a thick sound at the back of her throat and his dick twitched again, reminded of how it felt to have that hum against its head. She rubbed herself eagerly against him, slicking the underside of his shaft with her wet heat.

Gripping her thighs, he spread her wider. She flinched from the rope marks marring her inner thighs, but he didn't loosen his hold. He knew the pain only added to her pleasure. She confirmed it when her eyes glazed over and she licked her lips in anticipation of his possession.

Tugging the T-shirt over her head, he caught it at her elbows and tied a snug knot. With her hands immobilized behind her, he went to town on her beautiful small breasts. He licked, sucked and slapped her exquisite mounds until she begged him to finish her off.

Impaling her on his cock, he shouted at the first thrust. "Christ, you're so hot! So tight and silky."

She circled her hips in answer, her head thrown back in surrender of the insanity threatening to sweep them away. Noah attempted to slow things down...to gain a little clarity...to stop the rush of feeling that came with having this woman in his arms.

In the end, he closed his eyes and just rolled with it.

TWENTY-ONE

"Where's this place?"

Noah looked up from examining her newly re-bandaged wrist to the building the driver had parked in front of. He took his time to answer, kissing the inside of her wrist before laying it back on her lap. He nodded at the driver to open the door and turned to her.

"One Destiny Plaza is a new development. Twelve condos, two penthouse duplexes, each with a private gym, pool and a concierge service that means you don't have to leave the building unless you really, really want to."

"You sound like a realtor," she laughed.

"That's because I'm parroting mine. There's also a helipad at the top and I'm sure if you ask nicely, they'll build you a capsule to the moon or a stairway to heaven."

Grinning, she took the hand he held out to her. Her body brushed his when she stepped out of the car, and she heard his sharp intake of breath. Hiding her own flustered nerves, she returned the driver's smile and followed Noah, the man who made her heart race with very little effort.

Dressed in a navy blue shirt, tailored slacks and a grey jacket, Noah's commanding presence attracted attention the moment they walked into the building.

Female eyes checked her out, assessed the competition, calculated their chances and swung quickly back to him.

Not today, bitches, she felt like shouting out to them.

After fucking her twice more on his desk, he'd carried her into the bathroom and bathed her from head to toe. Then he'd set her down in front of the bathroom mirror and dried her hair. They'd shared a leisurely breakfast in his minimalist kitchen before he'd set her up with a spare laptop in his study.

He'd kept the conversation general and flowing and her throat had locked when she realized he was trying keep her mind off the impending auction deadline. He conferenced Tim and Harry every half hour, hammering them with questions about the strength of their trojan software until Leia had felt sorry for them.

Ten minutes before the deadline, he'd pulled her up from the sofa and onto his lap, his fingers playing over the area above her ear while his foot bounced with nervous energy.

His breath had punched out of his lungs when she'd circled her arms around his neck and planted a kiss on his jaw. "Noah?"

"Yeah?"

"Whatever happens, we'll deal with it together."

His foot had stopped for a moment, then resumed bouncing. "Too right we fucking will."

Her laptop had pinged with an email from her lawyers and the board, informing her they were on standby to deal with any media fallout should the auction go live.

She'd tensed at the one-line enquiry from one board member as to Warren's whereabouts.

Noah's jaw had tightened at Warren's response about taking a personal day, but he'd said nothing.

Midday had come and gone with no word from her stepfather. The boys' trojan had held, and Paddy called to say there was no suspicious activity at her office or any other place they were watching.

After another two hours, she'd begun to relax, allowing herself to believe they'd won this round. Thinking they'd be staying put for the day, Noah had surprised her by walking into the living room just before three, brandishing a box. It'd contained a gorgeous cobalt blue sundress with a visible leather-bordered zipper and underwear in fire-engine red. When she'd lifted her brows at the minuscule thong, he'd shrugged unapologetically.

He'd produced her shoes from the ball and lounged back to watch her dress in the living room. Next stop had been the private doctor waiting in Noah's office. The short, bald physician had declared her sprain healing, re-bandaged her wrists and given her painkillers to take when necessary.

Now, as she walked beside Noah through the stunning atrium designed to harness the best of Miami's year-round sunlight, the warmth of the day filled her heart. A futuristic-looking fountain gurgled quietly next to a pair of glass elevators, creating a sparkling reflection on the crushed glass and marble floor, as Noah walked her to the front desk and collected two keycards.

He inserted the first one into a slot in the sleek elevator and they shot up to the twenty-second floor. Trailing behind Noah, Leia glanced around the wide private hallway with interest. Everything looked beautifully designed and modern.

Noah opened the single heavy black door and stood back.

Crossing the threshold, she gasped. "Ohmigod, this place is stunning. Who lives here?"

Shutting the door behind him, he came forward and held out the key card to her. "It's one of the places I picked out for you to look at but judging by your reaction, I'm thinking this place is yours?"

Her mouth sagged open. "Are you serious?" She turned around and stared at the amazing living room. White leather sofas stood diagonal to black ones with a white scalloped rug completing the space. Above the seating area, a silver and crystal chandelier glinted, catching the sun's rays through wide rectangular windows.

She twirled and rushed to the opposite side of the room then screeched with delight at the less formal sitting area, complete with an Eames recliner, a floor-to-ceiling bookshelf and entertainment area.

She'd never given much thought to cooking her own meals or making her own coffee in the morning because Warren's housekeeper, Rita, had taken care of that. But now, the idea of total independence thrilled her into smiling broadly as she trailed her hand over the West African teak, which covered the center island. She imagined taking a gourmet cooking class and making a meal half as decent as the one Noah had cooked for her last week.

Checking out the rest of the Christopher Peacock designed kitchen, she walked through a short archway into a dining area. Beyond the chill-out space, sliding doors led outside to a huge balcony complete with a small pool and a set of white-cushioned lounge furniture.

Grinning, she turned to find Noah watching her, a smile on his face.

Walking over, she battered her eyelashes at him. "Oh Mr. Realtor, show me a bedroom with a skylight, and I'll be yours forever."

His smile faded. One hand slid over her nape and tugged her close. "Careful who you pledge yourself to, Miss Michaels. I understand you belong to a possessive motherfucker who doesn't like to even joke about imaginary assholes poaching what's his."

The atmosphere altered. Electricity and angst arched between them as Noah's hooded eyes pinned her. His head began to descend and she held her breath. Her mouth tingled, silently screaming for the kiss he'd denied her so far. He loomed closer until he filled her vision. At the last moment he twisted his head to one side and kissed the space below her ear.

Robbed of what she craved, Leia didn't hear his command to go until he tugged on her arm.

The rest of the two-bedroom condo was equally stunning, but her enthusiasm had waned. She made the right noises and even agreed to meet with the realtor but inside, her heart had turned to stone.

"You ready to go?" Noah asked after one final inspection.

She nodded and headed out of the kitchen.

He trapped her by the door and lifted her chin. "What's wrong?" he asked.

"You know what's wrong. I'm beginning to wonder what I need to do to get you to kiss me again."

His eyes dimmed. "You don't think I want to more than any goddamn thing in my existence?"

"Then do it. God, it's so easy. I'm right here..."

He laughed. "It's the most difficult thing in the world to kiss a woman who doesn't trust you...who doesn't think you're worth a call when she's in trouble."

His thick voice broke and ice drenched her. "Oh God, Noah. I didn't mean—"

He shut her up with a finger on her mouth. "I don't care what you *meant*. I only know that it ripped my guts out to know you chose to be alone in a goddamn hotel room rather than pick up the phone and call me after that asshole attacked you. You want me to kiss you? Show me that I'm worth something to you."

Dropping his hand from her lips, he stepped back and opened the door.

She stood frozen for a full minute after he walked away, blinking back stunned tears and the knowledge of how much she'd hurt him.

The sound of the elevator arriving galvanized her into movement. He waited with one hand on the door. When she reached him, they stared at one another for a long moment before he pulled her into his arms. They travelled in silence up another floor. She watched, puzzled as Noah went to a similar door and slotted in the keycard.

"Are we viewing another condo? I thought...the one downstairs is fine for me."

He threw the door open before answering her. "This one isn't for you."

"Then who...oh *you*?" she blurted.

"If it suits my needs."

A bolt of happiness shot through her, followed immediately by a well of despair. Aware that Noah was watching her, gauging her reaction like a hawk tracked its prey, she tried to neutralize her features. He shut the door and faced her and she knew she'd failed to fool him.

Long fingers traced her cheek. "You looked happy for a moment. But I'm guessing you let the monsters win yet again?" There was a heavy vein of sadness in his voice. "Does the thought of having me close distress you so much?"

She slid her arms around his waist and propped her chin on his chest. Preparing to bare herself to him made her heart hammer wildly. But she needed to take the step, or risk losing him sooner rather than later. "You want the truth?"

His nostrils flared. "Always."

"It scared me a little, I won't deny it. What we do to each other...it's powerful and untamable and reckless. I feel like I'm plugged into a live electric current every time I'm around you. It's exhilarating but I can't help wondering every now and then if won't...destroy us..." He started to respond but she shook her head. "That said, I'd rather have this, have a little of you for as long as you want this..." She attempted to smile around the painful throb in her chest. "I'm taking the condo downstairs, Noah. So you need to decide if you want this one."

His forefinger traced her mouth and he swallowed before he spoke. "It's already decided. I've had a duplicate keycard made for you for this place."

Her heart caught and happiness burst through her chest. "I'll have one made of mine for you, after I sign the lease."

"No need, it's already taken care of."

One corner of his mouth quirked at her affronted gasp. "The lease or the keycard?"

"Both."

"Do I need to waste my breath arguing with you on either issue?"

"Ah, baby, I wasn't really offering you a choice in the matter."

He grabbed her hand and guided her through the sprawling condo. It was easily twice the size of hers, with a larger pool, terrace and a hot tub. He groaned when they opened another door to a gaming room complete with roulette, pool and poker tables.

"The guys will never leave me in peace if they see this room."

She was wondering about his friends when he dragged her into the empty master bedroom and pulled down her zipper.

"I don't think I can call this place home until it's christened properly," he whispered in her ear. Her dress pooled at her feet and he lifted her out of it. Clad in just her panties and heels, she shivered at the fiery blaze in his eyes. "Will you help me christen it?"

"Yes, Noah."

Her throat dried as she watched him fumble to release his fly. His thick cock sprang free and she juddered in delight. Unable to wait, she pushed down her thong and kicked it away.

"Be a good girl and get on your knees."

TWENTY-TWO

They moved in gradually over the course of the week, a week during which Noah forbade her from leaving his side for all but the most important meetings. And even then, he'd argued that she relocate them to his offices. When she'd refused, Paddy's gruff and stoic presence had become a fixture in her office, along with goodness knew how many other minders that she couldn't see watching over her outside.

By mutual unspoken agreement, they didn't talk about Warren. Or Ashley. Or her stepfather, although she knew Noah had several video conferences day and night with Tim and Harry.

Warren had extended his leave of absence after the board had reluctantly taken the decision to delay floating the company on the stock market.

Then he'd abruptly sold his stake in La Carezza and resigned. Paddy had informed them that the Palm Beach house had been put on the market.

The ripple of Warren's sudden resignation had threatened to focus unwanted media attention on her, but Leia had put her foot down about delaying the launch of the new lingerie collection.

She refused to let Warren's sudden disappearance or Stephen Willoughby's black silence derail her life.

The auction website had stayed down. Its ominous threat worried her, but not enough to mar her happiness at having Noah close.

He'd hired a team of designers to deal with his condo, and at the times when the workmen got too loud, the two of them relocated to her apartment. While Noah wanted his place ready to be lived in immediately, she was content to take her time shopping for the right accessories for the furniture she had.

Her only compromise had been a bed large and sturdy enough to accommodate her lover's height and endless stamina. And seriously comfy and expensive bed linen that made her smile stupidly every time she burrowed into it.

Memories of cooking sausages and waffles with her father had triggered a visit to the grocery store, and she'd cooked her first meal in her new kitchen on their first weekend.

Noah had dutifully finished his plate of burnt waffles and undercooked sausages, then proceeded to express his 'gratitude' by spreading her out on the teak countertop and making her scream through several mind-altering orgasms.

Two weeks later, she walked into Noah's condo, excitement and a touch of anxiety bubbling in her chest.

He was in the kitchen, shirtless, stirring a bubbling pot on the stove. She paused in the doorway, completely arrested by the sight that never ceased to make her whole body quiver with delight.

"Dinner will be ready in fifteen minutes," he threw over his shoulder.

She nodded and walked to where he stood. Unable to resist, she placed a kiss between his shoulder blades, flicking her tongue out to taste his skin. He tensed and gave a tiny hiss before turning around to catch her in his arms. Bending down, he buried his face in her throat, then drifted his mouth to the point between her shoulder and neck. His teeth claimed her before he soothed the bite with his tongue.

Broad hands captured her ass and pulled her into his groin. "Hi," he growled.

"Hi," she answered. "I got you a house-warming present," she forced out, unwilling to spoil the moment with the painful knowledge that once again he'd avoided her mouth.

Noah hadn't kissed her in almost a month. Of all the punishments he delivered, this was the one that hurt the most. And the unshakeable certainty that it hurt him almost as much as it hurt her, killed her. She lowered her gaze as he released his hold and turned back to the stove.

"No need, you already gave me one," he said.

Leia frowned. "I'm pretty sure I'd have remembered that."

Setting down the black cardboard wrapped package next to the counter, she leaned next to him. Watching him cook was another major turn on. It really was bad for her heart that Noah King was so great at everything he did.

He shrugged, smiled, and offered her a taste of sauce from the ladle.

She tasted, groaned at the seriously good white wine sauce and pursed her lips. "Don't try and seduce me with your cooking, King. Where's this present, then? I want to see what I supposedly gave you."

"It's in the bedroom."

Still frowning, she dropped her bag and walked down the hallway to the bedroom, which took up the whole east wall of the building. Opening the door, she stared at the huge emperor-size bed, the nightstands and the dresser. Nothing.

Walking into the black-tiled bathroom, she peered on the shelves and in the drawers, then tried his walk-in closet. Striking out, she retraced her steps and found Noah in the middle of the room, an enigmatic smile on his face.

She threw out her arms. "Is it invisible?"

He laughed, and she tried not to dissolve in a puddle of hopeless need. He walked to his side of the bed and patted the middle. "Lie down."

Her eyes widened. "*I'm* the present? I was kinda looking for something along more...inanimate lines..."

"Shut up and park yourself on the bed," he growled playfully.

Tugging off her boots, she looked down at her short blue leather skirt and Chinese doll top. "Do I need to be naked?" she asked half-hopefully.

"Nudity is always appreciated but not necessary for this particular show."

Curbing her disappointment, she did as instructed.

He opened his nightstand drawer and took out a small electronic square with a dented middle. Lying down next to her, he aimed it at the far wall and pressed down with his thumb.

A soft whine proceeded movement on the wall opposite his bed. Two panels slid back and a painting rose slowly from below. It clicked into place and soft lights illuminated the large image.

Leaning on her elbows, Leia stared, open-mouthed.

"Ohmigod..." Chills chased up and down her body.

Stretching out next to her, he slid his arm around her and pulled her close. "I know how you felt about me having the picture on my phone, but I couldn't bring myself to delete it. This way, it stays hidden and only comes out for me."

"God, Noah, it's...it's..."

"Fucking beautiful. And for my eyes only," he whispered gruffly. He slid a hand into her hair and massaged her scalp, while his other drifted up and down her legs. "Do you like it?"

Struck dumb by the stunning piece, she could only nod.

Done in grey and red daguerreotype, the image of her welt-covered ass and thighs was sharply contrasted with the red garter belt in a breathtaking tableau. The strategically placed spotlights Noah had used to frame the picture created shadows and light that made the painting come alive.

It was unspeakably breathtaking. And the fact that he'd kept it private for his sole enjoyment made her heart swell. He moved against her, turning her head so he could read her expression.

Whatever he saw there made his mouth curve in a satisfied smile. She lifted her hand to caress his hair and he shifted even closer. Close enough for her to feel the iron-hard effect of his little exhibit. Moaning, she cupped his rigid length, sighing in delight when he thrust against her palm.

He slipped a hand between her legs and gave a loud groan when he encountered her wetness. "I knew we should've done this after dinner. Now my cock craves your tight little cunt more than my stomach wants food."

"I'm...I'm not that hungry either," she murmured.

When his fist tightened in her hair, her heart leapt. But he put a hand over hers on his crotch and lifted it. Kissing her palm, he moved away. "White wine sauce doesn't keep. Besides, I want to see my other present." He lunged out of bed and held out both hands to her. She let him help her up and gasped when he tugged her close. "But we come back here straight after dinner, and I get to fuck you long and hard with that picture for added stimulus."

She tilted her head. "Oh, are you getting to the stage where you need help keeping it up, King?" she teased.

A hard slap on her ass brought sweet, sweet pain and added wetness between her legs.

"Just for that, I'll make you sob for mercy."

"You mean you haven't noticed that I pretty much cry every time we have sex?"

His smile was steeped in wickedness. "Baby, tonight I want nothing short of ugly, clawing, head-banging tears. And no one will hear your excited screams when I whip your pretty little pussy because you'll have a ball-gag in your mouth. Now let's go open my present."

Noah bit the inside of his lip to keep from laughing at Leia's agitation. He'd deliberately drawn out dinner, fed her some more when she said she was full and made the most intricate dessert just to keep her on the edge. Scooping up another spoonful of freshly made chocolate mousse topped with lightly roasted shaved truffles and orange rinds, he held it to her lips.

Obediently, she closed her mouth over the decadent morsel. She looked at his untouched portion. "Aren't you going to eat yours?"

"You can feed me after I've fed you."

Eyes wide, she nodded. She ate another couple of mouthfuls, then cleared her throat. Again he swallowed a smile.

"Noah...about the...umm...ball-gag—"

"Shhh, we don't talk about the ball-gag during dinner."

She lifted a trembling hand to the newly shaved space above her ear.

His stomach muscles quivered as he flashed back to this morning. He'd asked her last week whether she would keep or shave the patch of hair. She'd wanted to wait until her wrist fully healed to decide.

He'd forgotten about it until he walked into the bathroom this morning and seen her holding out his electric shaver to him.

Get over it, Noah. It was such a simple thing. And yet, every time he saw that newly-shaved patch, something unfurled in his chest.

He captured her hand, kissed it and fed her another mouthful. With each bite, her spine grew stiffer and her breath puffed out.

God, was he a masochist to love her like this, all riled up and anticipating what he planned to do to her? Hell yeah. The hard-on he'd been unable to talk down since he'd shown her the painting throbbed harder.

Ten minutes later, he decided he would be better off not doing himself a permanent injury. He quickly fed her the last spoonful, tried to ignore the sexy little whimpers she'd been making for the last five minutes, and handed her his spoon.

Her hand trembled so badly he helped steady her first offered mouthful. He kept his eyes on her as the loaded spoon slid inside his mouth. Noah couldn't breathe at the open hunger and utter surrender in her eyes.

He wanted to believe, right then and there, that she would do anything he wanted...*be* anything he desired. And there was their problem. Outside of sex, he still wasn't sure he could trust her to accept him and everything in his life.

Hell, he was chicken enough that he'd avoided the subjects that really mattered, subjects which would rear their ugly heads sooner rather than later and smash the intimacy happening right here to fucking smithereens.

She gave a distressed whimper and he realized he'd squeezed her hand too tight. Slowly releasing her, he let her finish feeding him. By the time the spoon clattered to the countertop, her face was flushed and her thighs clenched and unclenched in uncontrollable spasms.

Reaching down to where she'd placed it earlier, he picked up the large wrapped package and propped it on his knees. "So what do we have here?"

Her beautiful eyes shifted nervously over the present. "O-open it."

He pulled the strings apart and tore away the wrapping. For several seconds he stared at the painting, then he frowned at her.

Her face fell. "You don't like it. I'm sorry...I just thought the color blocks would match the monochrome in the living room—"

"Are you fucking kidding me? You buy me a Mondrian and are surprised that I'm lost for words?"

"I didn't buy it exactly..."

His frown deepened. "You stole it?"

A tiny smile crept over her face. "Of course not. It belonged to my...father. After he died, my mom packed up all his art and stored them at the bank. But he left everything to me and I thought...I thought..."

Beyond its blinding worth, the exquisite art was breathtaking enough to rob him of further words. Knowing it had belonged to her father, a man she'd loved, made Noah's insides shake. He stared at the mostly white background, the precise lines, the blocks of blue, grey and red, and wondered when exactly he'd fallen in love with Leia Michaels.

He was still shaking when he hung the Mondrian over the white tiled fireplace in the living room. He didn't want to see her face, didn't want to watch that luscious mouth and give in to the craving slashing through him. When she curled her arms around her waist and smiled at the painting, Noah was sure he'd never wanted to kiss her more than at that moment.

She sighed. "It looks perfect there."

"Yeah," he said gruffly. "Thank you."

Her smile blew him away.

Turning her around and away from him, he clamped his arms around her waist and lifted her high. She curled her legs backward, hooked her arms around his neck and laid her head on his shoulder.

Fuck. So trusting sexually. He would give his right arm to have her trust him with everything she cared about. And maybe she did, maybe she didn't.

He was so confused right now, he couldn't think straight.

Taking a deep breath, he reined in his feelings and headed down the hall toward the bedroom.

One fucking step at a time.

Starting with making her sob with ecstasy as promised.

TWENTY-THREE

Vocalization had been a huge thing for them right from the start. So Leia was not sure how she felt about being gagged. Heck, *not sure* was the understatement of the millennia. Completely naked and perched on the side of the bed, her gaze followed Noah. As he disappeared inside the specially built room within his walk-in closet, she bit back the hysterical urge to yell *stop*.

Yelling *stop* would end more than a ball-gag in her mouth.

She loved Noah - yes, she was finally willing to admit that openly and honestly to herself - too much and too selfishly to jeopardize whatever time they had together. She passed a hand over the spot above her ear.

Watching him shave her this morning had been a singularly emotional moment for her. She'd dared to imagine them together like that in the far future, her love an open statement and not a secret guarded under lock and key in her heart.

At one point, his gaze had connected with hers in the mirror. She'd fooled herself into believing her emotions were reflected in his eyes. He'd looked away, and the foolish fantasy had disappeared.

Now, as he walked back into the room, her apprehension escalated, fluttered up to entwine with the excitement bubbling in her chest. Dropping the bullwhip, ball-gag and a velvet-wrapped package next to her, he stared down at her.

His blue eyes gleamed with savage intentions. "Any last requests?" he teased.

Unable to stem her jangling nerves, she licked her lips. "You like me vocal, Noah. I won't be able to talk with a gag in my mouth."

White teeth bared with a wicked grin. "I'm aware of that. We'll just have to find another way of communicating."

Slightly reassured, she watched him reef his black T-shirt over his head and drop it. Unbuckling his belt, he lowered his zipper and kicked his jeans away, leaving only his briefs on. With her fear slightly abated, hunger dug deeper furrows in her. Her fingers framed his cock and stroked him before he grabbed her hand and imprisoned it.

"Let's establish a few rules, sweetheart. You don't touch me until I give you permission."

She gasped. "But—"

"No buts...besides yours, which I want up on the bed, bent over and displayed to me. Right now."

The menace in his voice had her scrambling to obey. Kneeling, she rocked forward onto her hands and spread her knees.

Noah choked, then cursed fluently. "I can never get over how beautiful your pussy is." He cleared his throat. "But you're in the wrong position."

He moved to the foot of the bed and tapped the carved metal in the middle. Puzzled, she crawled toward him and only then noticed that the velvet cloth contained a pair of handcuffs.

Oh shit. She was about to gagged, handcuffed and whipped?

"Hold out your hands."

Retreat never crossed her mind. Her trust in him when they were like this was implicit. Pressing her wrists together, she offered them to him. His mouth parted and that look she'd imagined on his face in the mirror this morning made a brief appearance. It evaporated as he pulled her forward and lowered her bound hands to the bed.

She'd thought his intricately carved bed had been made with aesthetic appreciation in mind. Now she knew it served a greater purpose. Little hoops and hooks had been worked into the design. He curled his finger into the handcuff link and pulled her to the middle of the bed. One little click and her wrists were immobilized to the bed.

He produced a key, which he pressed into her palm. "You hang onto this tightly, baby. You drop it only if things get too much and you want me to stop. Okay?"

Her eyes widened in alarm.

He shook his head. "No, this *stop* halts whatever I'm doing to you right here." His gaze dropped for a moment before pinning her again. "The second *stop* comes without a gag. Understood?"

Her fist clenched over the key. "Yes, Noah."

That look again. This time it lingered on his face. Her heart stopped as she tried to decipher it. But he turned away and grabbed the gag.

Slipping his hand around her nape, he held the black ball an inch from her mouth. "Open," he rasped, his eyes darkening as he watched her mouth. Sensing his intense need to kiss her, she opened her mouth to beg him to do so. He inserted the ball in her mouth, choking her words. Palming the gag in place, he secured the leather ties behind her head and climbed onto the bed.

The lights in the room dimmed, bringing the picture of her ravaged behind into sharp focus.

Again she was struck with how stunningly Noah had depicted the image. Utterly captivated by it, she started when his stubble grazed her cheek.

"You know how many times I stroked myself off looking at that picture?" he asked in a low, deep voice.

She shook her head.

His husky laugh warmed her ear. "And you never will. Stand up."

The first lash of the whip struck a bare second later.

Leia screamed. Her hands jerked against the cuffs. All she felt was pain, no pleasure. A second later, Noah's hand cupped her breast and his fingers pulled at her nipple.

Oh, yes!

Pleasure exploded on the tails of the pain. She blinked back tears and sucked in desperate breaths. He released her breast and she twisted her head to watch him twirl the whip into his hand. The raw sexiness of it flooded her pussy with liquid heat.

He raised his hand. She squeezed her eyes shut in anticipation. The whip whistled through the air and her ass exploded in a trail of exquisite fire. The tip of the leather caught the edge of her pussy and this time pain and pleasure screamed through her blood. Two more, then he stopped. His arms closed around her, and he caressed her body from shoulder to knees and back up again. Just as her heartbeat lowered to mere palpitations, he dropped to his knees and slid the whip between her legs. The scent of leather and arousal thickened in the air. Expertly, he maneuvered the whip. Her hips pumped in time to his rhythm, her orgasm building to combustive levels.

"Are you going to come on my whip, baby?"

Incoherent sound gurgled around the gag.

He increased the friction, mercilessly pushing her to the edge. Her vision blurred. As the most intense orgasm she'd ever experienced tore through her body, she screamed. One strong arm propped her up through her convulsions, then lowered her to her knees. She was twitching through the last throes when another burst of fire streaked across her ass.

Electricity jolted through her body and her palm opened. She caught the key a second before it fell out of her hand. Squeaking with relief, she closed her fist around it then gave herself over to the sensation rippling through her.

Tears streamed down her face, caught the corner of her mouth and dribbled down to her chin. At some point, she'd forgotten to swallow and saliva had escaped.

She should've felt intense shame, but all Leia wanted was more of what Noah was doing to her.

After her third orgasm, Noah knotted his fist in her hair and pulled her head back. His other hand trailed up her inner thigh, caught the shameless evidence of her arousal.

"Holy hell, you're a fucking delicious mess," he crooned with deep satisfaction before he released her. The curl of his tongue on her skin a moment later snapped her head down.

He'd positioned himself between her thighs, staring up at her as he licked his way up her inner thigh. He stopped short of her swollen pussy.

Leia's body shook. Her tears spilled onto his mouth, mingled with her juices. He licked his lips and carried on with his torture until he'd lapped her clean.

With one long suck on her clit, he rose and kicked off his briefs.

He thrust into her hard, groaned deeply, then held himself still. Looping the bullwhip around her neck so the ends hung down her back, he began to ride her. Fast and deep, he pounded her through another climax, then shuddered roughly through his own powerful release.

Her hands were starting to go numb from being restrained for so long.

Still holding her, he rubbed at her closed fist before holding out his hand. Leia didn't want to let go.

He kissed her cheek and jaw, gently caressing her hand. "It's okay, baby."

Slowly, she unclenched her fist. He unlocked her and released the gag. As their eyes met, that connection she was sure wasn't just in her imagination anymore, arched between them.

In silence, he carried her to the bathroom. He washed her quickly, as if he knew she wouldn't last much longer on her feet. Back in bed, he curled himself around her back and massaged her melting limbs. As sleep swamped her, Leia wanted to embrace the bliss washing over her, but she knew it was false.

Noah's heart was closed to her, despite his strong arms wrapped around her body.

He still hadn't kissed her.

***

"Fuck it. Why the hell don't I learn to pick friends who understand the word *no*?"

Leia looked up from where she sat sketching on the sofa, and smiled. She'd arrived from work two hours before bursting with ideas for her spring collection.

Enjoying her creative energy, Noah had resisted the urge to disturb her the way he'd been dying to, choosing instead to drink a beer and watch her work.

"What's that...the fourth text in five minutes?" She quirked a sleek brow.

"The sixth. Those fuckers give thick and fast a new meaning." His finger hovered over the latest text as he considered deleting it.

"You blew them off for poker night last week." She shrugged. "Figures they're a little pissed."

"Pissed I can handle. Pissed and pushy is crossing the line," he grumbled. "They're threatening to come over unless I reply."

She dropped her pad and came over to kneel before him. Her hands on his thighs did amazingly powerful things to him. He caressed her cheek and felt his chest fill with that insane emotion again.

"Invite them over, I can work downstairs at my place for a while."

"No." The growl was a warning for her to drop the subject.

That beautiful mouth he wanted to kiss more than he wanted to breathe, pouted. "But I feel bad that I'm keeping your buddies from you—"

"You're not."

Her lips pursed. "Please, Noah. Do it for me."

His finger traced her lower lip. "What do I get out of this shitty deal?"

A peck on his finger followed a saucy smile. "I have two new pieces of lingerie downstairs. Have fun with your buddies. Let me work for a few hours, then I'll come back here and model them for you."

His heart pounded. "Or we can stay here, you work faster and we get to the modeling part quicker."

She drew back, plucked his phone from his lap and skipped to the other end of the living room. He watched, incredulous as she typed a response. Eyes shining with mischief, she hit send.

"Baby, you did not just do that."

His phone pinged a response seconds later. "They'll be here in a hour," she said.

Slamming his beer down, he prowled toward her. "So I have an hour to exact retribution for your insolence?"

Pleasure burst through him as her eyes darkened and his phone slipped uselessly out of her hand onto the sofa. God, he loved it when she reacted so viscerally to him.

She started to backtrack. He had her pinned against the wall in seconds. One minute later, she was minus her clothes, bent over the sofa and he was thrusting home.

Beautiful. God, she was so beautiful.

And so utterly his when they were like this.

He couldn't get enough of her. And he was fast reaching the point where he wondered how he'd survive the day when he demanded more...and she chose to walk away.

By the time his elevator delivered his unwanted guests, he was decent again, barely. He speared a hand through his hair and frowned at Leia's just-thoroughly-fucked appearance, which he'd have killed not to have his friends see. But she'd insisted on meeting them before she went to her condo and he...he was finding it damned difficult to deny her anything.

Gabe walked in first and slowed to a swagger the second he set eyes on Leia. Taking her hand, he kissed the back of it in true Lothario style. "Gabriel Antonelli. A pleasure to meet you at last."

Had Noah not known how crazy Gabe was about Angie, he'd have decked his friend right then and there.

Leia beamed. "You too, Gabe. Noah doesn't talk about you enough."

"Yeah, with good cause. He's afraid I'll steal you away," Gabe returned.

Sliding his hand around Leia's waist, Noah steered her out of his friend's path. And straight into Mike...who was imitating a puffer fish in his eagerness to introduce himself.

Shit.

"Hello, Gorgeous. I'm Mike," he supplied.

"Hey, Mike," Leia gave a wider smile and tilted her head toward Damian, who lounged in the doorway, surveying the scene with a resigned look.

"Don't mind these two knuckleheads," he said as he walked forward. "Some old bird with cataracts convinced them they were God's gift to chicks a long time ago. I haven't been able to restrain them since."

Leia laughed, and Damian's eyes widened.

Noah felt a growl rumbling from his chest. Leia slipped out of his hold and crossed to the sofa to gather her stuff.

His friends turned to watch her.

"Aren't you joining us for poker? It's not strictly a boys' thing. We'd love to have you," Mike coaxed.

"Yes. It is. And, seriously, you need to watch how you frame your words there, *buddy*." Noah fixed him with a deathly look.

Damian's shoulders shook with silent laughter.

Gabe's eyes narrowed and swung between him and Leia. Noah made a visible effort to relax as she walked toward him.

"It was good to meet you all." That stunning smile made another appearance.

"Yeah, see you around," Gabe said.

Noah led her out of the condo and into the waiting elevator.

"You don't need to come with me, Noah. You've got guests," she protested.

"I didn't invite them. They're big boys. They can take care of themselves for five minutes." Restlessness prowled through him. He glanced at his watch. "We'll be done in a couple of hours. I'll come and get you when they leave, okay?"

"Sure," she replied.

They reached her floor, and he spotted three packages sitting outside her door. "Expecting a delivery?" he asked unnecessarily.

"Yep, I ordered some bath stuff online last night."

For some reason that irritated him. "You aiming to take a lot of showers at your place?"

Her eyes grew a touch wary and she shrugged. "If I find myself in need of one when I'm home, yes."

Pursing his lips, he took her keycard and opened her door. About to help her with the packages, he stopped when she put a hand on his chest. "I'll get them in a minute, baby. Go back upstairs. The earlier you get your game going, the quicker I can come back."

Unable to argue that sound logic, he yanked her into his arms and drowned in her intoxicating scent. Then he reluctantly pulled away. "Two hours, tops. Ninety minutes if I can kick them out without them whining like spoiled brats," he promised as he backed away from her.

She laughed. "Yes, Noah."

Christ. Any more of those responses and he'd be begging her to let him stay, his friends be damned.

He returned upstairs to find the guys staring at the painting.

Mike was the first to spot him. "Is that a genuine Mondrian?"

Noah cocked a brow at his friend. "You're the only who deals with fakes, buddy."

The other two barked with laughter and Mike grimaced. "Shit, one girlfriend with fake tits and a guy can't live it down for love nor money."

"Shame Olga the Ogre took your love *and* your money!" Damian ribbed mercilessly.

Noah grabbed two six-packs from the fridge and headed for the gaming room. "I'd love to skewer you to death over that unfortunate, but entertaining, period of your life, buddy, but I'd rather kick your respective asses at poker as soon as possible and send you packing. So let's get this show on the road."

He was already missing Leia like crazy, and she'd been gone less than five minutes.

TWENTY-FOUR

Warren Snyder examined his closet with a sharp eye before settling on the charcoal grey pinstripe suit. Coupling it with a white shirt, he draped both over a sleek clothes press and moved to the mirror in his bathroom.

The bruises had faded. At least on the outside. But his jaw clicked when he moved it the wrong way. Or he chewed anything tougher than a rare chateaubriand.

According to his physician the sound might never go away.

That unquestionable blow to his pride was surpassed only by Leia's callous betrayal.

In the silent days, which followed the unfortunate event at the charity ball, locked away in the lake house no one knew about except him, he'd been fully intent on plotting to get her back. He'd deemed her worthy of one last attempt to salvage what she'd ruined. Just as he'd deemed his pride salvageable. With the right restitution.

His fingers paused over his still painful jaw. Flexing it delicately from side to side, he took a deep breath.

The breathing techniques had also failed him in the past several days while he'd been mired in fury. He was glad to experience the return of calm.

Changing his mind had been hard, but he hadn't come this far, removed the shackles of his unfortunate past, by being imprudent.

But that didn't mean the fire of revenge had abated.

No, far from it...

Timing himself, he dressed in precisely seven and a half minutes and tugged on his sleeves in satisfaction. Clarity of mind had always been his sharpest weapon. The enforced sabbatical had enabled him to see the forest for the trees.

Timing was everything. And he was now wealthy enough to make biding his time a non-hardship. The best chess moves came with patience. And precision—

His phone beeped with a message. He read it. He considered ignoring it. Then gave in and dialed the number.

"Miss Maitland, how may I help you?"

"I've been trying to reach you for days. I kept getting out of office replies."

"An appropriate response seeing that I *was* out of the office. Again, how may I help you?"

"Do you know that your little...are you aware that Noah and Leia are practically living together?" she asked through gritted teeth.

Warren strolled out his bedroom and entered the space he'd been using as a study. Pressing a button on his laptop, the screen flared to life. "For the sake of expediency, I'll say yes and suggest you get to the point."

"Don't you care?"

"Your point, if you please."

She laughed. "You must really enjoy leftovers from Noah King's table. Or you would have done something about our situation by now."

She wasn't worth the effort of him informing her he was doing something about it.

"I don't doubt that you and King deserve each other. After all, he's a thug and you're a hapless shrew. I'm not in the habit of revisiting failed ventures, Miss Maitland. But I suppose, if you insist on pursing your objectives..." he trailed off and waited.

"What?" she demanded after a minute.

He told her. And listened to her gloat. "This will be the last time we communicate. I strongly suggest you lose my number."

He hung up, placed the phone on his desk and clicked through the various electronic files until he located the one he needed. The puppet had responded to its master's command.

Flicking open the button of his single-breasted jacket, he sat at his desk, steepled his fingers, and watched the time.

The email pinged at the stroke of the hour.

He read it.

Warren smiled, his pride a touch placated.

TWENTY-FIVE

Regaining her focus after Noah left took a pathetically long time, but once Leia got into the swing of things again, excitement bubbled under her skin as her pencil flew over the sketchpad. After completing her sixth design, she got up from the sofa and stretched.

Going into her kitchen, Leia poured a glass of wine and eyed the clock. An hour and fifteen minutes since she'd said goodbye to him. She leaned against the sink and grimaced at the full scale yearning taking root inside her.

Hell, it had grown into more than a yearning. It was becoming a full-blown obsession. She craved Noah all the time. In bed, out of it. She even craved him when he was deep inside her, rocking her world the way only he knew how.

Was this how love was meant to be? Or was her particular brand a special strain because she knew she could lose him to his unborn child at any time?

Ashley...

She knew the other woman spoke to Noah from time to time. Noah always kept the conversation short, sometimes curt. But Leia couldn't hide from the fact that they had a relationship of sorts.

And always would.

Could she deal with that in the long term, *if* there was a long term for them?

She contemplated the other side of the coin—a life without Noah.

A spike of pain shot up her spine. Taking a deep breath, she pushed the thoughts away.

When the time came to deal with it, she'd dealt with it. Until then...

She walked into the living room and picked up her mobile. Catching her lower lip between her teeth, she contemplated what she was about to do. A wave of electricity sizzled through her belly as she started typing:

You have corrupted this fragile thing and brought out a writhing, mewling, bucking, wanton whore for your enjoyment and pleasure...hurry, your whore awaits :)

Taking a fortifying sip of wine, she pressed send. The reply came an excruciatingly long two minutes later:

Thanks for that. I just lost a very lucrative hand. If you think adding a smiley face to a paraphrased Sade quote is going to make me go easy on you for getting me so fucking hard I can't get up, think again.

She grinned and typed again:

Please show this newly deflowered sexter a little mercy.

Noah:

My mercy isn't little, baby. It's a huge, hungry motherfucker. You poked it. You get to appease it.

About to respond, she jumped when her phone rang. Only it wasn't her mobile, but her landline. Frowning, she crossed to the coffee table and picked up the receiver.

"Hi there, Miss Michaels. It's Alex from the concierge desk downstairs? I called earlier about your packages but there was no response, so I thought I'd double-check that you got them?"

"Oh...umm, yes." She grimaced. She'd totally forgotten about her deliveries. "I got them, thanks."

"You're welcome. We've had another delivery. If you're available now, I can bring it up?"

She reluctantly shut off the mobile and dropped it on the table. "Sure, thanks."

Hanging up, she went to the door and brought in the three packages. Opening up the first one, she stopped to sniff the expensive gel and lotion she'd had specially made from her favorite bespoke perfumery in Palm Beach. She was putting away the mood enchanting candles in her bathroom closet, when she heard the knock.

She opened the door and gestured to the coffee table. "Thanks, Alex. Can you put it on there?"

He nodded eagerly. He was about her age, decent looking, and she'd seen him check her out a couple of times. In another lifetime, she probably would've found him interesting enough to date.

But in this lifetime, she belonged to one man only.

Alex turned. "Do you need a hand with anything else?" he asked.

Leia eyed the large square box, wracking her brain to recall what else she'd ordered besides the bath stuff. "No, thanks. I'm good."

Alex let himself out, and she walked to the package. It was a large brown box, sturdy enough to indicate whatever it contained was heavy. Double-sealed with industrial strength tape, she would need a knife to open it. Grabbing one from the kitchen, she slid the blade under the lid, worked her way round and lifted it.

Horror engulfed her. The knife clattered to the floor as a scream gurgled in her throat, choking its way up before ripping through the air.

The three dolls were grotesquely life-like. But while the bodies were those of newborns, the heads were large and full-grown. And all three faces were as familiar to her as the nose on her face.

Shaking, Leia lurched to where she'd dropped her phone. A sob broke out as her fingers missed the dial button. Dashing her hand across her eyes to clear her vision, she tried again.

Noah's phone rang four times before he answered it. "Fuck, sweetheart, you have no idea how tough it is to walk with this hard—"

"Noah..." Her voice emerged a ragged croak.

"What the hell's wrong?" he snapped.

"Some...something arrived...a delivery." She shut her eyes as she caught the box from the corner of her eye. "Please, Noah...I need you." Another shudder ripped through her. She curled her body into a ball and wrapped her free arm around her knees.

"Stay on the phone, baby. I'll be right there." Chairs scraped hardwood floors. Pounding feet accompanied gruff male voices. Her heart hammered and her body shook as sobs rocked her.

"Ten seconds, baby. Hold on," Noah's voice was taut with anxiety.

A heartbeat later, the door slammed open and she was engulfed in strong arms. Phone slipping out of her hand, she threw her arms around his neck as he scooped her up.

"Are you hurt?" he demanded.

"N...no," she replied.

"Jesus, who the fuck would do this?" Damian growled.

Noah tensed and turned to see Gabe, Mike and Damian peering into the box. Leia closed her eyes, but images of the dolls were fixed on her retinas along with the labels attached to their chests.

Dead Papa Bear. Dead Mama Bear. Dead Whore Baby Bear.

The doll made in the image of her father, had a water-filled bag tied around its head and fishing net around its body. Her mother's doll had a bullet-sized hole in its chest. And Leia's doll had a filet knife inserted in her stomach.

"I'm calling the cops." Gabe pulled out his phone and dialed.

Noah carried her to the seat farthest away from the table and pushed his fingers through her hair. He kissed her temple and gently raised her chin. "Who delivered the box?"

"I don't know...Alex from the concierge's desk b-brought it up."

Noah's head reared up. "Get him up here, now!" he said to Mike.

Mike dashed for the phone and Noah looked into her eyes.

"Did he say who it was from?"

"I didn't ask...I thought it was one of the things I ordered online." Her lips pursed. Another shudder powered through her.

Noah pulled her tighter into his warmth. "I promise you, baby. I'll find the bastard and I'll tear him to pieces."

She squeezed her eyes shut and clung to him. Numbness closed around her, and the men's voices washed over her. What felt like minutes later, Paddy walked in, followed by a man in his fifties wearing a detective's badge.

Alex, who'd been summoned, looked nervously at the towering, bristling men in the room and swallowed before haltingly describing the man who'd made the delivery.

The detective looked at her. "Does that description ring any bells, Miss Michaels?"

She shook her head.

He eyed Noah, then Leia. "Paddy here gave me an abbreviated version of what's been going on. Is there any reason why you didn't report the blackmail threat to the police when it happened?"

Paddy clapped him on the shoulder. "Like I told you, they wanted to keep things...in-house. These days, everyone with a camera phone is a damn amateur tabloid hack. Not to mention an extortionist."

"You including cops in that *pointed* assertion?"

Paddy shrugged. "No offence."

The officer pursed his lips and turned to Noah. "And there have been no further threats for over two weeks?"

Noah's jaw tightened. "Not until tonight." He rose with Leia in his arms. "I think we're done here. If you need any more information, Paddy will fill you in. Or call me. He has my number."

The older man looked like he wanted to argue but sighed. "I'll take this down to the station, have the box dusted for prints," he said.

Noah was already walking away, followed by his friends.

All five of them crowded into the lift.

Gabe tucked a strand of hair behind her ear, ignoring Noah's low growl. "Easy, buddy. Shit, she's really pale. Want me to call the doctor?"

"I'm...I'm fine," Leia forced out through stiff lips. She felt Noah's probing gaze on her and looked up. Whatever he saw in her eyes made his own darken and his breath punch out.

"Noah..."

He shook his head, strode into his condo and headed straight for the bedroom.

Over his shoulder, Leia saw his friends' worried glances. She wanted to say something reassuring...but she was fresh out.

Noah settled her on the bed and drew her tight into his arms. A sharp knock on the door made him tense.

"Yeah?" Noah snapped.

Gabe walked in with a bottle of McCarran whiskey and two glasses. He placed them on the nightstand and looked down at them. "You need anything, you call. Before *or* after you do something stupid. We'll have your back either way." His gaze shifted to Leia and he sent her a crooked smile. "Good night, Princess."

He left quietly.

They lay in silence for several minutes, Noah passing his fingers through her hair and sliding his hand up and down her body, as if reassuring himself that she was all right. Against her breast, his heart thudded into his ribs.

She looked up to see his face contorted in a mask of anger.

"Noah, I'm okay," she ventured.

His fist slammed into the headboard. "He got to you, Leia. The bastard got to you right under my fucking nose."

She twisted in his arms and wrapped herself tight around him. "Please, don't do this to yourself."

He caught her by the shoulders and rolled her beneath him. His eyes blazed with fury and self-recrimination. "What if he'd talked his way around that idiot at the front desk? He could've entered your condo...*hurt you*..." his voice fractured.

She speared her hand through his hair, the other sliding around his waist. "But he didn't. He didn't get in. And I'm still safe. Here with you."

His hands shook uncontrollably as he cradled her face. "God, I don't know what I would've done if I'd lost you." A broken sound rumbled from his throat.

They stared at each other for a single heartbeat.

Then he was kissing her. Desperately. Ravenously. He devoured her like she was the answer to world famine, plunging his tongue into her mouth to dominate hers.

Her numbness fled, replaced by the blanketing heat and sustenance of Noah's attention. The pictures of the dolls flashed intermittently behind her lids, sending shudders through her body. At her gasp, Noah raised his head.

"Look at me. See only me," he commanded.

Nodding frantically, she raised her mouth to his. He offered her what she needed, pressing back the horrific images and replacing them with his essence. She tore at his clothes, and he helped her undress him. When he was naked, she clamped her thighs around him and scoured her nails up and down his back.

Rewarded with his predatory growl, she offered him more. Her mouth, her tongue, the wet hunger between her legs.

Her panties came away with one rough rip. Her top met the same treatment but, desperate for each other, he pulled up her skirt and thrust hard inside her. They held their breaths through the harsh storm of sensation, their eyes staring deeply into each other.

When her need clawed through her, she moved her hips.

He met her thrusts, slammed her repeatedly into the bed. One hand drifted down her side, seeking her tattoo. When he found it, he caressed the words.

He gritted his jaw, and clamped a hand around her throat. "I won't let him break us, Leia. I won't lose you. I won't."

TWENTY-SIX

Noah's eyes popped open a second before his phone beeped. Silencing it before it woke Leia, he read the message.

Terrace. Now.

Tugging on his jeans, he didn't bother to speculate on how his PI had gotten inside his condo. But he fully planned on tripling his security ASAP. Right after he tore a few heads off at the concierge desk in the morning.

Paddy sat in one of the deck chairs, cradling a glass of bourbon.

Noah took a seat across from him. The sky above was an inky black with a smattering of stars.

"Since you've helped yourself to my expensive booze, I'm assuming you have news?"

"You assume correctly. The cops actually came through. They found the delivery guy. Traffic cameras caught the idiot parking his motorcycle in an alley two blocks over. The plates were registered in his name."

The red rage threatened again. "We know who sent him?"

"He said some guy paid him two hundred bucks to deliver the package. He's been taken in for questioning. I have a friend at the precinct. We should have a description of whoever sent the package by morning."

"And if it's Willoughby?"

"Then it's good news. It means he's still in Florida and easier to track. It's likely he has very little cash and can't really go anywhere without the payday he was expecting. Unless..."

"Unless?" Noah demanded.

Paddy knocked back the rest of the drink and set the glass down. "The other thing you asked for. I have some info on that too. There's definitely a connection."

Noah tensed. *Snyder.* "Yes?"

"That name you gave me? He didn't always go by that name."

"What?"

"Who didn't go by what name?"

They both turned around.

Leia was leaning against the door, her arms folded crossed her midriff. She'd put on his Vassar T-shirt and her skirt from earlier but her hair was tousled and her mouth was red and swollen from the greedy kisses he'd demanded from her. He'd kissed her for a straight hour after they'd made love, and yet his need was as intense and insatiable as ever.

He held out a hand and she joined him, perching on his lap. His fingers drifted over her ear and she relaxed against him.

"You know much about Snyder's history, specifically when he met your dad?" Paddy asked.

She sat up. "Warren? My dad met him in college, I think. They were roommates."

"Your dad went to Yale, right?" he probed.

She nodded and glanced at Noah. "What's this about?"

His gut churned. Despite what Warren had done, he knew Leia still held out a tiny hope that the man who'd taken care of her after she'd lost her family, was redeemable. Noah had a feeling his suspicion that Snyder's actions hadn't been selfless right from the start was about to be confirmed.

Paddy stood and paced the terrace. "Snyder was a freshman at McGill University in Montreal two years before he transferred as a sophomore to Yale."

Noah's nape tingled. "Are you saying you don't know where he disappeared to for a whole year?"

"Oh, we know where he went. He was living on a farm in Montana with a family with the last name of Willoughby."

Leia paled. She swayed in his arms. Noah caught her before she slipped off his lap.

"Oh God. *Ohgodohgodohgod*," she whispered.

He pressed a hard kiss to her mouth, swallowed her horrified words. "Shhh, baby, it's going to be okay. We know what we're dealing with now so—"

"Do we?" Her face creased with pain. "He fooled us all. My dad, my mom...he brought that...that monster into our lives, and he sat back and watched him destroy my family." Her eyes widened into large, tormented pools. "Oh God, what if he was responsible for my dad...Warren was on the boat when the accident happened."

Noah tilted her face to his. "If he was, we'll find out. I give you my word."

Paddy cleared his throat. "Without evidence or Willoughby's corroboration, we won't have anything concrete against Snyder."

Pain ripped at his insides when her eyes filled with tears. Tucking her head against his chest, he looked over at Paddy. "Then find the asshole. Now!"

The older man gave a *message-received* nod and silently retreated.

Leia burst into tears.

His insides shredded at the sound of her sobs. Knowing she needed the release didn't make it any easier. He held her until her sobs turned to sniffles. Picking her up, he undressed them both and stepped into the heated tub with her. He cradled her in his arms until the sun rose and she woke from a light doze.

He suffered through watching her eyes cloud over as memory returned. Cupping her jaw, he stared down at her. "Do I have your permission to destroy the motherfucker now?" he rasped.

Her eyes lost a shade of distress and her jaw flexed against his fingers. "You find the deepest, darkest pit and I'll bring the shovel."

Paddy called just after midday. The description given by the delivery guy matched Stephen Willoughby. The detective, probably wanting to prove Paddy wrong for the incompetent dig, went at the case like a dog with a bone.

Not that Noah minded.

He had Tim and Harry on the case too, getting them to use their software to scour traffic camera footage within a ten-mile radius of the condo.

After this was all over, he was going to make those boys richer than their wildest dreams.

For the thousandth time, his gaze drifted to the sofa in his study where Leia was sleeping. His chest expanded at the sight of her relaxed faced and softly parted lips.

He loved her.

Fuck, he loved her so much, he didn't know how his body wasn't consuming itself with the force of his feelings.

After this was over...

He laughed under his breath. Yeah, after this was over he was going to do a hell of a lot of things. Starting with taking steps to make Leia Michaels permanently his.

Until then, he had two assholes to wrangle down.

Sucking in a deep breath, he clawed both hands through his hair, then tensed when his phone rang. Looking at the screen, he cursed under his breath.

Ashley.

He'd signed her up with a private OBGYN and the private chef she'd insisted she needed to maintain a healthy diet during the pregnancy. Beyond that, they communicated strictly by email because the sound of her voice filled him with loathing. And he was paranoid enough to imagine his unborn child could be adversely affected by hearing the anger he couldn't control every time he spoke to his ex-fiancé.

"I thought we agreed on a precise means of communication that did not involve me speaking to you?"

"Please don't be mean, Noah. I just...just wanted to hear your voice."

He swallowed his angry retort and took another breath. "Is everything all right?"

"With me or the baby?"

"Take the question at face value and answer it."

"We're both fine."

"In that case, there's nothing to talk about—"

"Wait!"

"What?"

"I have an appointment tomorrow. Will you come with me?"

He frowned. The OBGYN had sent him a schedule of everything *expectant parents* needed to do before the birth. He had nothing in his diary for tomorrow. "Is it routine?"

"No, but I felt a fluttering this morning and I want to check that everything is fine."

His boulder slammed into his chest. "Define fluttering," he ground out. He hadn't asked for this baby, but he couldn't dismiss the protectiveness he felt toward it.

"I don't know...a fluttering."

"You have a degree from Cornell, Ashley, and if you weren't telling one of your many lies, I believe your dad wasted a lot of money to send you to some fancy bullshit finishing school in Switzerland. Find the words."

A moment of silence. "Maybe it's nothing."

A needle of guilt pierced him, perversely making him angrier. "I'll call the doctor, tell her to swing by the condo." He paid enough for Dr. Franklin to make house calls.

"Thank you, Noah, I knew you—"

He hung up and threw the phone down. Dragging a hand over his face, he looked up to find Leia watching him.

They hadn't talked about Ashley or the baby since she'd moved in. His heart hammered as her eyes stayed on him.

"I'm sorry you had to hear that," he murmured, gauging her reaction. "That woman drives me to the fucking edge."

Without responding, she pushed aside the light blanket he'd thrown over her and stood. Expecting her to come to him, his eyes widened when she caught the hem of the short cream jersey dress and pulled it over her head.

No bra.

No panties.

His heart leapt into his throat. Leia's body. The ultimate distraction, panacea and paradise rolled into one. He stood and walked around to perch on the edge of his desk. His groin was already hard enough to cause him severe distress, but he stopped himself from reaching for her. He wanted to savor her, drown in the feeling thundering through him.

"Leia..."

She traced her fingers down her midriff to the top of her thighs. His breath stalled, then rushed out when she slid her fingers into her pussy. "If you come over here, I'll drive you to the edge, but in a good way."

His clothes came off in seconds.

Driving into her, he shuddered. "God, Leia...you make me...I feel..."

Her wet fingers drifted to his lips. "I know, baby," she whispered. "You don't need to find the words. This is our language. Express yourself."

Tim and Harry's traffic tracking program picked up Stephen Willoughby, returning to a seedy motel in South Beach, just before eight p.m. that evening. After congratulating them on a job well done, Noah left them hi-fiving each other and called Paddy.

"Call me once you confirm it's him," Noah instructed. "What I have to share with him won't take too long." Five minutes alone with the guy was all he needed.

"Understood."

He went into the bedroom.

Leia was packing her clothes away in the space he'd provided in his closet. She hadn't put up a fight when he'd had her stuff removed from her condo to his, thank God. Crossing to his side, he swapped his jeans and white T-shirt for a black turtleneck and black cargo pants. Leia's eyes widened when he opened a drawer and pulled out black leather gloves.

"Are we going out? And why do you need gloves—?" Her breath stalled. "You've found him?"

He gave a curt nod. "Paddy has a man stationed downstairs. He'll come up and stay with you until I come back—"

"No way. I'm coming with you."

"Hell no. I don't want you anywhere near that shithead."

She walked up to him and stared him in the eye. "I need this, Noah. You want me to be able to put all this behind me one day, I need to bring my shovel."

And there was his fucking conundrum. He loved her so desperately he didn't want her harmed in any way, but he loved her *because* of that steely determination and unquenchable fire which blazed through her.

"Okay, you can come, but you remain at my side at all fucking times. Understood?"

A solemn nod. "Yes, Noah."

He caught her nape and stamped his possession with a kiss. He watched her dress in tight black leather pants, a grey turtleneck and thigh-high boots. She was securing her hair in a ponytail, when his phone beeped.

He read the message with a satisfied nod. "Let's go."

The motel was two streets south of Collins Avenue. Noah parked his Maserati in front of a closed dry cleaners and handed his keys to one of Paddy's men.

"Room 332." The guy nodded at the two-story building across the street.

Noah grabbed Leia's arm and led her to the motel.

Paddy was waiting and opened the door. They walked in, and Noah stopped in front of the guy seated on the only chair in the room.

Willoughby had dirty blond hair and had once been passably handsome in a way that Noah supposed could turn heads when he was cleaned up. And not overweight from eating too much shitty prison food. The arms restrained behind him showed cheap prison tattoos. When he saw Leia's name in red ink down the bastard's neck, Noah's stomach roiled.

Paddy had already introduced him to a few fist sandwiches, judging by the thick cut on his upper lip.

An upper lip that curled in a sneer when he saw Leia. "There's my little baby whore—"

Noah's foot, propelled into the Willoughby's chest, stopped him from finishing the sentence. He crashed into the wall. The back of his head gave a sickening crutch when it connected with hard concrete. Taking a couple more steps, Noah placed his booted foot on the guy's throat and leaned over him. "Now, is that the way to greet your stepdaughter?"

Willoughby's eyes bulged, and he tried to wriggle away.

Noah picked him up and slammed him back down. "Let's try again, shall we?"

Wheezing, Willoughby spat out blood and stared at Leia. "Did you feed him the same lies you fed the court?" He switched his gaze to Noah. "She wanted it. Same as her mama, this one. Cock-hungry little—"

Leia's boot caught him in the nuts.

Willoughby squealed.

She smiled. "I think I'll let you get up so we can catch up properly." She stood back. When he just grunted, Paddy grabbed him by his arms and hauled him up. The moment the PI let him go, Willoughby lunged at her.

Noah moved to intercept, but Leia was faster.

She crouched, spun on her heel and slammed her elbow in her stepfather's face, followed by a sharp jab in the ribs. Noah barely managed to stop himself from applauding. When Willoughby crumpled into a heap, she bent down and spat in his face. "This time when they lock you up, I hope they throw away the key."

She was trembling when she walked into Noah's arms, but the remorseless fire in her eyes made his heart sing.

She would be okay.

And if they were lucky, *they* would be okay.

He turned to Paddy. "Make sure he hands over every copy of the pictures and videos. Then find out everything he knows about Snyder, whether he sent those dolls, and where we can find him. And do it before our detective friend gets here, in case he decides to play hard to get later."

Paddy smiled and nodded.

Halfway across the parking lot, they heard Willoughby squealing for mercy.

TWENTY-SEVEN

"I have to fly out of town for business this weekend."

Noah's heart leapt in his chest. How in the hell did his world stop just from those simple words?

Hoping his panic didn't show, he tucked his hands behind his head and watched Leia from the bed. She crossed from the bathroom to the closet in nothing but an ice blue garter and matching thong. "When and for how long?" he asked.

"I leave on Sunday night and get back on Wednesday morning."

Today was Friday. He'd planned a leisurely weekend for them, perhaps even a double date with Damon and his wife, Birdie, since Gabe and Angela were fighting again and had headed out of town to fuck knows where.

Now, he was supposed to contemplate four days without Leia? No fucking way was that going to happen. "Where are you going?" he asked nonchalantly.

"Hong Kong. Production hit a snafu. I need to make sure things get back on track ASAP. The launch is creeping up fast. I can't afford to sit back and let the stupid bureaucracy sort itself out."

Unable to lie there and pretend he was okay with it, he got up from the bed and paced to his closet. Pulling out a pair of shorts, he stepped into them.

"Is there any reason you're attacking your shorts like you want to rip them apart?"

He whirled to face her. At the amused smile on her face, he exhaled. "Yes, dammit, I can't keep an eye on you from halfway across the world."

She dropped the silk shirt in her hand and slid her arms around his waist. "Noah, my stepfather's back in prison. We don't need to keep our guards up so much anymore—"

"Yeah, but Snyder's still out there. He wouldn't have gone underground if he didn't suspect we knew he orchestrated that fucked up delivery to your place. Wishing he's gone quietly into the night will be fucking naive." Worry made his voice harsh.

She leaned back and glared at him. "I get that, but don't bite my head off for wishing the danger was over, Noah."

He forced calm into his body. Waking up to her this morning, sexily tousled, warm and so fucking ravishing, he'd let himself entertain that same wish. But wishing was foolish when the reality was so much more unsettling.

During the police investigation, before he'd been sent back to jail a week ago, it had become clear very quickly that Willoughby had been a puppet controlled by Snyder.

When Stephen was sixteen, Warren Snyder had turned up out of the blue at the Willoughby's family ranch looking for work. Willoughby Senior had offered him a job as a ranch hand.

Within months, the Willoughby family had been destroyed. Stephen's mother had walked out and his father had hung himself. Snyder had taken Willoughby under his wing. It was during that time that another underage girl had been sexually assaulted. The cops had never managed to pin it on Willoughby. Snyder had stuck around until the inheritance money ran out and then disappeared overnight.

He'd only contacted Stephen again after Logan Michaels died. He hadn't directly introduced them, but he'd made sure Stephen was well-positioned to meet the newly widowed Mrs. Michaels.

The psychopathic long game he'd played, was what made Noah wary of Snyder.

With him still out there, no way in hell was Noah letting Leia out of his sight.

"What exactly is going on with production?" he asked.

She relaxed back against him, her long nails lazily raking his back. "I'm not sure. My last half a dozen emails and phone calls have gone unanswered. I know there was some sort of labor strike last week but indications are that it's over. Besides, the strike had nothing to do with La Carezza or any overseas company as far as my people could tell. Which is what's puzzling about the whole thing."

He leaned down and brushed her lips with his. "I have contacts out there. Want me to sniff things out, see what I can find?"

Her tongue snuck out and brushed his. His body thrummed and he almost groaned when she pulled away. "I'd rather go see for myself what's going on."

"Hmmm, but you do know there's no way I'm letting you go on your own, don't you?"

A mutinous look entered her eyes. "Noah…"

He clenched a hand in her hair and pulled it tight. "It's non-negotiable, sweetheart. I come with or you're not going."

Her mouth dropped open in surprise. "*You*? I thought you were going to sic me with Paddy again."

Noah chuckled. "I wouldn't do that to Paddy. He hates to fly."

Her answering laugh warmed his heart. "Small mercies, I guess." She gave a long moan when he massaged her scalp. "Can you really come with me?"

Bending his head, he trailed his mouth down her throat, then lower to graze the top of her breast. "It'll be a good opportunity to test the waters for new deals by day and indulge my insatiable sex slave by night." He caught her nipple into his mouth and suckled. Her whole body shuddered.

"I think I can...work with that." Her nails dug deeper as she tried to hold on.

Noah smiled and flicked the hard nub. "Great, I'll make the arrangements."

About sixty hours later, Leia rolled over in bed, sat up and was hit by another skewed sense of déjà vu.

She was back in Noah's suite on the Indigo Lounge jet. He handed her a glass of champagne, then sipped his whiskey while flicking through the list of onboard and off-board activities on the screen.

When he said he'd make the arrangements, she thought they'd fly to the Far East on his private jet or even commercial. Another trip on the Indigo Lounge had been an unexpected and thrilling surprise.

"Are you scheduling in any sleep into this trip at all, or are we going to survive on sex and booze?"

He turned his magnificent body toward her. "We never finished our list of highs. If we time it right, we can work the last three in there somewhere." His grin was wicked and borderline savage.

Leia wondered which ailment she'd expire from first - overwhelming love or wall-to-wall sex with Noah. She raised her glass and took another mouthful. Either way, she supposed it was a good way to die.

A bout of turbulence hit the plane, and he laid a hand on her thigh to steady her.

Her heart lurched with elation. Noah took care of her in big, possessive ways, but it was the little, almost absent-minded, gestures of protectiveness that she treasured most.

He made a selection and clicked. She peered around his broad shoulder, but the screen disappeared.

"What was that?"

"If you didn't see it, then it'll remain a surprise. Wanna order in?"

About to nod, she tilted her head. "Have we actually had dinner out before? I mean with other people in a restaurant, like normal—" She stopped when she realized what she'd been about to say.

Dropping the remote, he turned to fully face her. "The masked ball dinner in Prague doesn't count?"

She grimaced. "I was too nervous about how you'd react to my past to enjoy it."

He shrugged. "Then we'll dress up, go out and pretend like we're normal."

"You mean we're not?"

He winked at her. "Baby, we're fucking extraordinary. But we won't tell anyone."

She dressed in a long, black leather-sleeved dress with a thigh high slit and strappy silver Louboutin heels. Noah chose a silvery grey shirt, which did incredible things to his blue eyes, dark pants and a black jacket. Foregoing a tie, he left the two top buttons of his shirt undone. His hair had grown an inch longer and gave him a rakish look that made her heart stutter.

"Ready?"

Watching his long sexy stride as he crossed to where she waited by the door, she swallowed, unable to pry her eyes from his arresting body.

"Umm hmm."

Smiling, he offered her his arm.

The Indigo Lush restaurant was as normal as one could get on a flying sex palace. Cozy privacy booths with white linen tablecloths and exquisite silverware made her feel like she was on a proper dinner date with Noah. Until she sat down and realized the booth held a compartment housing sex toys, and that the candle set into the solid silver candelabra was giving off a scent that made her head swim and her pussy clench with ravenous need.

"What *is* that candle?" she blurted, after five minutes spent talking herself down from jumping Noah and humping him like a wild rabbit.

His strained smile indicated he hadn't escaped the effects of the aphrodisiac. Picking up the candelabra, he brought it to his nose, sniffed, and set it back with a deep chuckle.

"What?" she demanded.

"I detect a distinct whiff of a certain weed."

Her eyes widened. "Oh my God. Is that why...?"

"You suddenly feel like my cock is the only meal you want to devour?" he rasped.

She looked down at his crotch—his very full and tight crotch—and nodded jerkily.

"I'm sure there are other mood enhancing properties in there, but yes. You've never tried weed before?"

"No. I took half an E once, when I was sixteen. All it did was make me horribly thirsty and not-in-a-good-way spaced out."

A loud crash sounded behind their booth.

A good-looking couple, clearly feeling the effects of their surroundings, were letting their inhibitions fly. The woman lay naked and spread eagled on the table, her nipples clamped with tiny silver pegs, while her partner drove into her with thick grunts.

Two waiters approached, swept away the broken china on the floor, then discreetly withdrew.

A sharp tap on her wrist snapped her round. Her face flamed at Noah's narrow-eyed look. Swallowing, Leia tried to block out what was happening behind her.

Noah beckoned a waiter over, gave their food and wine order, and sat back, watching her with hooded eyes.

"We're going to enjoy our meal like a *normal* couple, then I'm going to take you back to our room and introduce you to your surprise."

TWENTY-EIGHT

She took a deep breath, and immediately wished she hadn't when heat flared to her crotch and exploded throughout her body. Her nipples tightened painfully, and she gasped as her clit swelled and throbbed.

Noah's eyes met hers and burned with dark, dangerous promise. "You're desperate to be fucked, aren't you?"

"Yes," she moaned.

He nodded and just watched her.

Once again, turbulent feelings rampaging through her ruined her enjoyment of the meal. All she could think of was getting through dinner and getting him alone. She polished off her lemon thyme tortellini, refused coffee and dessert and gulped down her wine.

Noah abandoned his roast veal halfway through dinner and switched to throwing back his red wine with one hand firmly cupping his crotch. The moment she laid her cutlery down, he discarded his glass and surged to his feet.

As soon as they entered their suite, he kicked the door shut and shoved her against the wall. Bunching her dress at her waist, he pulled her thong to one side and drove hard inside her.

"Fuck!"

"Yes! Oh God, Noah!"

Her knees buckled with the force of his possession. He clamped an arm around her waist and drove deeper, shouting his pleasure and worshiping her body with thick, incoherent words.

Her orgasm left her limp and useless, barely able to keep her eyes open as he picked her up and walked into the bedroom. Undressing her, he pulled back the sheets and laid her down. Then he disrobed and got in beside her.

"Time for some shut-eye."

Her mind circled something important. "No...I want my surprise."

He chuckled. "You'll get it when you wake up." He kissed her long and deep before tucking her head beneath his chin.

Her dream was delicious...

Warm, clever fingers massaged her back...her sides...her hips...down to her ass. They squeezed, plumped, worked her ass muscles until she was humming into her pillow. Silky, liquid heat dribbled onto her back and the scent of potent oils drifted into her relaxed senses.

A middle finger eased between her crack and gently probed her anus. Her eyes popped open, her body no longer relaxed.

"Noah?" she asked breathlessly.

A slow circling of her sensitive hole. "Your surprise is ready," he whispered in her ear. "Look behind you."

She looked over her shoulder, then her gaze snapped upward.

The device was less of a swing and more of a suspended harness. Two broad horizontal leather straps were connected with a vertical one about three feet long. On either side of the lower strap, smaller straps extended along a chain link. And the whole thing was intricately connected to a pulley hooked into the ceiling. Beneath the harness, a pair of black finger gloves rested.

She gulped. "What...? Umm..."

Merciless teeth caught her earlobe, then grazed down her neck, nipping and biting along the way.

"You're about to be ass-fucked at thirty-three thousand feet, baby. Welcome to high number five."

His finger, coated in some sort of oil, circled her back entrance again. Electricity zapped through her body, but it wasn't the white-hot lightning kind, more a blanketing sizzle...

Oh. My. God.

She realized she'd said the words aloud when he laughed.

"I was so desperate for you earlier, I didn't finish my meal. I can't think of anything better than to feast on you right now." He suckled the pulse at her throat.

Her skin tightened at the dark promise. He worked the tight bundle of nerves until the tip of his middle finger probed inside her. Sensation burst along her nerve endings. She clutched the pillow and moaned as he pushed in deeper.

"I need you to relax, baby," he crooned. "Trust me to make this good for you."

"It's already good. That's what I'm afraid of," she said in a rush.

Another deep laugh that unraveled her. He pushed and withdrew.

Push.

Withdraw.

Each time her empty pussy clenched and her temperature climbed higher. Her hips started to roll, pushing back against his finger, seeking a deeper, thicker presence. He curled his finger downward and she screamed as a surprise orgasm stormed through her. The harsh bite of his teeth on her neck prolonged her pleasure and she surfaced, gasping and jerking to find herself on her back.

"What was that?" she asked in a daze.

His smile was shamelessly smug. "I take it you enjoyed that?"

"I love everything you do to me." *I love you. I love you. I love you.*

Leia swallowed hard. It was only a matter of time before the words tumbled out. She knew it. And even though it scared her rigid, she was beginning to be okay with it. Noah may not love her, but he cared about her. Enough that maybe he wouldn't mind that she loved him...

"...baby?"

"Yes?"

His eyes narrowed. "Do you need a session with my belt to keep you in the present?"

She pouted. "But I was thinking about you."

The hard look dissipated. "Nice save." He indicated the lowered harness. "Get up here."

She stood up and he guided her into position. The top strap supported her shoulder, the middle strap her spine, and the bottom strap took the weight of her lower body, leaving her ass hanging over the edge. Noah tied the remaining straps around her thighs and calves, then pulled on one part of the harness. The linked chain widened her legs, leaving her wide open to his gaze.

She grabbed the chain connected to the shoulder strap and used it to raise herself slightly. A dark flush covered his face. He stroked his cock as he sat back and stared at her.

"Each time I think you can't get any more spectacular, you fucking floor me," he whispered darkly.

Licking her lips, she watched his cock thicken further in his grip. Hunger clawed through her. "I need you, Noah."

Adam's apple bobbing on a thick swallow, he grabbed the oil and dribbled it onto her stomach. He massaged it all over before spreading it into her pussy and back hole.

After lubing himself, he discarded it and slid onto the bed directly beneath her.

"Rest your head on my shoulder, baby. I need you not to be tense," he coaxed thickly.

She obeyed and her stomach and back muscles relaxed. The oil had left her muscles languid. When he grabbed her chin and turned for a long kiss, her bones completely melted.

Still kissing her, he steadied her with a hand at her waist and positioned his cock against her back passage with the other.

The first push burned.

Tears sprang to her eyes and she tore her mouth from his.

Gasping, she looked at him.

Reassurance blazed from his gorgeous blue eyes. "It'll be so fucking worth it, baby. Just trust me."

Nodding, she fought to relax. Another probe. A deeper, longer burn. The head of his cock popped in, and she shuddered. Both hands gripped her waist and he rolled his pelvis. She screamed at the thickness invading her. He pulled out slowly and sensation exploded up her spine.

"Oh God!" The chains rattled with her shuddering. He pulled on another part of the harness and her shoulders lifted a few inches.

"Christ, you look so fucking amazing from down here, baby. I could come right now just from this incredible picture." With infinite patience he fed his cock inside her, inch by delicious inch. The burning had receded, overcome by insanely intense pleasure every time he pulled out.

"How do you feel, sweetheart?" he asked when he'd worked half his cock inside her.

She groaned and shook her head.

"Vocalize, baby."

"It's...oh God, it's...I feel like I'm drowning in pleasure. It's too much!" She cried out as he pushed back in.

"Want me to stop?"

"No! Don't you dare!"

"Want more?" He pushed another inch.

"Oh!" Pain exploded alongside pleasure.

Noah grunted. "I think you've reached your limit. Now here comes the great part."

He fucked her ass with long, delicious rolls of his hips. Once he established a firm rhythm, he released her waist slipped on the gloves.

Her sides, her stomach, her nipples tingled under the most electrifying stimulation.

Certain she was about to pass out from the flood of sensation, she squeezed her eyes shut.

"Noah, I can't...I can't..."

One hand fisted her hair and turned her to meet his kiss. The other slipped between her legs. Two gloved fingers filled her pussy and his thumb circled her clit, delivering tiny currents to her swollen nub. Tugging her head away after a deep kiss, Noah stared deep into her eyes, his own glittering with stormy emotions.

"Surrender to me, my beautiful angel. Show me your soul. Come apart for me," he whispered gruffly.

"Y-yes, Noah."

The plane bounced, seating him deeper inside her. A final hoarse cry ripped from her throat.

Then she was falling, the center of her world spinning on its axis. She was still spinning when he slackened the harness and rolled them onto their side.

He waited until her breathing calmed.

Then he really made her soar.

TWENTY-NINE

Considering the incredible heights they'd achieved, the plummet was almost inevitable.

It began as she stood at the picturesque window of their suite at the Indigo Lounge HK. The view over Hong Kong Island was breathtaking, with myriad lights from skyscrapers reflected over Victoria Harbor.

Behind her, Noah was taking a shower.

They'd arrived late on Monday night and crashed. Now she was wide awake in the early hours, unable to shake the stone of anxiety wedged in her gut.

None of her staff at La Carezza had been able to reach the manufacturers. And since Warren had taken direct responsibility for fostering a relationship with the Hong Kong part of her business, she was operating in the dark, with the threat of his evil presence lingering.

She turned from the view and smiled at the sound of running water. Noah had probably fallen asleep leaning against the shower wall. The stamina he'd demonstrated during the flight had been nothing short of Olympic. She hadn't been surprised when he'd fallen into a coma-like sleep minutes after they'd checked in. Grimacing that her anxiety was what had woken him, she crossed the suite to go check on him and stopped when she saw his wallet on the floor.

Picking it up, she walked to the dresser, her fingers caressing the expensive leather. Almost unbidden, Ashley's smug voice exploded from deep within her subconscious.

...he asked for a copy of the scan to keep in his wallet...

She bit her lip. What she was contemplating was wrong, but her fingers moved anyway. She opened his wallet and plucked out the ultrasound scan before she could stop herself. Hands shaking, she held it up to the light.

The arms, legs and head were distinguishable but the rest was still a blob.

A desperately precious blob...a piece of Noah she would never be able to create with him... Knowing he would be a brilliant father made her heart swell with joy for him.

Even while savage pain ripped through her soul.

"What are you doing?" Noah's deep voice vibrated from behind her.

She jumped, dropping the scan and wallet.

Slowly, he bent and picked up the photo. His eyes narrowed at her. "How did you know this was in there?"

"Ashley..."

His nostrils flared. "She told you about it the day she came to see you?"

"Yes," she replied.

He looked down at the picture for a moment, then back at her. "What else did she say?"

"She said you were going to commit to her and the baby sooner or later and I was...standing in your way."

He cursed. "That's why you cancelled on me that night?"

Her breath shuddered out. Suddenly cold, she folded her arms.

"I told myself I was just coming to you for the sex, but even then I knew it was a lie. Just as I knew right from the start that it was wrong to dream of any sort of future with you. But I went ahead and did it anyway. Her visit reminded me that I could never give you this, that I would never hold your babies... It didn't matter whether you would want that with me or not. All I could see was the black hole of nothingness..." A sob escaped before she could stop it. "It kills me, Noah. And when you told me you wanted to be a father... It was foolish, I know. God, we'd only known each other less than a week and I was already building you into my future, had already imprinted you so indelibly into my life that I ignored the one thing I could never ask you to overlook."

"Leia..."

She closed her eyes and squeezed the words out. "It's okay. You have that now..."

"Just shut the fuck up for a minute—"

She shook her head. "You have a baby on the way. Anytime this gets too heavy for you, just tell me and I'll...I'll step aside."

He inhaled sharply. "You'd walk away from me? Again?"

"If that's what you want. I know I can never be a whole woman for you."

"Leia." The rough gravity in his voice made her eyes pop open. He'd paled and his face was a mask of tortured resignation.

"If *I* couldn't give you children, would you walk away from me?" he asked bleakly.

She frowned. "What? Of course not..."

He shook his head in despair. "You're determined to be so fucking noble. Did you ever stop to think of how this would play out if our positions were reversed?"

She shook her head. "But it's not," she cried. "I'm the one—"

"Who has to make all the sacrifices? Even more than you've already done?"

"You don't understand—"

"Then educate me. Or actually don't. I've had it up to my back teeth with you falling on your sword for everyone but yourself." He stepped forward and grabbed her arms. "Be selfish for goddamn once. Demand what you want. Take what you need and to hell with everyone else. You want me. Take me, dammit. Don't apologize or make excuses not to have me."

Her eyes rounded when he held up the scan. "I didn't plan for this, but I'm making room in my life for it because I have no choice. You have a choice to make room in your life for me. Do you want to?"

She squeezed her eyes shut for a blessed second. "Yes. Yes, I do."

His eyes narrowed. "You said yes to me once, and I dared to believe you meant it. You better make sure you mean it this time."

"I mean it. If you want me, Noah, I'm yours."

He stared at her for a long time before he exhaled harshly. Crushing her in his arm, he muttered, "God, you drive me crazy. I have no metaphorical toes left from dancing to your insane tune."

Her heart hammered as she sought the words she needed to say. "Noah, about...about the baby."

He stiffened. "Yes?"

"You know what I said about not wanting to be saddled...I didn't mean it. If you want me to be part of you and the baby's life, I'll—"

They both startled as the phone rang. She knew the moment Noah realized what she was thinking.

Phone calls in the middle of the night were never a good sign.

"Leave it," she pleaded.

Noah soothed her shiver with warm hands. "Okay, if that's what you want."

The ringing stopped. Then started again almost immediately.

"No," she whispered under her breath.

"Hey." He lifted her chin and pressed a kiss to her lips. "Whatever it is, we'll deal with it."

Gritting her teeth, she nodded.

He picked up the phone, listened, and looked over at her. His closed face set her heart racing. "It's for you. From your office."

She gave a sigh of relief. Business problems she could deal with, although finally talking to Noah about Ashley and the baby hadn't gone too badly.

She answered the phone, her mind on that last, most important thing she needed to say to Noah.

At first, her PA's words barely trickled through. Then she clutched the phone and fought the icy shivers dancing up her nape.

"Hang on, Celia, could you repeat that?"

"I'm sorry, Miss Michaels..." her PA's voice shook.

"Stop apologizing and tell me what's going on."

"I...I managed to track down the manager from our manufacturing outfit in Hong Kong. The reason they've been out of touch with us...well, the manager says the warehouse burned down. We've lost the whole collection."

THIRTY

Noah dialed his assistant director in charge of overseas ventures. "Gus, get me a list of all the clothes manufacturing ventures we're involved in, primarily in Asia. Yeah, KL is good. Email me the name of the point person, would you?" Waiting for the email to come through, he kept a close eye on Leia as she paced the living room.

She spun the other way and her earpiece glinted. "Did we confirm that there were no casualties in the fire?" she asked.

Watching her take the news of her destroyed collection like a champ, Noah had never felt more proud of her. Or loved her more. Or been more furious on her behalf.

Whatever gods were supposed to be watching over her were doing a piss-poor job thus far. Which was why he intended to take over the job on a full-time basis.

He heard her audible sigh of relief. "Good. Make sure the compensation scheme La Carezza has in place is activated immediately." She nodded to whatever response she got and executed another tight turn.

Her eyes caught his and she stopped.

He crooked a forefinger. She came toward him. Bending forward, he kissed her, quick and hard. She lifted her hand and traced his eyebrow with her fingers, then mouthed *thank you*.

"Thank you, Celia. I'm about to contact our nano-tech people in Kyoto. Send me the list of other manufacturers as soon as you have it." She hung up and massaged the back of her neck.

Stepping forward, Noah brushed her hand away and took over the massage. "I'll go and rustle up some lunch while you call Japan, then we'll hit the list of manufacturers, okay?"

She nodded, then moaned when he kneaded a particularly difficult knot. "Noah?" Her voice was hushed, small enough to make his insides twist.

"Yeah, baby?"

"You're...you're the reason I haven't fallen apart over this..." Her breath caught and she sniffed loudly. "I don't know what I would've done if you weren't here," she finished.

He curled his arm around her shoulders, pulled her back into his body and kissed her temple. "You're mine. I'll go to hell and back for what's mine. But you haven't fallen apart because *you're strong*. Much stronger than you know. It breaks my heart that you don't recognize your own strength. Until you do, lean on me all you want, baby. I'm not going anywhere."

Leia watched him stroll to the door. Unable to hold it in anymore, she took a deep breath. "Noah?"

He stopped. Turned. "Yeah?"

"I love you."

Her words visibly rocked him. He stumbled against the door, caught himself. Gaped at her. In quick strides, he crossed the room to her and caught her nape. His eyes sparkled with a thousand raw emotions. His hand trembled. Hell, his whole body shook as his chest rose and fell in short pants.

"Only you would throw such a beautiful, life-changing earthquake into my world when we're in the middle of a crisis," he growled fiercely.

Her phone rang. She ignored it. "Do you want me to take it back?" she asked anxiously.

"Are you fucking kidding me?" he asked hoarsely. He kissed her, plunged his tongue between her lips and ravaged her mouth. All the while the phone rang.

"Dammit!" He sucked in an unsteady breath. "Answer the phone. I'll go order our lunch. We'll pick this up later."

They didn't get a chance to pick it up for twenty-four hours. Noah flew in manufacturers from Kuala Lumpur to meet with Leia, and then they flew to Japan to consult with the nano-tech team on how quickly they could produce the spec for a new collection. Luckily, with the template already in place from the previous production, a new batch was promised for the next week. Between Leia's team and Noah's connections, they managed to find two manufacturers willing to combine their resources to reproduce the collection.

With the agreement of the US retailers, Leia pushed back the launch by a week.

Because they'd missed the return trip on the IL jet, Noah had his jet flown in. They were scheduled to fly back to Miami tonight.

"The world can hold on for one damn minute while I take you to dinner," Noah had snarled earlier in the evening after they'd fielded yet another phone call.

Now she walked into the living room in a sleeveless burnt orange dress with matching shoes and a black leather bolero, which she carried over her arm. She'd worn her hair up and completed the look with gold chandelier earrings and a long gold necklace.

Noah was waiting for her. He turned from the view and his breath visibly stalled. "Shit. Maybe we should stay in..." His voice was severely strained.

She gave a nervous laugh. "I look that bad?"

"You look like heaven, wrapped in sin, wrapped in a thousand dreams come true."

She melted. "Oh, Noah."

He laughed huskily and slid a hand through his hair. "Fuck, you've got me all sappy now. Let's go before it gets worse."

He held her hand in the car, kissing the back of it every few minutes. The restaurant he'd chosen sat at the top of a stunning skyscraper in Kowloon, overlooking the harbor. They were led past the lushly decorated main dining floor to a private room upstairs. Their exclusive chef served freshly prepared Shanghai noodles with braised lamb for her and grouper fillet for Noah. They fed each other bits of their food, his eyes burning hot each time he looked at her. When their waiter delivered their coffee, Noah pulled out his wallet and slid him several hundred dollars, murmuring something she didn't understand.

The waiter smiled widely, bowed and left.

"I didn't know you spoke Mandarin."

"I do a lot of business in China. Knowing the language cuts through a lot of bullshit." He stood and held out his hand to her. The heat in his eyes had grown wilder, primal.

Heart pumping, she rose. "What did you say to him?"

"That we would look after ourselves and we're not to be disturbed."

The lights dimmed and soft strains of music filled the air. She gasped as she recognized *Fused Realms'* slowest song. "Oh, Noah."

He pulled her into his arms and swayed with her across the room. "Those two words, aside from *Yes, Noah* are my top three favorite phrases."

"What's your other favorite?"

He stopped at the door to their private room and locked it. "The ones you spoke this afternoon. The ones I'm terrified were a figment of my imagination." Blue eyes blazed down at her, vulnerable, yet possessive. His eyes searched hers with an intensity that stopped her breath.

Her heart climbed into her throat as she put everything she had out there. "They weren't, Noah. I love you. More than I can find adequate words for. I think I loved you from the moment I saw you. I knew I loved you when you kicked my ass the first time I let the monsters win. I'm sorry I let you down then and I can't promise I won't—"

"Shhh, don't ruin the moment, baby. You love me. You love me despite all *my* baggage." He shook his head in wonder. "You know how fucking honored I feel to know that? You didn't flinch when you were slapped around the face with what I did in New York—"

"Because I know she drove you to it. We've both been victims of mind-fuck experts."

He nodded. "But I choose to believe it's made us stronger. Strong enough to know what a beautiful thing we have going here. I love you, Leia. You turn me inside out every time I look at you. Every day I wake up with you in my arms, promises to be the best day of my life. I never want that to stop. It tore me apart when I thought I'd lost you. I'll protect you and that precious love with everything I've got, if you'll let me. Please, sweetheart. Please say yes."

She blinked back gulping tears. "Yes, Noah."

Their kiss was long, deep and heart melding. When he lifted his head, she swayed to a little more than the music. "Why did you lock the door?"

"I booked an all-night dining experience that ends at midnight. We're done eating, our bags are packed and already at the airport, but we don't need to be there for another..." he glanced at his watch, "two hours. So I thought I'd let you...enjoy the view." He slanted her a crazy wicked grin.

"Enjoy the view, huh? And what will you be doing?"

"I'll be enjoying the view too...of your naked body and how it feels with my cock in it." He winked.

Laughing, she looked around the room. It was spacious and beautifully decorated. But it severely lacked anything remotely resembling comfort.

She also knew the man she loved was nothing if not inventive.

When he picked up a dining chair and placed it in front of the wide floor-to-ceiling window, she lifted her eyebrow. "That's it?"

"That's it."

He stepped behind her and drew down her zipper. Her dress fell to the floor, revealing black panties. Removing his jacket, he sat down and patted his lap. She climbed aboard and leaned in for another kiss. Lifting his hips, he freed his cock and removed her panties.

"Place your hand on the window, baby."

She obeyed, then groaned as he slid slowly inside her. "I love you, Noah."

The fierce awe that washed over his face would be forever seared in her memory. "I love you too, my beautiful Leia," he replied gruffly. His hands framed her hips and squeezed her ass. "I'm going to make love to you long and slow. And you're going to try and point out every landmark you see."

Her breath hitched. "What's my prize for right guesses?"

"For each one you get right, I'll let you come."

She got four right and Noah threw in a bonus just for laughs.

Which was part of the reason she wore a broad smile as they were driven to the airport. "Counting tonight, we've only had six highs, not seven."

Noah kissed their linked hands. "You told me you love me. That's the high to end all highs for me. But if you insist on being pedantic about it, I have a private jet fuelled and waiting. And I'm not afraid to use it."

THIRTY-ONE

"Noah?"

"Yes, sweetheart?"

"Tell me about this T-shirt."

They'd been back in Miami for less than a day, and it looked like Leia had found her favorite item of clothing again. And fuck if Noah didn't feel stupidly light-headed with happiness from seeing her in it.

His heart thumped hard at her beauty framed in the early morning light. He held out his hand to her. When she reached where he sat on the terrace, he pulled her into his lap.

Clearing his throat, he played with the soft hair above her ear. "It's my father's. He wore it the day he proposed to my mom. He wore it the days my brother and I were born. He jokes that if it could withstand not being ripped apart by my mom when she was in labor with me, it can survive anything." Noah shrugged. "It's his lucky shirt."

Her fingers traced his brow. "Why do you have it?"

"He...he gave it to me the day I left New York two years ago. I guess he could tell I was in a dark place and needed something to hold on to. I didn't want to take it, but he insisted, said I needed it more than he did. And he was right. It brought me luck. It brought me you." He nuzzled her cheek and she melted into him.

Noah was sure in that moment there was nothing more beautiful in the world than the woman in his arms.

She took his face in her hands and kissed him. "I'm so glad."

He reluctantly pulled away when things started to get heated. "You need to get dressed, baby."

"Why?"

"Paddy's on his way over. Or he's probably already inside, helping himself to my most expensive booze again."

She yelped and jumped off his lap. Peering cautiously into the living room, she looked back at him with relief before disappearing inside.

Paddy walked out onto the terrace three minutes later.

Noah sighed. "You do know that the day you see Leia anything less than fully dressed is the day you die, right?"

His PI grunted. "Relax, I have impeccable timing." He sat down and patted his pockets restlessly.

"You lost something?" Noah asked.

"Yeah, the Marlboros I quit smoking five years ago."

"Any reason you want to light up now?"

Paddy shrugged. "According to my daughter, every time I take a drink before noon, a fucking hamster dies."

Noah's brow rose. "And you happen to love hamsters?"

"Yeah, go figure."

"We have coffee," Leia said, as she walked back onto the terrace. She'd taken his T-shirt off and replaced it with jeans and a tank top. Her hair hung loose and silky around her face. She sat next to him and put a hand on his thigh. His heart swelled larger. "You have news for us?" she asked Paddy.

He nodded. "We're almost sure we've tracked Snyder down to a lake house in Maine."

"Almost?" Noah asked.

"He's also been spotted in Montreal, Canada, where he's originally from. Snyder was his mother's maiden name. His real name is William Bouchard. He grew up on the streets of Montreal and got caught up in a crime syndicate there. He disappeared real quick after suspect funds went missing."

Leia's hand trembled and Noah covered it with his own. "You've informed the detective?"

Paddy nodded. "From the information Willoughby gave us, he thinks there's enough to arrest Snyder, but it would be better all round if he's arrested on US soil. We have people watching both residences."

"Be careful. He's...clever," Leia cautioned. Noah knew she was blaming herself from being fooled for so long by the man she'd called her savior.

The PI rose. "He may think he's clever, but I'm badass." He stared down at Leia for a moment. "Sorry to hear about your production issues. Do you want me to look into it?"

Her eyes widened. "You think it's suspicious?"

"Everything's suspicious. Until it isn't." He left as silently as he'd arrived.

Noah saw the anxiety on Leia's face and silently cursed his PI. It was clear Paddy had a soft spot for Leia. Which made his veiled implication grate on Noah's nerves.

"You think he's right?" she asked.

"Paddy's suspicious about his own shadow. He'll look into it whether we want him to or not. If he finds something, he'll report it."

She nodded. "I have to go into the office for a while, make sure everyone knows what's going on."

Noah rose with her. "I'll drive you. I'm headed into the office too."

They left after a quick breakfast. He spent an inadequate ten minutes double parked outside her building, kissing her goodbye. She was blushing profusely by the time she slid out of his Maserati.

"I'll pick you up at five. Dinner at Pietro's?"

She gave him another of those spectacular smiles. "Yes. I love you, Noah."

"I love you." Three simple words that filled him with awe, trepidation and endless happiness.

He strode into his office with a huge grin and ploughed through the mountain of work that had piled up in his absence, starting with drawing up a contract for Tim and Harry. The boys' effusive chatter when they received his email made his grin widen until Noah thought his face would crack.

His desk was clear by four. On a whim, he grabbed his keys and headed down to the private garage. His phone beeped as he gunned the engine. Ignoring it, he floored the car all the way to Leia's office. As he alighted, his phone beeped again.

Deciding to wait for Leia outside, he leaned against his hood and pulled his phone out of his pocket.

Missed call from Dr. Franklin, Ashley's OBGYN.

A shiver raced over his skull.

He dialed.

"Mr. King, thanks for calling me back—"

"What's wrong?" he cut across her.

"It may be something, it may be nothing, but I had a call from a colleague at a private clinic in West Palm Beach. It seems Ashley checked herself in this morning for a procedure. I only know because she listed me as her physician."

His blood ran cold. "What sort of procedure?"

Silence.

"What sort of procedure?"

"Mr. King…Noah, I suggest you get over there as soon as possible." She rattled off the name of the clinic and hung up.

God no. His vision swam and he closed his eyes.

"Noah?" Leia stood in front of him, her face creased in worry. "What's wrong?"

He shook his head. "I think..." he stopped and swallowed. "I think Ashley checked herself into a clinic this morning to get rid of my child."

Noah had little memory of driving to the clinic and virtually no memory of calling his attorney. But Sam Ferranti was waiting for him outside the exclusive clinic when he arrived with Leia.

"Sam?" He frantically searched the other man's face.

His lawyer's expression confirmed his worst fears. "I'm sorry, Noah."

First he went numb. Then a well of hatred and fury cannonballed through his chest. "Is she here?" he rasped.

Sam nodded.

"What room?"

"I don't think they'll let you—"

"The bitch just aborted my child. She'll damn well see me!"

"She's upstairs. Room 21. We'll go together just in case..."

Noah's feet pounded up the stairs. He had a vague notion that Leia trailed him with Sam, but his mind was refusing to work properly. And the ache taking root in his heart grew by the second.

He located the private suite and yanked the door open.

Ashley lay in bed with her face turned toward the window, her expression as serene as a mountain lake. At his entry, she turned her head and her eyes bulged in alarm.

"You. Fucking. Bitch."

"Do you blame me? When you can't do anything right?" she snarled.

He struggled to speak through the tentacles of pain and anger. "Excuse me?"

She shook her head. "I told you there was something wrong. While you were gallivanting all over the world with your little whore, I had the baby checked out. Turns out there was a five percent chance it would've been born with birth defects."

"What the hell are you talking about? Dr. Franklin never mentioned anything—"

"She wanted me to *wait and see*," Ashley sneered. "As if I wanted to be saddled with a defective kid. I really don't know why I chose to overlook the fact that you're not normal. I think I fooled myself into thinking you were worth considering for a relationship. I supposed after Taylor died, I panicked. I was the last of my family. It made me forget that there's something broken in you. Hell, your genes aren't even up to creating anything but a deformed baby!"

He sucked in a shocked breath. "My God, *are you for real?*"

"I don't know what my brother saw in you, but before he died, he convinced me to give you a second chance. God, how I wish I hadn't. I've wasted far too much time on you. I'm going back to New York. You can carry on hiding away here where everyone around you is just as depraved as you are. Was that the attraction to moving into this godforsaken city in the first place?" she mocked.

"For the love of Christ, do you hear yourself? Are you even sorry for anything you've done?"

Her smile held razor-sharp calculation. "I have nothing to be sorry for. You didn't want me here. I'll get out of your hair as soon as we reach a financial understanding."

Noah waited for the punch line. None came. "You really are serious, aren't you?"

"As a heart attack. You've ruined my life for long enough. I'm not going to go quietly into the night." She folded her hands calmly over the satin sheet.

"Oh no?" He smiled. And it must have been one worthy of a horror flick because she recoiled just a tiny bit and lost a little of her bravado. Keeping his eyes on her, he withdrew his phone from his pocket. His call was answered immediately. "Sam, can you come in please?"

Sam walked in with Leia. Ashley's face turned more vicious. "Ah, there's your little trollop." She tilted her head to get a better view of Leia. "I hear your warehouse burned to the ground, taking all your ghastly collection with it. What a shame."

Noah froze.

Leia stepped beside him. "How the hell did you know about that?" she asked.

Ashley flicked her hand. "Word gets around..."

"No, it doesn't. Only a handful of people know what happened at the manufacturer's in Singapore," Leia said.

"*Singapore*? But the guy Warren had me bribe was in Hong—?" She froze, her eyes widening in consternation before she clamped her mouth shut.

"*Gotcha*," Leia murmured with a smile.

Noah kept his eyes on the vile creature perched on the bed. "Sam, did you catch that?"

"I did."

"Do you also remember how we decided to go easy on Ashley because she was carrying my child?"

"I do."

"Consider that request unquestionably revoked. Throw the book at her. Everything you have. Oh and ideally, I want her arrested and charged within the hour."

Ashley gasped, her eyes rounding as she lost all color. "You can't!"

"Watch me. And Sam, I think Leia will have charges of her own to add. I'll have my PI dig up some details for you within the next twenty-four hours."

"Understood," Sam replied. "I'll go tell the administrator that she's not allowed to leave. I'll make sure he organizes enough security so she doesn't accidentally find her way out of this charming facility."

"Noah! Let's talk about this—"

He took Leia's hand and headed toward the door.

"You can't do this!" Her voice trembled.

Against his better judgment, he turned around. Despite the fake tears streaming down her face, her eyes shot pure venom at him. He opened his mouth to speak, but Leia beat him to it.

"I told you that you were stupid to try and come after something that never belonged to you in the first place. You should've listened to me and scurried back to New York when you had the chance. Now you get to accessorize orange jumpsuits for the next decade. Enjoy prison, bitch."

They ordered food from Pietro's but picked at it until it went cold. Noah couldn't think straight. He alternated between impotent rage and a numb sense of loss. When Leia suggested an early bedtime, he nodded and walked out of the kitchen.

His skin ached, as if he'd been flayed from the inside. Undressing, he got into bed and threw his arm over his eyes.

He heard Leia walk in and undress. Craving her warmth, he turned toward her, but she was heading to the bathroom. For several minutes, he lay on his side, listening to the shower...and the faint sound of sobs.

Frowning, he rushed into the bathroom. She stood under the spray, her slender shoulders shaking.

Fear overtook every other emotion warring inside him. "Leia, baby what's wrong?"

She turned and clamped her arms around his waist. "I'm sorry, Noah. So, so sorry." Her tears mingled in the spray, her eyes dark pools of sorrow.

"For God's sake, what for?"

"This was your chance to be a father. And that...that bitch took it away from you! I'd give anything to not have you go through this."

Noah's throat closed up. He kissed her cheeks, her eyes, her mouth. Tried to get himself under control enough to speak. "Oh God, Leia. I love you. I love you so much, baby. But don't cry for me. I don't deserve it. I'm the guy who doesn't know how to mourn a baby he didn't know existed until a month ago. A part of me is relieved that the child will never know a mother like Ashley." His eyes clouded over. "I've been asking myself what special kind of monster that makes me for the last few hours."

Her hand framed his cheek. "Oh Noah, there's nothing wrong with you. Remember what you said to me when I blamed my mother for leaving me? What you're feeling is human. But..." She shook her head. "I wanted this for you." Her voice broke.

His heart splintered, for her and for him, but the healing power of love soon staunched the pain. "And we will have it. *You and I.* The way it should be. It may not be naturally, but we have options, baby. Many, many options."

Her anguish started to dissipate. "I'm afraid to hope."

"Then have faith instead. Have faith that I love you and will stop at nothing to give you your heart's desire."

She trembled in his arms. "I can do faith, and I can certainly do the loving you back thing in spades."

He kissed the tip of her nose. "Good. But to make it happen, we need to do things in the right order, baby."

Her eyes returned to the alluring shade of grey, which had captured his heart, body and mind the moment he saw her. "What order is that?"

"First, I make love to you, right here, right now. Then I get on my knees and ask you to marry me. You say yes. Then I make love to you again. Then we get engaged, have lots and lots of sex between then and whenever we decide to get married...and when we're ready, we decide how to have a baby."

She tilted her head to one side, her eyes shining. "I really want to find a flaw in that plan..."

He smiled. "But?"

"But I can't," she whispered and curled her arms around his neck.

EPILOGUE

Seven months later

Leia opened the front door to the condo to find Noah pacing the living room where she'd left him two hours before.

He caught sight of her and changed course, taking her in his arms the moment he reached her.

"Show me," he demanded hoarsely.

"I'm still really sore, Noah. Can't you wait till this evening?" She couldn't resist a light tease.

He caught her left hand and meshed it with his. Her enormous square-cut diamond engagement ring glinted in the sun. "Oh baby, did it hurt a lot? I chose that place because they're supposed to be the best. Shit, I knew I should've come with you."

"Noah!"

He grimaced. "Sorry. This no cursing rule is fu...messing with my head. Please show me, I promise I'll be really gentle."

Fighting laughter, Leia turned and headed for the bedroom. Dropping her purse on the bed, she faced him.

"Ready?"

He nodded.

She slowly unzipped the blue and white summer dress and dropped it to the floor. Raising her arm, she angled her body toward him.

He fell to his knees and read the new words etched into her skin.

From A Broken Acorn...
...The King of Oaks And Owner Of My Heart

He looked up, his eyes glistening. "Darling, it's beautiful."

He gently kissed the words, his mouth trailing his name over and over. She handed him a bottle of antiseptic. As he gently applied it, she watched beautifully turbulent emotions wash over his face.

God, she loved this man...

"So, the tattoo artist who did this was a woman, right?" he asked with deceptive nonchalance. Another kiss, this time on her hipbone. He capped the bottle and handed it to her.

Suppressing a smile, she spoke the word that would sooth her alpha beast. "Yes." And then because she couldn't resist teasing, "But she had these huge tattoos on her arms of women in various forms of undress. I may be wrong, but I think she's into chicks—"

His growl of warning made her dissolve into giggles.

"If you think that this unbelievable miracle happening in our lives," he caressed a hand reverently over her four-months pregnant belly, "excuses you from punishment, baby, think again." He kissed her stomach and Leia felt the tiniest kick, a fluttering really.

Blinking back tears, she watched the man of her dreams shower their unborn baby with love.

When further exploration had revealed that her damaged tube was only partially blocked, they'd been cautiously optimistic about natural conception. And with her pill-taking regimen having bitten the dust amid the turmoil in her life, Noah had encouraged her to stop taking them altogether.

Leia had fallen pregnant two months after she'd come off the pill.

Noah's happiness at the news had been incomparable and every day she grew more amazed at the depths of his love and devotion.

She slid her fingers through his hair and tightened her fist. His low hiss before his eyes connected with hers was music to her ears.

"I think the artist was heavily into girls. What are you going to do about it, Noah?"

Slowly he rose to his feet, dislodged her grip and pulled both of her hands behind her back. Stormy blue eyes locked on hers. "You need me to remind who you belong to. Is that right, baby?"

Breath fleeing her lungs, she nodded jerkily.

She took her punishment like a thoroughly loved and adored champ. Two hours later, they entered the living room to find Paddy in residence, his customary glass in his hand.

"Fuck. That's it, baby. We're moving," Noah griped.

He earned an elbow in his ribs for swearing around the baby. He wondered how much it'd cost him to throw his PI over the balcony.

"Turn on the TV," Paddy said. "Channel Four."

Noah grunted. "You help yourself to my booze. Why not add watching TV? That way we can adopt you into this family."

Leia laughed and found the remote. All laughter ceased as they watched breaking news of William Bouchard aka Warren Snyder being led away in handcuffs.

"He was found with an underage girl at the lake house in Maine. She'd been missing from her family home in Florida for the past six months and she'd been badly..." His gaze flicked to Leia, "manhandled. I called in a few favors and I'm fairly certain his trial will be held here. If we can pull the right strings, he could end up in the same place as Willoughby. I have a few friends on standby to give them both a reunion party they won't forget."

Noah's teeth bared in a savage grin, and he shook hands with Paddy. "I'll foot the bill for the party streamers and any other entertainment required."

A look of brutal understanding passed between the men.

Paddy left and she stared at Noah.

"What?" he asked, his voice soft, deep and filled with love again.

"On the day I complete my tattoo, we finally close the circle. Warren gets arrested. Ashley is already doing twelve years for stealing the embryos, her part in burning down my warehouse, and for embezzling from the art gallery in New York, and my stepfather won't see the light of day for twenty years, minimum. So..." she caressed his mouth with the tips of her fingers, "you get one free pass to get as sappy and swear-y as you want."

He caught her fingers in his hand and stared deep into her eyes. "Leia, baby...I love you. I'll always protect you and our baby. But I'm glad we don't have to look over our shoulders any more. So yeah, life is Fucking A right now. Don't you agree?"

"Yes, Noah."

Fucking A...

THE END

Dear Reader

Thank you so much for taking the time to read SOAR! If you have a moment, I'd really appreciate a review of this book at a review platform of your choice. Reviews are the lifeblood of indie authors like me, so thank you so much for your help in advance.
If you'd like to keep in touch:
Join my NEWSLETTER for up to date news on books, book tours, signings and general mayhem!
Friend me on FACEBOOK or go one step further and join ZACH'S HUSSIES, my Street Team - that's where the real naughties come to play!! I'm also on TWITTER, GOODREADS and INSTAGRAM: @ZaraCoxWriter

COMING SOON

FREEFALL
(THE INDIGO LOUNGE SERIES) #5
BY
ZARA COX

MORE ABOUT FREEFALL...

Keely Benson:

Nineteen. The age I threw my life away.

Twenty-Five. The age I decided to do it a second time.

Twenty-Five plus one day. The age Benedict Mason Sinclair III walked into my life.

Mason Sinclair III:

She was a curse.

A sex bomb.

A perfect reminder that *not* having a heart was the best choice I ever made.

Other Books By Zara Cox
HIGH (The Indigo Lounge Series) #1
HIGHER (The Indigo Lounge Series) #2
SPIRAL (The Indigo Lounge Series) #3
WRECKLESS

Acknowledgements

First of all to Kate Reed, my friend, my crit partner and my editor (the perfect trifecta). You continue to inspire and blow me away with your friendship and support. I couldn't have done this without you!

To my Gorgeous Minxes, and the reason for at least a dozen smiles each day. I love you guys! I'm so very grateful for you.

To my readers who, amazingly, keep asking for more books! I never thought this series would be so well received. Your support means the world to me. Thank you!

Last but not least, to my husband and kids (who're breathing a sigh of relief that THE BOOK is finished!), I love and adore you for your patience, your care and your unfailing support.

Copyright

Copyright © 2014 Zara Cox
Edited by Kate Reed
Cover by Angela Oltmann
All rights reserved. No part of this e-book may be reproduced in any form other than that in which it was purchased and without the written permission of the author.

This e-book is licensed for your personal enjoyment only. This e-book may not be re-sold or given away to other people. If you would like to share this book with another person, please purchase an additional copy for each recipient. If you're reading this book and did not purchase it, or it was not purchased for your use only, then please return it to the retailer and purchase your own copy. Thank you for respecting the hard work of this author.

About Author

Zara Cox has been writing for almost twenty-five years but it wasn't until nine years ago that she decided to share her love of writing sexy, gritty stories with anyone outside her close family (the over 18s anyway!). The Indigo Lounge Series is Zara's next step in her erotic romance-writing journey and she would love to hear your thoughts. Visit her Facebook Page - Zara-Cox-Writer or connect with her on Twitter (www.twitter.com/zcoxbooks), Instagram or Goodreads.

Don't miss out!

Click the button below and you can sign up to receive emails whenever Zara Cox publishes a new book. There's no charge and no obligation.

Sign Me Up!

https://books2read.com/r/B-A-EQL-NMYC

BOOKS 2 READ

Connecting independent readers to independent writers.

Did you love *SOAR*? Then you should read *High* by Zara Cox!

Welcome to The Indigo Lounge, the scandalously sexy sky-high playground where anything can happen...

Flirty, dirty and utterly delicious, HIGH is the perfect next read for lovers of the internationally renowned This Man series from Jodi Ellen Malpas & Sylvia Day's Crossfire series.

Zachary Savage is a man accustomed to getting whatever and whoever he wants. He's buried his demons and risen from the ashes to become the playboy owner of the internationally renowned Indigo Lounge, a fleet of ultra-exclusive sky-high pleasure palaces.

He has everything he wants, until he sets eyes on Bethany Green. One look is all it takes ~ she has to be his.

Bethany Green has endured the worst year of her life; bad luck and heartbreak at every turn. Karma swings wildly in her favour when a money-can't-buy golden ticket lands in her lap - an invitation to experience the scandalously sexy Indigo Lounge for herself.

Green by name and green by nature, is she brave enough to accept the hottest ticket in town?

One glimpse of Zachary Savage is enough to convince her that she isn't cosmopolitan enough to play in his glamorous, sinfully sexy world. But they're already in the air, and reality is a long way behind them. The only way is up.

The Indigo Lounge. Step aboard and check your inhibitions at the door.

Praise for High:

Wow! The naughtiest book I've read this year, so hot it made ME blush! **Zara Cox** is a sizzling new voice in the erotic fiction world. **Kitty French, USA Today best selling erotic author of The Knight Series.**

Warning This book contains explicit sexual scenarios that will make your pulse explode. 18+ only.

Also by Zara Cox

The Indigo Lounge Series
High
Higher
Spiral
SOAR
Freefall
Indigo Velvet
The Indigo Lounge Box Set
Spin

About the Author

Zara Cox has been writing for almost twenty-five years but it wasn't until seven years ago that she decided to share her love of writing sexy, gritty stories with anyone besides her close family (the over 18s anyway!). The Indigo Lounge Series is Zara's next step in her erotic romance-writing journey and she hopes you'll take the journey with her.

Printed in Dunstable, United Kingdom